SCATTERLINGS

SCATTERLINGS

A Novel

REŠOKETŠWE MANENZHE

HarperVia

An Imprint of HarperCollins*Publishers*

Excerpt on page vii from "Scatterlings of Africa," written by Johnny Clegg. Published by Scatterlings Pty Ltd. Used by permission.

Originally published as *Scatterlings* in South Africa in 2020 by Jacana Media (Pty) Ltd.

FIRST HARPERVIA EDITION PUBLISHED 2022

Designed by SBI Book Arts, LLC

Library of Congress Cataloging-in-Publication Data has been applied for.

ISBN 978-0-6-326411-3

22 23 24 25 26   FRS   10 9 8 7 6 5 4 3 2 1

Dear Selina,

I wish you'd lived; but since you didn't, I like to think the sun doesn't set where you are. I'm sending these words so you can know where the story stopped for some time; it hasn't ended yet, but I think the sun has been rising on me too.

I think I should thank you now, and let you go back to resting. The sun will be over the horizon soon, so I need to go back and finish the story.

scatterling

/ˈskætəlɪŋ/

noun (plural: scatterlings)
1. *a person without a fixed home; a wanderer.*

"Scatterlings and fugitives, hooded eyes and weary brows,
seek refuge in the night."

—"Scatterlings of Africa," Johnny Clegg

PART ONE

Children of the First Gods

The Stars of the Milky Way

I t was first told by the San people that, in the blackness of night, a girl took roasting roots and ashes from a fire and threw them into the sky. Thus the stars were born. A path was made in the sky, and hunters who were lost followed it home.

The San were an old people. They might have been the first people. And so, when the wind took their tale through the summers, its whisperings breathed new facts into the story. The Basotho said that the children of the first Gods had walked the path in the sky to reach the place of the rising sun, where Molalatladi, the Lightning Bird, rested in eternity.

That was long ago. It was when people sat around fires to recall the world's past with each other. There was no time for that anymore. People now told their stories while passing each other.

As for the girl who made the stars, people had forgotten her. Besides, the sky was since partitioned: where walked the San and

Basotho now lay under the southern stars. It was a dry place for miles and miles, for when not calling the stars of harvesttime, the sun was a thing of death. It was a vast place; unlike Amsterdam, where boats parted rivers or ships were hammered into being; nor was it like the hurried hubbub of London, immersed in all its cacophonies.

The San were a nomad people, always taking from the earth only what it was willing to yield and then moving on to other plains and valleys; and before settlers drove them entirely to the inner deserts and near-deserts, factions of their tribe had taken to wandering near the sea. There, a foreign silver light tainted the world, for the sky, merging its endlessness with that sea, looked bluer than ordinary. The Basotho had settled deeper into Africa, and hence saw the plains in the golden light of sun, for the sun shone brighter there.

The seasons were dull. They shifted within themselves like a melody, dancing languidly between the Karoo and the savannah, and summer was nearly the same as winter. Maybe that was the reason the colonists believed they could own the place, for it was dry and hot and looked to be dead. Not knowing that no place was dead, they planted a flag on some hill, declared it for their king, and proceeded to forget the ancient names sounding in the crags.

Africa, being rich and generous and unpretentious, easily yielded to the partitioning of her face; the morphing of Ngola to Angola; the cutting of the Gold Coast and Johannesburg from her womb; the death of the quagga, the burying of her Gods, and so forth. Maybe that was another reason the colonists believed themselves to own her. Africa had bent easily. Ethiopia, with her rebellion to Italian annexation, was an anomaly. Africa was, over-all, so malleable.

By the year 1927, and possibly for the sake of her own survival, Africa had begun to bend herself into irony. That was how it came to be told by Alisa van Zijl, who had herself bent her name from Alisa Miller, which she had bent from the mononym Alisa; that is how it came to be told by this Alisa to her daughters, that once a suckling child was thrown from the breast of a god-woman. Gushing milk sprung from the god-woman's breast and into the sky. Thus the stars of the Milky Way were born.

That was how this story ended.

Now, this is how it started.

This Silent Interlude

There was a madman who, it was said, had war in his blood. His grandfather had fought in the First Boer War, his father had fought in the second, and he, in an upward trajectory of tragedy, or glory, had outdone them in the Great War of Europe. It was expected that, should renewed freedom of the Witwatersrand mines from the British Empire be imagined, or Europe begin another conflict, the man's son would continue that bloody legacy so efficiently inherited from his forefathers.

But as it was on 29 March, 1927, which was a sunless day filled with many omens, the man didn't yet have a son. It was hoped that the world and South Africa might hold off from any pending revolutions so the man might have enough time to rear that fated son, and thus complete his earthly role.

His name was John Ashby, and most times he could be found in the city, near the auction house at the corner of Burg Street, hawking newspapers to those passing by. Abram van Zijl found him there. "What does the governor-general say today?" said Abram.

"Good morning, Mr. Van Zijl."

Remembering his manners, Abram conceded a greeting, and the man read from the placard he brandished: "Immorality Act assented. House of Assembly prohibits illicit carnal intercourse between Europeans and natives."

A motor car turned up dust as it swerved around the corner, and several pedestrians were left to scold the recklessness of the driver, and to ponder the general decay of morality the city was enduring. Abram had clutched at his chest, but recovered himself.

"Let me see," he said, reaching for coins in his pocket. In return, John gave him a newspaper, and Abram immediately scanned it until he finally came to page 14, where the headline read: ACT NO. 5 OF 1927. TO PROHIBIT ILLICT CARNAL INTERCOURSE BETWEEN EUROPEANS AND NATIVES AND OTHER ACTS IN RELATION THERETO.

With those words, Abram's life tumbled into chaos. The rising foreboding with which much else had happened before then seemed to culminate rather quickly, as though the omens had grown impatient. So there stood Abram with a madman saying to him, "I hear the governor-general will be bringing the guillotine."

The man's voice was an echo to Abram. He heard it as though remembering a dream, a bad dream. From this, he had to wake up. "Thank you, John," he said, shaking his head, then tipping his hat in farewell. "I'll be heading home now."

"It was a pleasure, sir," said John, he, too, tipping his hat.

Abram crossed the street to where Farouk, one of his workers, waited for him with the car. "Where to, sir?"

It was still morning, and Abram had intended to go to Parliament. But his heart failed him. Now that it was broken, he couldn't face the world. He felt that he shouldn't cower where observing eyes might be unsympathetic. So: "Home."

Farouk nodded and started the car.

The city unfolded itself like a history book. The buildings were like chapters, each telling of a different era of immigration or fashion. As the old world poured itself into Cape Town, so too had Gothic churches, hotels that mimicked the façades of Victorian London, pale Dutch parodies that had swiftly become characteristic of the Cape—they lined the city like models in a museum, like suggestions of how to reconcile clashing cultures. In short, the city spread itself like an exhibition of evolution.

Main Road would be smoother, with fewer turns and less cause for worldly worries. But the path leading past the Castle of Good Hope, out towards the foot of Devil's Peak—where the University of Cape Town was to be re-rooted—past Mostert's Mill and so forth, until depositing them in Constantia Valley, would be quieter, with fewer acquaintances and less cause for existential worries. "Farouk," said Abram, "not through Main Road."

Without quibble, Farouk kept Table Mountain on their right and mounted the hills, slight and steep. The mountain rose impressively into the sky, heralding its own magnificence. A wind blew from the southeast and with it, a cloud-cloth formed to drape itself atop the plateau. At dusk, when the dying light of the sun wafted away from the mountain, the mountain would be darkened against the sky. Its pine-draped slopes would be hidden behind a mist of things known only by the scientists. It would look like a silhouette of itself then as, as though by some unchangeable fate, it yielded to the decay of day. Abram had lived in Cape Town for over two decades and this simple wonder still awed him.

Presently there was a bump in the road and Abram was woken from his reverie. There were times when the car felt to be alive with annoyance and protest, though they went on steadily. All the while Abram formed and destroyed and reformed what he would say to his wife. She had become a difficult woman, Alisa. Whatever he said would be an act of villainy in her eyes. What he didn't say, or rather, what she would want him to say, was more important still. So he formed and destroyed and reformed his words.

They wound their way into the lush expanse at the foot of Constantiaberg. Here, the world dipped from the mountaintop to the sprawling farms with a convergence of several unique vegetations, a mock-tropic that came alive with breeds that couldn't be found anywhere else in the world. But a mockery is, of course, a mockery, and it must have deficiencies that set it apart from an absolute or an original. Such was the case with the valley; the rains preferred to fall in winter and the summers were hot and dry—in short, these splendid vegetations that spread themselves in that odd corner of the world were forced into resilience. The fynbos, being more resilient than the rest, had spread itself in several variations of shrubbery and heather.

Turning east from Constantiaberg, they entered the parade of wine farms littering the slopes. The Van Zijl Estate was nestled near the edge of the litter. The driveway leading to the manor was flanked by imposing oak trees, their shadows meeting in the middle to dull the sun's potency. As the manor, with its pristine whitewashed walls unknowing of his fate, rose before him, Abram still hadn't settled on what to tell his wife.

As he had expected, Alisa sat under the weeping willow. Unexpectedly, she wasn't writing in her journal. She faced the vineyards with her head leaning on the tree trunk, her eyes closed, and her hands clasped on her lap. She could have been sleeping; but sensing him, she looked around and their eyes locked.

When they first met, those eyes had been a darker shade of brown that sparkled when she smiled. Through the years, her incessant tears seemed to have washed them, diluted them some-how. What was left was a dull brown, so pale and worn, and so quick to show pain. Abram swallowed and walked to her.

She stood and, almost smiling, said, "The Act has been passed, hasn't it?"

Abram nodded. Alisa slid back to the ground. She settled on her knees and tears quickly sprung into her eyes. Abram slid, too, to his knees, and held her hands. "Look." He opened the news-paper for a second time, turning to page 14. "Look, Clause Five says if we can prove we're married, there won't be trouble for us."

Alisa read where he pointed. Then, shaking her head, she pointed to a clause of her own: "It says if we can't prove we're married then we can be deemed unmarried. The penalty will be five years imprisonment for you, four for me, and the children . . ." There, her wits failed her. She slumped further into herself, and could only utter formless sentimentalities. "Oh, the children, Bram. The children . . ." She grew more incomprehensible, her weeping more erratic. But most significant was the hug she gave Abram. She fully submitted herself into his arms—rested her head on his shoulder, then wept and wept.

It had been so long since she last touched him. Her skin, once so familiar to him, now estranged, felt fickle, brittle. She trembled so freely. And as if afraid she would disintegrate where they were, she hugged him closer. "Oh, Bram," she said.

Baffled by the abundance of an affectionate wife, Abram found himself echoing her sentimentalities back to her. "It will be all right, Alisa." When that didn't seem enough, for she trembled more vigorously, he complemented it with this: "They won't take our children from us. The Act says nothing about children. They won't take them, my love. The children are safe."

Perhaps because he was unsure what else to do, he slipped into memories, into habits once familiar to him. He rested his chin on her head and mumbled promises, protections he could give to both her and the children. And foolishly, Abram began to dream of a reconciliation. He began to hope.

. . .

Once the sun had set and risen again without delay, it started to seem that his life's routine couldn't be so easily shaken by something as abstract as the Immorality Act. Abram began to indulge himself with further forms of foolishness.

He and Alisa presently strolled down the vineyard path leading from her weeping willow. The intimacy of yesterday had dissipated. They walked apart from one another, and yet it seemed to Abram that Alisa longed to be nearer to him. Her pride, however, would not allow her to concede affection, not without the excuse of shock.

She had her arms folded behind her. Every once in a while Abram stole a glance at her and smiled to himself. She, however, dedicated her gaze to the ground. The wide-brimmed hat she wore to shield herself from the sun shielded, in turn, the full view of her face from him. Maybe she wore it for fashion, he concluded—indeed, the effect was remarkable. The pallid pink of the hat and the white of the flowers sewn along the top made her seem gentle, tame.

They endured this silent interlude for nearly a minute. Then as usual, Alisa broke the peace: "There isn't a chance Parliament will reverse the law, is there?" she said.

Abram shook his head. "There isn't. But we don't need to worry. The law is for people who aren't married. That isn't the case for us. Truly, we have nothing to fear, Alisa."

They entered another interlude, and Abram took the chance to admire the golden hue of the slopes stretching before them.

"We can't trust that," said Alisa. She stopped walking and faced him. He was also compelled to stop. Her face was beseeching, and from under the hat's shadow, he saw a flash of fear in her eyes. "We have to do something, Bram. How can we sit and do nothing? We can't simply hope that things will work out, you know."

This was the reason she had burst into his room, then. It wasn't just a walk that she wanted to enjoy. She wanted to discuss the implications of the so-called Immorality Act, to infect him with the panic she seemed so eager to carry. Well, at least he had enjoyed a morning walk with her, a walk that *she* had asked for, even if her intentions were clearly far from pure. He had even savoured the silent interludes, for they had seemed filled with a gentle sort of solidarity.

But like the vineyards endlessly winding in and away from the estate, in and away from them, Abram and Alisa had trod the path of fraught pleasantness so tirelessly. He could, by then, predict any and all arguments she might make, for she had recited these woes countless times. He submitted himself to the wind of hope and foolishness that had swept through him since yesterday. He made the argument for her. "We must leave," he said. "We must leave the Cape, South Africa. If you're afraid, Alisa, we must leave."

"And go where?"

"Anywhere you like," he said, simply.

Without even thinking about her answer, or so it seemed to Abram, Alisa said, "The Soviet Union."

By then she had resumed her fascination with the ground. She didn't look up, so she didn't see the shadow passing over his face. Such was Alisa's carelessness with these things—she didn't ask him where he might want to go.

The Soviet Union, she had said so easily, as though her mind was already there, the words lingering, waiting to be said, and all he had to do was ask the question and they'd tumble from her mouth like rain that had long been yearned for. Ah, such was her carelessness. And perhaps because she had confessed her heart's desire so easily, Abram decided right then that if there was a place whose air he would never breathe, it was the Soviet Union.

The Existence of Things
as They Existed

The chaos of having one's life upturned is never entirely ended. Abram was sorry to discover this as the days wore on. The sequence of events was progressing rather quickly. It was disconcerting. Firstly, his children had to be taken out of school. This sorry business was entirely inspired by Alisa's panic. But when all was said and done, Abram couldn't rightfully resent her for this. In fact, he felt that he might need to be on her side.

This was how things started: their daughters attended a girls' school for their English education. Alisa was never happy about this from the start. But Abram had insisted, and she had conceded only because she wanted the girls to have friends apart from one another. Then she had complained about the sorry standard of things at the school, that the nuns were limited in their thinking, that the boys' school taught advanced mathematics and the sciences, that they dissected the classical languages and literary works more thoughtfully, more reliably, and so on.

How Alisa knew what was being taught at the boys' school, she never said to Abram, and he never wasted his time with asking. The key point was this: more needed to be done for their daughters. As Abram understood it, he was meant to be doing this "more" that she wanted. "Yes, yes," he nodded. "Things could be better."

"Dido is a precocious child," Alisa had said. Dido was their eldest. "The things she says sometimes, Bram, she's far too clever for that place. The school isn't enough for her."

There, the ordeal couldn't be helped. Dido *was* rather clever, but she couldn't very well go to the boys' school. And so, through the years Abram had been forced to listen to Alisa as she lamented the sorry state of things at the school, the uselessness of it all—and, by extension and more importantly, his own uselessness in the matter.

Abram missed Alisa's old complaints, for he now realised they used to be far more mundane. Her disdain had evolved. But again, he was obligated to be on her side.

Yesterday their daughters had come home early. With them was a letter that summoned Abram to the school. When he got there, he was told by Sister Elizabeth, the headmistress, that a rather strange thing had happened. A man from the House of Assembly had come to the school and asked to be shown the Van Zijl girls. "We thought it might be for Dido," Sister Elizabeth had said. "I've been meaning to tell you—we'd thought of running a trial with our companions at the boys' school, you see."

"As you know, the university's done it and it's not ended badly for those women. Sister Alice and I thought we'd do it for our girls. Oh, don't worry, it wouldn't be anything scandalous. The girls would still take their classes here. But we'd thought of getting a teacher for more advanced mathematics . . . just five girls. Dido's so bright, we'd thought of including her, you see. I thought that might be it, Mr. Van Zijl. But it wasn't. Oh, it wasn't."

Sister Elizabeth had sighed and pulled her habit closer about her. Then she had relayed the strange happening: the assemblyman had wanted simply to see Abram's daughters. "That was all," she had said. "I don't imagine myself a frivolous woman, Mr. Van Zijl. I'm old, I'm impatient with trivial things, you see. But this wasn't a trivial thing. I don't mean to alarm you, but I didn't like the look of that man. I'd thought not to mention it, for fear of needlessly alarming you. But strange laws are being passed, I hear, and small things aren't small things these days."

"A man was sent to their school, Bram," said Alisa, the panic and sorrow of her voice disrupting the memory.

It had rained in the night, and in the sky, there were still clouds lingering as if unsure of whether to shake off their burden or pass on. It was dark and cold and not a day to be sitting under a tree. So naturally, that was just the thing Alisa had chosen to do.

"I know," said Abram. "But the air is cold. Please come inside. We can talk there." He didn't look at her as he spoke. Instead, he tried to distract himself with the nothingness of the world, the existence of things as they existed—the pungency of the salt and sulphur of the wailing sea, the flashing bolt of lightning that suddenly split the sky. Thunder, being a faithful crony, soon followed with a resounding clap.

Abram was a man very easily carried by winds. Winds of

existentialism, winds somewhat unreal, proverbial winds of the times and change and other truisms—these were things that easily lifted him into private instances of revolution and, sometimes, entanglements he had no business entangling himself in. Lately he was carried by that wind of hope that started blowing on the 29th of March. A gale it was, a steady gale that wouldn't die, or couldn't, for he couldn't quite unlove Alisa. Just then her face was soft with longing, and her head slanted to follow the breeze.

Abram pointed to where lightning had split the gloom of early evening; it was such a rare thing in this part of the world. He couldn't help but smile. He couldn't help but say: "Do you want to go back to the Indies? We can leave if you want. We can stay if that's what you want. But for now, please come inside." He knelt at her feet, took her hands in his and kissed them. "I'm tired of fighting, Alisa. Please. I am one man. If nothing else, can you not forgive me that?"

She didn't meet his eyes. She looked into the distance as though, in the fabric of the world, she could see a secret that was denied to him by his stubbornness. Plunged into solemnity as she was, it was to that distance she spoke. She sighed. She did so deeply, as though, if she could, she would sigh him away. But she chose not to, and so Abram teetered as if at the edge of a storm.

Losing her patience, she promptly delved into familiar things. "These are not easy things to say, Bram. You think me your enemy for saying them. I don't want to burden you. And I don't want you to hate me."

So strong and steady was the gale sweeping him that Abram kissed Alisa's hands again. "You don't burden me," he said. "I don't hate you. I love you. You know I do. Now please, Alisa, come inside." Finally, she took his hand and followed him to the house.

. . .

It was noon when the man named Daniel Ross zoomed through the gate. The clouds had relieved themselves of only the lightest of their load, which fizzled with little protest when the sun decided the sky might be worthy to carry its full might, after all. Tired of their effort, which had seemed so basic to Abram but was apparently labourious to the clouds, they quickly scattered, perhaps in shame.

Such was the indecisiveness of the weather in this place. The sky never committed itself too seriously to a stance one way or the other. If the sun became lazy or unwilling or shy to shine, the sky yielded; it quickly summoned such gloomy things as rain. If the sun became selfish and demanded complete attention, the sky yielded, still. Like Abram, the Cape was a place that was easily carried by the winds and other such truisms.

And so, it was a bright hot noon when the man named Daniel Ross zoomed through the gate. His car, black, turned up enough dust to shroud him in mystery for several moments after he alighted. When the dust had settled, the man was revealed to be short and thickset, and clothed in a brown woollen suit with a neat hat to match it.

In a twist of irony, the dust had clung to him. He was thus preoccupied with beating that dust out of his suit. When the chore was done, he set off to the manor.

Abram received him in the library, where the man with the brown suit vehemently insisted on standing, because, as he said loudly and often, "I won't be staying long. No, no! Not long at all."

They descended into an embroidery of greetings and pleasantries, during which the man declared himself as Daniel Ross, an officer of the House of Assembly.

"But you know, Mr. Van Zijl," said the man, "we're only making sure everything is all right. I go around the estates, the farms and wineries and all that. I go around to check business and such. That is all." He flung his hands this way and that and winked, and wagged his finger like an old friend telling a private joke. "That is all."

Feeling that he was expected to smile, Abram did so. "I understand," he said.

Daniel Ross placed his hands over his heart, and with a face conveying sympathy, went on. "If we don't do this kind of thing, things fall apart, eh. There's been trouble up in the north, up in the Transvaal. Troublesome place it is, the north. People doing as they please. You know they found a native with more money in his bank than all the white men there. Just nonsense, Mr. Van Zijl. Nonsense! The sort of thing that needs to be cut out, eh."

"Of course," nodded Abram.

"I'll be needing to see the rest of the house, eh. The cellar, the yards, not much, really. I'll just need to see everything. I won't take too much of your time, no time at all and I'll be gone." The man carried on into further inanities and contradictions that, when all was said and done, said one thing: the Van Zijl Estate was being surveyed, possibly for seizure by the government. If not that, then something worse, and there, Abram allowed his imagination to hover blankly. "But I'm a citizen," he said at last, interrupting Mr. Ross.

Mr. Ross nodded, as though he had expected just this sort of trouble, having seen it before. "Ah, but you see, sir," he said, "it's like I said: we like to make sure everything is up to scratch—" Before Abram could interrupt again, the man was immersed in another soliloquy. This time, he held up his hand to indicate that he didn't want to be interrupted. "I take it Mrs. Van Zijl is here, eh? The children too. How many is that, two daughters? No son yet, eh, and Mrs. Van Zijl not in her prime? No heir. A shame, really. A tragedy."

He swept the room with his eyes, Daniel Ross, often lingering on the cabinet of antiquities where, from behind glass, a seventeenth-century map of the known world loomed over a clutter of sundials, coins, and other souvenirs Abram had collected in the places he'd visited. Near it was the cabinet supporting the tattered stacks of newspapers, journals, letters, and other documents he had discreetly liberated from his father's library. Most of the more personal of these belonged to long-dead seafarers, some to men who fought in the Great War, and a few to the rare literate ancestors of slaves once bound to the Constantia Valley.

Abram himself sat in an oaken chair opposite these. Over him and all around loomed Alisa's Greek and Latin classics, tomes and plays and novels of the Haitian Revolution, the Russian Revolution, histories of the British Colonies, and the like. He realised that the library was his only in name. Alisa had filled it with pieces of herself, and banished him to the mere two cabinets he sat facing.

Was that the reason Daniel Ross flicked his eyes there? The

rest of the library was a neat set of spines that boldly told the story of the world; yet there, in a corner that never caught light from the window, crouched an assortment so feeble and decrepit that it seemed ashamed to confess the stories it might know. Was his estrangement from Alisa so apparent that an unpractised stranger could identify the symptoms with a mere glance?

And this talk of the lack of an heir—were the old rumours rising again? Out beyond their taciturn peace, somewhere in the past, unkind things had been whispered about Alisa. She had, of course, brought the entire thing on herself. For being her husband, Abram was naturally dragged into the ordeal. More precisely, his manhood was put on trial, and it was decided that it must be lacking. Why else would his wife—though she was of native blood—stray so far from morality?

Now here was Daniel Ross, a man apparently sent by the Province to unfurl these pasts best left behind—to unravel Abram's tragedies, to tally and trade them back to the Province, for, like his soul, a man's peace could be sold. The man could decide whether he wanted it sold to another or himself, but it could be sold nonetheless.

Abram's mind fumbled through several things all at once. Firstly, had Daniel Ross asked rhetorical questions, or did he want answers? Secondly, could Abram lie or hide what he chose? This led him to a unique conundrum: precisely what details of his life did Daniel Ross know? What did he know about Alisa and the children? What did he assume? And more importantly, what could be saved, what could not?

Abram was unsettled by what was unfolding. It was clear that something had gone terribly awry and worse things would follow. He felt, for a moment, that he couldn't breathe. He felt that he was racing against something he didn't quite understand, and he couldn't breathe.

· · ·

At that same moment Alisa was being told by Gloria, the children's nanny, that a man from the House of Assembly was in the library with her husband.

"What does he want?" she asked. Gloria didn't know, and said as much. "What did the man say?" continued Alisa.

Gloria said, "He greeted me. He asked for the *baas*. The *baas* greeted him and took him to the library."

Alisa had been reading *Oliver Twist; or, The Parish Boy's Progress* to her daughters. They sat near the pond, where, as a symptom of autumn, the ducks congregated to siphon off the last sunrays, preventing them sifting uselessly into the passing wind. There were voices in the distance, not quite choral, but there and calming. The farm workers sometimes sang to pass time, to siphon some of their toil off to the passing wind.

When Gloria came running to the tree to speak of the assemblyman, the near-chorus scattered itself into a booming discord—a violent invasion of Alisa's senses.

Quickly, she stood up. She had nearly reached the manor threshold when she realised the absurdity and abruptness of this chaotic sequence. She turned back to Gloria, who still stood stunned near the pond. She said, "Please take the children to my room. Keep them there." Then she resumed her panic and fled to the library.

· · ·

Gloria took the children by the hand to lead them to the far quarter of the manor, the eastern, their mother's refuge. "Here," she said, leading them to their mother's bed, "I'll go to the kitchen to get cake for you. Dido, my child, look after your sister. I'll be back now-now. Look after your sister, heh?" She nodded, and Dido nodded too. "Don't leave the room, heh." Again, Gloria nodded, and so did Dido.

As soon as Gloria locked the room, Emilia, who was the younger of Abram and Alisa's daughters, promptly succumbed to tears. Dido was the elder by a mere two years—yet still, it fell to her to take Emilia's hand and chide: "Oh, Emilia, why are you crying?"

"Mama was crying," said Emilia.

Dido was still a child herself. It was a habit between the girls that when one cried the other would soon follow. "No, she wasn't," said Dido.

"Yes, she was. I think a bad man's come, Dido. Mama wouldn't cry."

"There's no bad man here. Come." She hugged her sister as they waited for the door to open, for Nanny Gloria to bring them cake.

. . .

When she dashed into the library, Abram was forced to exit his reverie, his wallowing. The race, it seemed, was escalating; it seemed it had entered a second phase.

"Ah, good!" said Mr. Ross. "I'm so glad to meet you, Mrs. Van Zijl. Ah, I forgot to say, eh. I forgot to say but remember, Mr. Van Zijl, remember the funny business that's been happening in the

Transvaal? All sorts of things up there. All sorts! You know men and women have been caught living in sin? Respectable men at that, eh. Good men, living in sin! We can't have that. No, no! We can't have that. I forgot to say but I'll need to see the marriage certificate, eh. Not much, just proof of the marriage. Simple matter, really. Simple matter. Just to keep things right, eh."

Before Abram or Alisa could speak, Daniel Ross had apparently remembered something else. Again, he flicked his hands and wagged his finger. "You know they found a man who did this sort of thing, eh. Lived with a girl. Native, the girl was, of course. No shame, no shame at all. The magistrate called him up and right there, he goes up and says he wants to marry the girl. But ah, says the magistrate, that kind of thing isn't right, eh. A sin can't be taken back. No, no! The crime was done. That sort of thing can't be taken back. The crime was done. You take my meaning, Mr. Van Zijl?"

Abram took his meaning well enough, and judging from the way Alisa's lips trembled ever so slightly, right there at the corner, she took his meaning too.

"Anyhow," said Daniel Ross, clapping his hands, "we need to be done with the business of the, eh . . . I suppose it's right to call it a survey. No? Yes, yes, let's call it a survey of the estate. That sounds right. Sounds right to me."

As simply as that, the wool of foolishness was clawed from Abram's eyes. Ah, how quickly it all happened. By the time the sun set and rose again, all his hope was gone.

PART TWO

The Gift of Bonds for These Orphan People

And Weeds Sprouted
in Disarray

Dido's mother never truly smiled—not freely, and not merrily. She liked to sit under the weeping willow and write in her journal. If not the journal, then endless letters to Grandmother and Grandfather, both of whom lived across the Atlantic Ocean, all the way in England. And if not that, then she simply sat under the tree as though guarding it.

Her skin shimmered in the stream of midday sunlight, which scattered into a kaleidoscope of colours that danced on her skin—scattering and mixing and dissolving again, then quickly folding back into her dark complexion. The sunrays moved through the tree canopy like raindrops, touching here but not there, over there but not here; then the branches fluttered and the light shifted as well, painting her mother in sunlight and darkness, illuminating her pallid dress, her hat, and even her solemn eyes—smoothly drifting across her like a wave.

She rested her head on the tree trunk, stretched her legs, and closed her eyes as though in prayer. She looked at peace then, almost smiling. The falling leaves fluttered around her reverently, like acolytes—floating in the breeze until at last they touched the ground in obedience. Some settled on her shoulders and some on her head, all of them gently, leisurely, like birds in a trance.

Summer was newly departed, gone with the moon. The turn of autumn had turned the leaves golden, and their hue made her mother seem a queen.

Dido liked to sit behind the kanferboom tree and watch her mother, taking care to go unnoticed. When the omnipresent Emilia promised to be quiet, Dido allowed her to join her under the kanferboom in this strange vigil. It was a dull thing, and much too often, Emilia broke her promise and complained of the boredom. "This is no fun," she said. "Let's play a game."

The break in Dido's focus was like falling in a dream; it woke her too suddenly. "In a moment," she said.

"The sun will set soon," protested Emilia.

"There is still tomorrow."

"But I don't want to play tomorrow," said Emilia. "Pleeease." She stretched the word, further bending it with the whistling lisp born of her missing teeth, and ending on a high inflection that, ever since she lost those teeth, had become typical of her speech. "I promise I won't want to play tomorrow," she said. "We'll do whatever you want."

"Anything?"

"Well, let me see—"

"Because that's the only way I'm leaving this tree to play with you."

"Okay, okay," said Emilia. "But last time you wanted us to catch a bird. That was only fun at first. This time we have to do something I can do too." Her eyes squinted when she emphasised her words, and her left foot rose and fell in a rhythm. "You have to promise me that."

"But we can't know what you can do unless we try."

"I know I can't catch a bird, or swim the entire Breede River, or climb all the way to the top of the house. So we can't do those."

"I promise."

"Thank you," said Emilia, kneeling to kiss Dido on the cheek. Then she dropped her voice to a whisper, as if that was the thing to do once her knees touched the ground. "Do you think if we tried we could make it to the top of Table Mountain to see if Captain Van Hunks and the Devil are really there?"

"Just climbing the house made you tired—"

"Only because I knew Nanny Gloria was watching us!"

"She wasn't," said Dido. "You couldn't breathe and we had to climb down."

"If she didn't see then she would have seen later. My shoes were muddy—"

"And that was the reason I took mine off. Listen, it doesn't matter now. I don't think we can even make it to the foot of the mountain. We'll be in worse trouble than when we swam in the river."

"I only thought . . ." Emilia's words trailed into silence. Failing to think of an adventure unique, daring, and feasible, she slumped into herself, with her small, pretty face receding into sadness. She resembled their mother acutely at that moment—sombre, silent, and apparently serving at the foot of some wilting tree.

To calm her, Dido said: "I think when we're older, when I'm thirteen or so, we can ask for Father's permission."

"That's still . . ."

Emilia tried to do the sum in her head, but Dido completed it for her. "Four years away," she said.

"Do you promise to remember?"

"I promise to remember."

"Okay," agreed Emilia, her head bobbing up and down.

"What game do you want to play now?"

Emilia shrugged. "I don't know. I just want to play with you."

Dido smiled. She jumped out from under the tree and cried: "I bet you'll never catch me. Not today, not in a thousand years!"

Emilia sprang up in pursuit. It fell to Nanny Gloria, as it always did, to remind them to be careful. "Watch where you run!" she screamed, wagging her finger.

Their mother woke from her reverie to see the girls chasing one another like two mad people. She, too, shook her head, though only in mild disapproval. And seeing that Nanny Gloria kept watch over the girls, she muttered something Dido couldn't hear and closed her eyes again. Unaware of their mother's fleeting alertness, Emilia continued to shriek with glee. To maintain her sister's obliviousness, Dido ran west, away from the willow and towards the cellar and the ponds. The vines receded behind them and slowly the manor came into view; and to the east, a mist cloud danced around the Boland Mountains.

Dido skipped around Emilia like their mother's falling leaves. She veered right, and Emilia followed; then she turned left, and still Emilia followed, moving swiftly, nimbly, lifting her legs tirelessly, but still missing her sister's skirt by a heartbeat.

"You're cheating," protested Emilia. "You aren't meant to pretend to go one way and then move another."

Dido laughed. "You're meant to run faster," she said.

"Yes, but you're tricking me."

"Are you admitting I've defeated you?"

"No!"

"Then prove it."

"I will."

They resumed their dance with renewed zest; spiralling their way around the false olives, to the grey tree pincushion standing stunted near the manor. In summer, the huge flowers opened and the sunbirds chirped their thankfulness. Autumn had wilted that too.

As Dido ran and Emilia followed, their feet loosened the soil, and the grains were cast into the intermittent breeze wafting from the sea, then floated unto some foreign plain, slowly, in infinite sums. The breeze eroded their footprints. They stepped in new places, shuffled more sands. Around and around they went, until their dance led them to where the eastern gable of the manor rose to the sky. Then swiftly, for the path back sloped down, they returned their dance to the kanferboom tree.

It was there it ended. "I've caught you," declared Emilia, her hand pulling Dido's arm. "It didn't take a thousand years, not even a single day!"

"I let you catch me," said Dido.

"You always say that," said Emilia, "but I know it isn't true. If you chased me, I bet you'd need more than a thousand years to catch me." With that, she sprang away, towards their mother's willow tree. As Emilia ran, she laughed heartily, and Dido decided against ending the game.

Emilia stopped by the red alder and said, "See, if you don't catch me in the next minute, I win. There must be a reward for the winner."

Dido saw that their mother, unlikely to find quiet while the girls played, had woken up again. She had reopened her journal to continue her writing. Dido watched her carefully, forgetting that her sister waited for an answer. Just then, a gust much stronger than the breeze blew up the slopes, causing Mother's pages to flutter uncontrollably and her face to contort with annoyance.

"Dido," said Emilia. "Dido, did you hear me?"

"I did," said Dido, looking away from their mother. "But I don't think we should decide the reward now. I think we should do it after you lose."

"I'm not going to lose," said Emilia.

"We'll see."

Emilia laughed, and then their mother said to them: "Whoever wins can choose tonight's story. I was going to tell one of cannibals in a world beneath this one, of giants that feast on children, of witches and golems and all things foul. It's grim, I tell you, and you won't sleep a wink after hearing it. The fear alone will eat you, just as the giants would." She paused and shrugged. "I might decide against that until later, when you're older and not easily frightened. In the meantime, the winner can choose your stories for a week." Then, very strangely to Dido, her mother smiled most sweetly. "Do you accept?"

Emilia nodded profusely. "Will you let us have orange juice too? And sweets, and whatever else we think of later?"

"Agreed," said Mother. "Dido, do you agree as well?"

"Yes," said Dido.

"Before we start," said Emilia, "can I ask what you'll choose if you win, Dido?"

"The one with giants and witches and golems and all things foul, of course."

Emilia looked at the sky, her hands folded behind her back and her forehead wrinkled in great thought. Satisfied with her decision, she said: "I was going to let you win. I don't think I'll do that now. I don't want to hear about cannibal giants."

"It's not cannibalism when giants eat children," countered Dido.

"Giants are people. Big people. But they're people."

"No, they're not. They're giants."

"Ma," said Emilia, turning to their mother, "aren't giants people?"

Their mother shrugged. "Who knows? All I can say is this: if Dido wins, I might have the answer. If she loses, however"—she shrugged again—"well, we might never know."

"I'm curious," said Emilia, "but also frightened."

"Do we have it, then?" said Dido to Emilia. "Are you going to *let* me win?"

"We'll see," retorted Emilia, restarting her sprint. Like before, she laughed as she ran. She darted through the trees as nimbly as a squirrel, swishing from the assegai to the willow tree, to the red alder, then to the gulley where proteas, fynbos, keurboom, and weeds sprouted in disarray; then past that and all the way to the vineyard, where the slopes rose and fell seamlessly, and the yellows and browns and golds of autumn endlessly painted the fields.

The ribbons in Emilia's hair came loose and departed with the wind, her curls streaming wild behind her. Her laughter grew more hysterical. Then briefly, Dido heard her mother laughing as well. That was when she stopped her chase and looked back to the willow tree, where her mother stood, cheering and laughing.

"You're losing, Dido," said Emilia. "You're almost out of time."

"I know," she whispered to herself. "I don't care."

The hard part now lay in dodging Emilia for as long as possible, but without making her aware of the trick. And so, as she followed her sister, Dido took her time winding through the vines. Every once in a while they veered down the slopes, back in the direction of the willow, and Dido stole a glance at the tree to make sure her mother's glee wasn't a fantasy. Her heart leapt every time she found that it wasn't. Oh, how sweet it was to see, how happy her father would be when Dido told him about it. How happy he would be to know that Mother's sadness was healing again.

Dido knew it could end as abruptly as every time in the past. It would go around and around until the bitter silence returned, the way it always did. It would consume her mother—plunge her into a cloud of loneliness. It would all return, maybe more strongly, knew Dido. But that didn't matter just then; in that moment, her mother was happy.

Tale of the Swan Princess

With her head against the bedpost and her legs tucked beneath the blankets, Mother flipped through the pages of her journal very tenderly. She narrated the tale of the Swan Princess and her exploits across the mythical nations of the moon.

Emilia sat to Mother's right, with her head rested on her bosom and her legs half on Mother's lap. Her thumb in her mouth and her arm linked to Mother's, she looked the picture of serenity. Dido had chosen the edge of the bed for herself. She crouched on her knees and elbows, holding her head in her clenched hands. She watched her mother with joy stomping the depths of her heart; listening, but without truly hearing. The candlelight, with the soft dance of its flame, painted her mother's face with a golden glow that swam over her, better illuminating her improved temper. This was the thirteenth telling of the tale that Dido had endured.

Her mother narrated: "When she found the tribes of the black deserts, she saw they were a gentle people. They said to the Swan Princess: 'Bring you more wars to our people, new traveller? Bring you more thieves to steal our treasures?' The princess kneeled before the chief in penance.

"She said to him: 'I bring no wars, great chief, no thieves and new calamities to plague your people. I am a life seeker. I seek forgiveness for the crimes of those who came before me. I beg you heed my tidings. I beg you grant me passage across the river.' That was how—" Seeing that Emilia, who had drunk three glasses of orange juice, had fallen asleep from fullness, their mother stopped her narration.

"Your sister has given in to her tiredness," she said. "Are you sure you don't want more juice, Dido?" As she spoke, she yawned from her own tiredness.

"No, thank you," said Dido.

"Right," said her mother. She then looked at Dido strangely, with concern, it seemed. Dido grew shy from the stare and looked away. Her mother leaned forwards and gently raised Dido's chin to face her. "You're most like me," she said, "more than your sister. You've inherited my melancholy. Nothing escapes your eyes. You dwell too much in your memories, be they good or not. I had hoped differently. I hoped you would belong here. But alas, here we are."

Dido looked at her mother and saw that the joy of mere moments before had dissipated. In its place had settled the familiar desolation that so diligently afflicted her. Dido cried; her father hadn't seen Mother's bliss for himself. He wouldn't believe her even if Emilia and Gloria said it too. Oh, how quickly the tide had turned, and how completely.

She felt tears fall unbidden, her eyes sting with pain, and her heart quicken with melancholy of her own. "I'm sorry, Mama," she said. "I didn't mean to make you sad. I'll drink more orange juice. I don't mean to be rude. I never meant to—"

Her mother shook her head and patted her lap for Dido to sit. Then she wiped Dido's tears and hugged her. "You've brought me joy, Dido," she said. "You've loved me. I have loved you. And for a while, I was worthy of you. This is not what I wanted to be. Please believe me."

Dido couldn't speak if she tried. Her throat, now only capable of breathing and producing a small wail, could barely be relied on to say to her mother, *Please don't be sad again.* In the end all she could do, all that she did, was snuggle against her mother's chest and try to catch her breath.

"There you go, my darling," said her mother. "Rest now."

Dido nodded into her mother's chest and tried blinking the tears from her eyes.

There was a painting on the wall. It showed a large hut fenced from the rest of its world by an uneven, wooden *kraal*. Near the hut was a file of a dozen young men who, except for the strings of beads crossing their torsos and the cowhide concealing their privates, were entirely nude. Their skin was red from being adorned with a ritual balm called *leszoghu* by Nanny Gloria. Their heads were bowed, and their hands clasped as if to help where the cowhide guarding their dignity might fail. Another young man, more heavily clothed than his red companions, led the file with an ornate fighting club raised to the sky, challenging anyone who dared confront his charges.

That leader had been caught in song, thought Dido. His vacant eyes seemed indifferent to what lay ahead and instead simply gazed beyond the canvas in eternal stoicism—his riddling thoughts forever trapped by the painter's brush. Bringing up the rear was another similarly dressed young man. He too was caught in a song that couldn't be heard.

Dido had once asked her mother about those red young men. They were Nanny Gloria's people. They were newly returned from the mountains, where, in the heart of the coldest winter of their generation, they were taught the ways of men. As Nanny Gloria told it, the song sung by the keepers was a secret spell of sorts. It was a sacred rite inherited by virtue of manhood, a promise of courage and love, cast into time and space and all the things of the world.

Dido's tears dried as she admired the art. Her eyes slowly closed and her thoughts wove stories about the red young men. Had she been the painter, she might have lifted the men's heads to show their faces. She might have painted happiness into their eyes, hope and pride too; for what else could they feel upon achieving that prized gift of adulthood?

Her young men would know every mystery about their people and any people that lived. One day, years and years away, another child would look upon those gleeful faces and think, *Only a wise painter could free her children from the brush.* Dido felt herself smile at the thought. But she couldn't be sure. Her mind drifted in and out of oblivion. Did she see the red young men, or did she dream them?

The fantasy of the young child—she of years and years away—swam in and out of her mind, again and again, morphing in and out of the dreams that deeply lulled Dido into the comfort of her mother's hands. Bit by bit, Dido swallowed away the hiccoughs that had risen from her sobs. "Okay, Mama," she whispered. Soon, without meaning to do so, she fell into a deep sleep.

. . .

It was the smoke that woke Dido. The smell of it made her lungs and eyes burn even worse than poison ivy. The heat of the flames made her skin sweat, and try as she could, she couldn't call to her mother and Emilia. She coughed and coughed until she thought she had surely died from all the burning and coughing.

Her blood felt like it was leaving her body; and her head, it didn't feel like it belonged to her. It was heavy on her shoulders, the same way her body was growing too heavy for her to lift off the bed. She tried to scream, to call out, but her mouth only produced another bout of violent coughing. She opened her eyes to find her mother and sister, to rouse them with her hands.

Everything in the room was on fire. Even the red young men had turned to ash. All that remained was the golden frame that once held them in place. For a moment in the unending nightmare, it had seemed as though Emilia and her mother were afire as well. Dido blinked and opened her eyes anew. Her heart leapt to see that her imagination had tricked her. There they lay, whole and unburnt.

Although they both looked as still as the dead cat she and Emilia once found near the river, they were not as red as the flames and embers and the thatch in the roof and the bedpost and curtains and falling ashes and everything else that burned.

It was then that her mother coughed and Dido saw blood lining her lips. She opened her eyes, briefly and painfully, and in them Dido saw a ghastly plea that frightened her. There was no doubt then, looking at the stillness of those eyes, that her mother was stricken by pain more severe than her usual anguish. She was dying.

"We're burning," said Dido, hoping to frighten her mother out of the stupor that so mercilessly arrested her. In response, her mother closed her eyes again. Try as she did, Dido couldn't reawaken her. In heightened fear, Dido returned to Emilia. She desperately tried to shake her sister back to life. "Please wake up, Emilia. We're burning," she repeated, through coughs and wheezes and torrents of tears drenching her face. "Please wake up," she pled. Emilia didn't stir.

It was another dream, felt Dido. It was all a horrid dream, and the drowsy sensation she felt was the proof. She hoped to tell her mother about it, once they all woke up.

Her eyes closed again. She tried to keep them open but it didn't matter. It was a dream, and when morning came they would all live again. It felt like her lungs stopped breathing.

The dream grew dimmer . . . fading into the depths of her mind . . . her mother's lips didn't bleed anymore. Emilia didn't lie still and the dream the dream the dream . . . it was a dream—

. . .

Someone . . . Dido wasn't sure, but someone somewhere was chopping her mother's door with something. An axe, yes. That someone also shouted and called for someone else, someone who was somewhere, somewhere doing something he wasn't sup-posed to be doing, something that wasn't supposed to be done just then. Her father's voice was there as well. He shouted the loudest to tell the many someones to do as *he* instructed.

There were too many voices, too many languages, and far too much creaking and breaking and crackling for any of it to make any sense to Dido. And someone somewhere . . . it sounded like Nanny Gloria but Dido wasn't sure of that either. But there Nanny Gloria was, among the men and doing what she wasn't supposed to be doing. She was screaming instructions of her own, crying, assuring Father of something, something Dido couldn't understand, and screaming some more, adding more confusion to the cacophony.

It must have been her father who carried Dido from the bed, she later realised. She tried to tell him about Mother's bleeding and Emilia's grave silence. But her head was heavy, and she felt like she was dreaming again.

The burning had finally stopped. That was good, she thought. There was no falling ash blinding her eyes and the acid in her lungs had become duller in her sleep. But somewhere on the periphery of her awareness, someone had lit a candle whose flame shadows danced the way her mother's candle had done.

The sight made her wish for the oblivion of moments before. At least there, in silence and darkness, she was not afraid of the spread of the fire and the roaring of the flames.

She thought she heard her father cry, scream, cry again, curse, scream, and cry some more. It was endless and grotesque. He was such a gentle soul, her father. To see him so upset was nearly as frightening as her mother's silent plea. Oh, how she wanted to beg that he stop. How she wanted to lift his sadness as well. But it was a dream and Dido still couldn't open her mouth. There was something stuck in her throat, not quite something . . . a feeling, a feeling. She couldn't open her mouth and the feeling made her want to cry again.

Finally, near the end of her wakefulness, her father whispered something to her. "Please wake up," she heard, she thought. In response, and just as she had done with her mother, Dido snuggled against him and drifted into oblivion.

Cinder and Sludge

There was an hour near dawn that was colder than any other. The sky was black with night and the night silent as the grave. If a man found the patience to endure that hour and mark the majestic birth of the sun, he would be rewarded with other splendours too. The flurry of life as it filled the world was like an orchestra. The roosters led the symphony, heralding the waking of things as the darkness of night lifted away.

Other birds took the call and spread their wings. The chill of the air scattered with the mists. In summer, the colours of mountains and fields and people bloomed anew; and in winter, it was the colours of seas and deserts that did so. They were birthed again like the sun, generously gifted to that patient man who endured the cold hour of dawn.

When Abram was still a man drunk with love and heartened by youth, he travelled to every place his wife wanted to visit. They went north to greet the tribes near the border of Southern

Rhodesia; then farther north, to places across the edge of the Sahara, where desert people drove their caravans to greener pastures eternally elusive. He travelled even to the colony of India, to every place she desired and every one that would receive her. That cold hour, when a man might ponder, with grief, the failures and achievements of his life, was, as far as Abram could conclude, common to every place. It was for the second time in that week that, at that precise hour, he sat on his bed and made a reckoning of all he had achieved. By his count, his failures far outweighed his victories.

The fire still raged outside. The men ran from the dam with pails to quench the flames, and so the flames raged with dying passion. A wind blew from the northwesterly direction. Abram had feared it would fan the fire and spread it from his wife's wing to the far side of the house, where he presently sat in both mourning and guardianship. It had not. Instead, the gust had beaten the rising flames to the ground, or so it had looked to Abram. The wind had fed the flames to excess and killed each of those that, in their excited dance, had threatened to escape their cradle and spread their destruction.

The wind had then departed, summoning drizzle from the sparse clouds that roamed above. Gloria had dared call it an intervention of the Ancestors, for it was not known for wind to kill fire, to summon rain from scant clouds, and to leave only the weak, infant-flames of a fire. Some of the men had nodded their agreement. Abram, on the other hand, had not.

"The papers you want couldn't be found, *Meneer*," said Gloria, entering the room and rousing Abram from his musings. "Every document in the east wing burnt. The fire seems to have started where Miss Alisa kept her papers."

He saw that her eyes, usually bright with joy, were red with grief and fatigue. The smoke had cloaked her in a blanket of soot. The sweat of the labour caused her dress to cling to her, and where her dress didn't reach—her arms and neck and face—that sweat shone like a balm of happier times. She had discarded her head-covering and allowed her coarse hair to become sprinkled with ash, dust, and all the symptoms of fire.

"Nothing was saved?" he asked, as always when he spoke with her, in tentative Afrikaans interrupted in places by Dutch. It made his speech stiff and all too formal for his liking, but it was the best he could do. And this wasn't the time to fret over language.

Gloria nodded. "What wasn't burnt was ruined by the water," she returned in fluent Afrikaans, which she was far more comfortable with than English, maybe because it was a kitchen language that had sprouted as slaves and servants adapted to their servitude. Out of need, innovation, and a dozen or so cultures, they'd brewed a language. They recognised parts of themselves in it. They were loyal to it. "Everything is gone. It all turned to cinder and sludge, *Meneer.*" Her words sounded like a memory, like the echo of a nightmare. Try as Abram did, he couldn't wake from it. "Will the fire spread?" he said.

"No, *Meneer,*" said Gloria. "The drizzle is turning into rain. It will cool the ash and stop that from spreading too. But if the rain doesn't come the men are prepared in other ways. There is water in the dam. Farouk and his shift will keep watch till dawn. Tariq and *his* men will take the guard from then on."

"Thank you, Gloria."

"There was no trouble to it," she said.

"No trouble," Abram repeated to himself, shaking his head in a futile attempt to clear his thoughts. "Gloria, do you think I am the villain of this tragedy?"

Gloria looked at him as though waiting for more to be said. When that did not happen, she took two paces, stopped at a distance she judged to be appropriate, and said: "I'm not sure I understand."

Abram said: "Here I sit, with one child and not another, guarding *her* and not the other. It is a simple thing. Yet, a grand declaration. I can assure you that my wife was not one to miss such slights. She wallowed in every crime committed against her, trivial and not, true or not. She saw it all and imagined it as momentous as the rising of the sun or the changing of the seasons.

"She saw me as the author of her misery. This, it seems, is the conclusion of her tale. I was the villain while she lived. It must then stand, by her elaborate calculation, that I am the villain even now. So I ask you: what do you think?"

"*Meneer*," said Gloria, "I don't think you are an evil man. In times such as these all men are tied at the hands. But where another might have broken from pain, you found courage to lift your daughter from flames. There she is now, alive. Such a man cannot be accused of villainy."

"To lift her from fire was an ordinary thing. It says nothing about my villainy, or lack of it."

When Gloria spoke, she gestured to Dido. Her eyes were filled with love and longing, as though *she* were his daughter's mother. Abram knew the pain he felt was in Gloria's heart too— pounding, pounding till all that remained were aching and remorse, remorse for crimes he was afraid he wouldn't fully grasp until the day he died.

She said: "When the child wakes up she will ask, 'Who saved

me from the burning that nearly stole me from this world? Who breathed life into my lungs?' We will say to the child: 'It was your father. He loves you beyond his own life.' These words will fill her with joy. There will be sadness when she is told the tale whole. But the joy will be there, etched in her heart.

"If that isn't a truth you want, then think of this: what good can it do to guard a daughter who is un-alive, while in the same moment another daughter lies tenderly tethered to the realm of the living, and tethered on the other side, to the spirit world? No good, I say. No good," she finished, shaking her head.

"That is what you believe?"

Gloria nodded. "That is what I believe. You don't trust my words?"

"I trust that you believe those words to be true. Whether they are, in fact, true, I must decide for myself."

Dido gave a soft cough. She was sprawled on her bed and bargaining for her life with whatever angel sought to steal her from him. Abram felt bile rise from deep within him. It rudely reawakened him and completely confirmed Alisa's wickedness. After relentlessly threatening to leave him to return to the West Indies, she had at last arrived at an irreversible decision. It couldn't be said that she was a determined woman. No. She had easily started projects that she just as easily abandoned. She had done everything else in her life half-heartedly. But in her death, she had been most thorough, achieving both flair and dramatics.

She first poisoned herself, it seemed. The blood lining her lips suggested as much. Then, taking inspiration from the tragedy of a fire that decimated the neighbouring Groot Constantia manor house two years before, she set the east wing of the house, which she had occupied since their estrangement, on fire, ensuring her death beyond all forms of resurrection. But like everything else in her life, she hadn't quite succeeded in what she set out to do; it seemed that the poison had killed her before the fire had a chance to touch her body.

One day Abram would be able to tell these things to Dido so that she might better grasp the circumstances of her near-death. But then again, she might not. She might instead realise his motives, and think of him as that which he feared more than anything else—the author of Alisa's misery. Alisa was never loved by anyone, not in her mind. To her the world was filled with foes designed by some malevolent deity who sought only to torment her. In the end she believed him to be that devil. Her sadness was born and nursed until, at last, she inflicted her cowardice on his daughters. Dido might inherit her mother's nature. She might believe herself unloved. She might hate Abram as Alisa did in the end.

He hesitated before saying his next words, for he was afraid that his grief was steering him into territories best left unmapped. But if a man can't be allowed moments of impropriety while in the cold clutches of grief, when can he? Thus, granting himself that forbidden boon, to allow himself the will to carry on, in desperation he said to Gloria: "Dido will know that I love her, won't she?"

Gloria plunged them further into indecency by placing her hand on his shoulder. Abram felt himself nod. He felt himself wipe a tear from his right eye. And he wished, even then, that he could have heard himself speak the word itself, but he found that he couldn't; so he nodded his own answer and hoped it was enough.

"She will," said Gloria. Abram was comforted by that. He wanted to be soaked in the fleeting reprieve Gloria offered, for fleeting it was, and perished it would be in the next moment. He sank deeper into helplessness. "Emilia—" As he said the name, tears fell from his eyes. His voice cracked before his courage could allow him to complete his thought. He hung his head and wiped those wretched tears.

Gloria had, by then, succumbed to tears of her own. Abram closed his eyes at that. He might have also said a prayer, he couldn't be sure. He had prayed only once in his life, when his mother neared her death. In the end she had died in what the doctor deemed a peaceful sleep. It seemed fitting that the senseless death of his youngest daughter, his sweet, gentle Emilia, be marked just as pointlessly.

Gloria, who had recovered from her helplessness more quickly, now gently elaborated the extent of his tragedy. Abram tried to listen, to record it faithfully; but with every morsel of strength he gave, his heart broke, his spirit left him, and the pounding pain returned to overwhelm him. If only he could reverse it. If only he could prove it was all a grotesque fantasy, he might breathe easy again. "Does Tariq still keep watch over Emilia?" he asked. Upon Gloria nodding, he added, "Please stay here with Dido. I must sit with Emilia now. I feel . . . I feel I must see her."

"Emilia must first be cleaned, *Meneer*," said Gloria. "Your hands must be rubbed with salt. You must not touch Emilia now, lest the omen of death follow you to your end."

"She's my daughter—"

"And no longer of this world, *Meneer*. Please bear that I speak with respect. You must not pay vigil to the dead child and return to the living one unprotected. If this thing you do, then the living child will also fall into misfortune."

"Then bring the bloody salt!" he shouted.

Gloria flinched from him. But being a professional woman,

she quickly masked her reaction. Stoically, she bowed to him, as though this ordeal remained respectable, and gracefully exited the room.

"And bring back the doctor!" he shouted at her back, yet just as quickly regretted his impatience. His failures were not hers to carry. And she had loved Emilia. Falling tears still marked the pain she felt. "Gloria," he called, hoping she was still near. "Please come back."

"Yes, *Meneer*?" she said, entering the room again.

"Thank you. You have been . . ." He tried to find a fitting word but felt as though his head were being pierced by a thousand knives. He sighed deeply and gave it another go: "You have been . . . to call you useful would cheapen your worth. But in this trying time, it is the only word remaining to my befuddled mind. Know that I say it only from fatigue. Were it a simpler time, I might be kinder to you, perhaps as kind as you have been to me."

She nodded. "There is no trouble to it, *Meneer*," she said.

"No trouble," he repeated to himself, shaking his head to clear his mind. That cold hour, when a man might ponder his life, was a plague Abram couldn't escape.

The sky was black with night, and the night silent as the grave. If he found the courage to endure that hour and mark the harsh birth of the sun, then he was sure to be tormented by the persistence of other trivialities: the flutter of life as it filled the world, that would not mark the death of his child. The roosters led the symphony, heralding the waking of lesser things as the darkness of night lifted away.

It was morning. And the pain still throbbed and throbbed and throbbed away.

A Clash of Contradictions

There was a hill beyond the vineyards that was the highest point on the estate. When he stood on it, Abram saw all around him—where the valley carved itself into hidden coves of shy breeds, flowers not named; where it unfurled again and stretched itself like a child finding life; where it yielded itself to the order of agriculture and toiled away as the vineyards, till it reached the cellar, then rose, terribly, as the half-charred remains of his home.

If he shaded his eyes and looked to the east, he saw shadows of the mountains where, once upon a time in the foothills, he had hunted eland. He'd taken Dido along. Emilia had been too young, too gentle, and the mountains so far. That seemed so long ago now. The hill itself felt like a phantom Abram couldn't quite grasp. It was like a sentinel—it saw everything and, save for the burnt house, everything around it was beautiful. It was a good place to lay a child to rest. Sadly, because the child was a child, it was a good place to lay her mother to rest too.

All the workers came. Save for Farouk and Gloria, none of them had been close to Alisa. But they all looked sombre and some cried. They mourned for Emilia, of course, for, as they lamented, the death of a child was an exceedingly unnatural thing.

However, as the service went on it became apparent from the way they spoke about her that despite the distance they had kept, they had nonetheless felt a form of kinship to Alisa. Most of them were descended from slaves, from the East Indies, India, Angola, and other far places they'd heard in the telling of stories. Sometimes the name of a place was all they knew. The somewhat more fortunate were those descended from the San, the Khoi, and the various Bantu tribes scattered in that corner of the world; they could at least estimate where the bones of their ancestors were buried, which seemed important to some of them.

Farouk, who had emerged as a leader of sorts for the Muslim field workers, asked Abram if those who could, would please say something about Alisa. How could Abram say no to this third defeat? Here were the children of slaves burying a child of slaves; even he, who believed in very little good about the world and found that he could, in fact, hate Alisa, couldn't deny this last obligation. He nodded his consent.

Father Benedict shook his head gravely. Abram took it to mean that he disapproved. But there was nothing regular about the whole affair. The letter sent to Alisa's parents was likely still on its way to England, and so they didn't know their daughter had died. Secondly, those in attendance were a ramshackle assortment: there was Sister Alice and Sister Elizabeth from the girls' school, the priest, the farm workers, Dr. Mason and his wife, and Abram himself.

Dido was ill. Although she was otherwise a healthy child, she'd taken in too much smoke, said Dr. Mason. She had bouts of coughing, a mild cold, and was therefore left in the surviving manor wing with Nurse Thomas. Abram didn't protest her absence. She was at least spared the ordeal of watching as the earth greedily swallowed Emilia. Emilia—who thought the sun went around the world, who had to be reminded the sun was a star and big and very far away, whose missing front teeth never grew back, whose lisp never faded with adulthood . . . Emilia, whom time, like the ground, had taken. "Oh!" was the cry that escaped Abram's mouth, was the cry that was swallowed by Hafsah's eulogy.

"Miss Alisa was a gentle soul," said Hafsah, one of the farm-hands. "If she saw a pretty flower she didn't know, Miss Alisa asked what it was called. If no one knew what the flower was called, she named it there and there." This was followed by subdued laughter. Hafsah herself wiped a tear on her cheek and sighed deeply. "First time she asked me about flowers I went and thought to myself, *Oh now, who goes around wasting time with flowers?*" Here, too, there was laughter. It was louder, merrier, and Hafsah conceded a smile.

"Oh," she continued, "I think Miss Alisa saw I wasn't the kind to waste time with flowers and she said, she looked at me and said right there and there, 'What do you know about the world that I don't, Hafsah?' First I thought she was being a snob, you know. I started to feel small because I thought she might have thought there wasn't much to me. She corrected me quick-quick. 'I'm not from here,' she said. But now I'm thinking she might have said something longer, you know, something fancier. You all know she liked to carry on with words, our Miss Alisa." There was a hum of agreement at this.

"Ah," continued Hafsah, "I taught her about the vines." She stood straighter as she said this, as though a surge of pride coursed through her. "Oh yes, it was me who taught her about the vines right there and there. I said to her, 'You know vines don't need bees to pollinate. They pollinate themselves most times.' Our Miss Alisa didn't know that. I was the first to tell her . . ." Here, Hafsah finally succumbed to her tears. She had to be taken back to her seat.

Samson spoke next. His story detailed Alisa's brief foray into grape tasting and sorting. She had apparently wanted to separate the very sweet grapes, usually reserved for eating, from the sourer kind, meant for winemaking. After only a week, she decided that all grapes were the same, that they tasted the same, and gave up the project.

Abram noted that Samson, too, spoke of "our Miss Alisa." When Farouk and Gloria and all the others followed, they also spoke of "our Miss Alisa." Each of the stories followed Hafsah's lead. They narrated some brief and merry adventure Alisa had undertaken—some fleeting history to be now remembered fondly, to induce shy, quiet laughter, then reduce the narrator to longing and, finally, to reluctant tears.

There settled something like shame at the root of Abram's heart. Although he was the bereaved to whom everyone looked when sparing their pity, he felt like an imposter too. He was relieved when the string of eulogies teetered somewhat, then steadily declined into a few mumbled utterances about Alisa's kindness and the general evilness of death. Father Benedict, with palpable relief, quickly progressed to the lowering of the coffins.

No one seemed to know what to say about the second soul being laid to rest. She was a child whom everyone met, loved; whom it was fair to say was loved more than Alisa. Such was the irony of death, that people found it harder to speak about her.

No one could say, *It was her time*, for it wasn't. She was killed by her mother. But to say the circumstances of her death would contradict Alisa's admirable whimsy, which had been narrated only moments before by the same people who must now renounce her. Emilia's passing could only be mourned incompletely, as though by some unfathomable twist of circumstance, she had simply died. No one and nothing had killed her. But there she was, being buried.

And so, as the eulogies teetered into depletion, Abram found that he was also relieved. It was fleeting, however. Now came the thing Abram was glad Dido didn't have to endure—the coffins' descent into the ground. Someone, likely Gloria, moved Abram's hand so it could fling soil onto the coffins. There was a thud and then many, then the thuds died as the gravediggers, who had seemingly materialised from nowhere, filled the graves. Then there was silence.

Then Abram had to remember to breathe. Then he had to remember to move. But he couldn't quite remember where he had to go, so he submitted himself to Gloria's guidance. Once he got to where he was supposed to be he didn't quite know how to go on being; he had to remember to breathe again, and wipe his tears, and say to Dido, "I'm here. I'm sorry. I love you." Such simple things these were, but he had to be guided to remember them.

. . .

Dido wanted to plant a tree behind the graves. She said the hill was too open to the sky, that in summer her mother and sister would need shade from the sun. Gloria thought it was a sweet thing to do and together they went about planting a weeping willow with a stem they took from Alisa's old tree. As Dido saw it, her mother had liked to rest under the tree when alive, and would therefore love to rest under it even in her death. Here, too, Abram was forced to concede.

The trouble was that weeping willows were notorious for their gluttony of water. There wasn't a river or lake near the hill. Quickly, Gloria volunteered to carry a bucket of water to nourish the thing, and every day, Dido followed behind with a meagre pail of her own to pour into the ground. She kneeled and brushed debris away. Pointing at an offshoot that was likely some breed of weed or grass, she said, "I think it's starting to come out."

"Yes, yes, we will see," said Gloria.

But that would have to wait, as here came Farouk, huffing and puffing his way up the hill. Abram wondered why a heavy man like Farouk would burden himself with running when clearly his legs were not meant for the sport. Before anyone could ask Farouk the reason, he wheezed the answer: "Man from Assembly . . . coming!"

He hunched over, hands on his knees and chest heaving, while everyone else tried to wrestle meaning out of what he'd just said. No one spoke, however, so Farouk was forced to catch his breath more swiftly, or, as evidenced by the gulps he took between words, make do without it for the meantime. He said,

"The assemblyman . . . the assemblyman who came before . . . to look around . . . the man . . . he's coming." He looked behind him and wheezed again, "He's here!"

Farouk's prophecy now conveyed, the man it concerned emerged. He rose, it seemed, like a summoned angel, or demon, all too suddenly over the horizon. He wore his brown woollen suit and neat hat, and walked so briskly that he seemed to be gliding. Abram decided he *must* be a demon. "Oh dear," howled the man, as he was still some distance away. "Oh dear! It's a walk from the house, isn't it? Oh, it's a walk, all right!"

Though he had a better time than Farouk of battling the hill, Daniel Ross was just as spent when he reached the top. The labour humbled him, for, much like Farouk, he was forced to take in his air in greedy gulps. And so it was that for the first time since Daniel Ross blackened the Van Zijl Estate with his presence, he was rendered completely speechless.

Everyone else was still too confused to speak, however, so Daniel Ross quickly recovered his pomposity. "A sorry business, this. A sorry business, eh. If I knew I would have waited for your boy to call you down. But oh, it couldn't be helped. No, no! It couldn't be helped at all. Time doesn't wait for an idling man, eh. Time is money, say the Americans!"

Gloria took the opportunity of a very transient instance of silence to signal to Farouk, and to say to Abram, "Might be about time for lunch, *Meneer*. I'll be taking Dido with me."

Not one to let a thing he hadn't examined and re-examined pass by without his input, Daniel Ross took his own transitory opportunity. "Ah, this must be one of your daughters, Mr. Van Zijl," he said. "Which one is she?"

Seeing as the episode was developing so quickly, with little of it making any sense to him, Abram chose that moment to reverse things and start the whole affair again. For his contribution to the madness, he chose a greeting. "Ah, Mr. Ross!" he said. "How are you this afternoon?"

Guffawing and shaking his head, Daniel Ross said, "Ah, Mr. Van Zijl, please forgive my rudeness. Ah yes, yes. These things sometimes happen. Busy man, you see. Busy man, eh. Never a moment to rest. Ah, not one. Please forgive my rudeness." The rudeness forgiven, he asked if Abram had heard of a man from the north who had gotten himself entangled in some unfortunate business.

"The man who got rung up by the magistrate for living with a native girl?" said Abram.

Daniel Ross confirmed that he was speaking of that very man. "He got himself in more trouble, eh," he said. "Oh, Mr. Van Zijl, we live in troubled times. Troubled times."

Farouk, Gloria, and Dido still stood where Daniel Ross had found them, arrested by the unfolding scene. It seemed he would not be the one to release them, for now when he spoke he looked at Dido. He looked at her like a man might look at a bird whose colours he'd never seen, or a cloud whose shape he wanted to morph into something else.

Suddenly, Daniel Ross smiled and returned his gaze to Abram. "I've always said it was lucky you had children, Mr. Van Zijl," he said. "Oh, so lucky. Ah, I think she'll want her lunch now, no? The maid said it. Now she'll only think of lunch."

"Make sure she finishes her food," Abram said to Gloria, and she, Dido, and Farouk hurried down the hill.

"You know when I was here in March you didn't bring me to this hill?" said Daniel Ross.

"Like you said, Mr. Ross, you're a man with much to do," said Abram.

"Ah, that *is* true. True enough." He nodded. He swept his gaze east and west and everywhere, shook his head, and sighed. He fanned himself with his hat, put his left hand in his pocket, and looked again at Abram. Before, he had smiled at Abram with the hint of a wink in his eyes, as though they both knew a secret that no one else did, as though a deep camaraderie existed between them, and there wasn't a need for words. But now, Abram saw that there was something else in that smile.

"You know the man up north, in the Transvaal," said Daniel Ross. "People living in sin, sir. You, yourself . . . oh! But I shouldn't say these things, eh. Vulgar things. Vulgar things, really. It's a lucky thing you have children. A very lucky thing, eh. You take my meaning, Mr. Van Zijl?"

Abram took his meaning well enough. This proverbial delinquent Daniel Ross spoke of, this unlucky man who seemed to be unnaturally tethered to the north, was, of course, entirely hypothetical, amalgamated by Daniel Ross from a collection of rumours and whispers carried south by winds and trains. This northerner man, he was designed to frighten Abram into a precise epiphany—for his crimes against the State, he had to surrender the estate or suffer something else.

The way Abram saw it, Daniel Ross was such a man as might say to a person, *Your mother has died*—with a smile, and without malice. It couldn't be easy to be such a man. That might have been the reason the veins of his face seemed to want to burst; that when he took his hat off, his hair stood on its ends as if, if it could, it would climb out of his head and into the sky. He seemed to always be covered in sweat. His words left his mouth too rapidly. His hands flapped about, and his eyes . . . when he looked at Abram, Abram imagined that every secret in his heart felt compelled to paint itself on his face, for it wanted to be seen by those eyes gazing at it.

One could be forgiven for thinking that he was a frivolous man, a fool. But that would be a gross lapse in judgement. There was nothing frivolous or foolish about Daniel Ross. Abram now realised that everything was deliberate. Mr. Ross hadn't worn the same suit because he didn't have another, he'd done so because he imagined himself to be a rather memorable character in some great unfolding saga. One day when he told the story of how he'd done a hard job for the House of Assembly, he wanted to remember the precise details, then decide whether to bend them with poetry and imagination, or shroud them in ominous hypotheticals.

Abram imagined that if his own story was ever told back to him by Daniel Ross, he wouldn't recognise the details of his own life. In fact, he imagined the story would feature a man who lived in Mr. Ross's favoured, notorious north and dabbled in several acts of recklessness. This northern depravity would unfold until, suddenly, Mr. Ross was called to put a stop to it. He was a man living out a fate he intended to see to the end, Daniel Ross. At least, that was what Abram, in irritation, concluded.

With all that said, the second reason for the suit was what troubled Abram. It was simple and sinister enough, and it was this: the deliberate man that he was, Mr. Ross *wanted* to be thought of as a frivolous fool. It couldn't be a coincidence that he repeated everything he said ad nauseum. His greetings, an opponent's name, mundane details of things—he recited them over and over. And so, when he repeated something as kindly as, *It's a lucky thing you have children*, to drive his point home, he had to say, too, *You take my meaning?*

And this was his meaning: if Abram didn't quietly surrender his estate, his punishment could be worse than imprisonment. His manhood, once put on trial and judged to be lacking, was now being sentenced so as to complete the trial. By the Union of South Africa's account of things, it could be said that Alisa van Zijl was guilty of certain indiscretions. It could further be said from this that Abram had fathered no children from her. Further still, it could be decided that given his deviance, he couldn't be trusted to father children from any woman.

The threat was whispered at first. Rumours that on Robben Island, men's manhoods were taken from them; they were shocked with electricity or cut away. No, whispered someone else, the place was up north, where the problem of racial mis-cegenation was rampant. In Pretoria, that was how the Union hoped to keep the Transvaal in line. Oh no, said someone new. The place was unknown, completely secret. In the end it didn't matter where "the place" was. What mattered was that the Union wouldn't take the contravention of its laws lightly.

"My daughter is a citizen," said Abram, desperation prompting him to bravery. "She was born here. She belongs here." His lips might have trembled, he would never know. What he knew, what he would remember, was this: the old race that started when he first met Daniel Ross was headed here. It was clear to Abram that there was no escaping it. So all he could do in the end was say a thing that now, as he looked at Daniel Ross's widening smile, he began to doubt. "Both my daughters were born here," he said. "They both belong here."

"Oh yes, Mr. Van Zijl," said the other man, "I'm sure they were born here. I'm sure you'll say that. I'm sure you'll say that, eh. This isn't a simple matter, though. A small thing to you. A small thing, eh, but that isn't how things are done. You know this, Mr. Van Zijl." The truth was Abram did know this.

By the Union's account of things, Abram's tragedy had unfolded entirely as a result of his own recklessness. For its part, the Union had tried to prevent this. The four colonies, now provinces of one country, had merged with a clash of contradictions that would surely muddle governance. For instance, only civil men could be citizens; only *they* were granted the franchise for government and matters of administration. Further, all white men, by virtue of their race and gender, were civilised. This was true enough in the northern provinces.

The Cape and Natal were troublesome, however. Here, any man, whether white, coloured, or native, so long as he owned or rented property, could sign his name, and earned fifty pounds in a year, could be trusted with the responsibility of a vote. In short, any person, so long as he was a man, could acquire civility and thus citizenship. This was all well and good, but the trouble came when African men started to migrate in droves to work in the farms and cities. They threatened to overwhelm the voting franchise and reduce white men to a minority. *This* was a simple problem that could be solved by raising such requirements as the yearly earnings of a potential voter.

But here the Union was faced with the uncomfortable issue of the poor white population. It reasoned that poor white men tended to be unemployed, without property, and idle; as a consequence of the last trait, this class easily fell into temptations of crime and other immoral acts. They were content to settle as the economic and social equals of the vast majority of Africans, freely mingling with natives and other races. This became so ingrained in their character, so irreversible, that ultimately, it was inherited by their children. Thus the confines of civility were blurred. Poor white men couldn't be trusted to live like white men. Put simply, they were the enemy within.

Women were a problem too, especially white women, regardless of class. They organised themselves in factions that deviated from each other along the lines of religion, marital status, or language, or a combination of all three. They were unreasonably numerous and diverse, which ensured that even if a woman didn't agree strongly with one group or their dogma, she would surely identify with the next. And although on the surface the factions seemed to clash, they were, in fact, united in one thing—white women, too, wanted the vote.

They were a persistent pestilence for the Union, but the Union figured that it needed to deal with one annoyance at a time, and the annoyance of poor white men was a rather immediate one. It would see to the women later, for theirs was a frivolous cause that could be easily appeased.

It was thus concluded, after much debate, that the only way to remedy the issue of poor whites was to simply disenfranchise African men as a whole, regardless of class, and at the same time raise poor white men to a respectable standard of living. It could, of course, be argued that to revoke the vote from African men would remove their incentive to better themselves, for if not afforded a say in government, how might they lift themselves above the disadvantages of their race? But for the Union to survive, it had to be done. The rules had to be absolute.

That was Abram's crime: the Union had bent its laws too far for too long to untangle several such contradictions from each other.

Yet here Abram was, introducing another complexity. He had flouted the natural responsibility bestowed to him by his race, gender, and class. He had flouted civility, morality. The Union was kind enough to indict him unambiguously in this regard; immorality was his crime, and so the Immorality Act cornered him.

Even he had to admit it was an elegant web that caught him. There was nothing personal about it, nothing petty. It was only a symptom of a changing world. There was nothing left to be said. He had to bow out. What was left for him was to sort out his life and at least try to escape. The thirtieth of September, which was when the Immorality Act would take effect, was just five months away. All in all, there wasn't much time for this planned escape.

And She Was Un-human

There were those who thought the affair of Alisa's death tragic. Abram saw reason in select aspects of the argument: his surviving child was motherless, and the only proof of her legitimacy (and of her birth) had burnt to ashes. He had searched through the documents remaining in his wing, and even in the dregs of his wife's refuge. He found only those cursed ashes. It seemed like the wind carried them everywhere. The very blood of his veins was polluted by those ashes. Once the fire died completely, Gloria once again sieved through the cinder and sludge, only to reap the same harvest. As far as Abram could tell, Alisa had fully intended to erase all proof of Dido's and Emilia's lives, as though she wished to deny him his daughters even in their deaths.

Yes, Abram saw reason in aspects of the argument. It was just the last aspect he could not reckon a tragedy—Alisa's death itself. He found that he could neither mourn nor forgive it, not while the several consequences of her selfishness continued to reveal themselves with such severity.

"Time will take the pain, *Meneer*," said Gloria, unceremoniously releasing him from the solitude of his thoughts. He raised his head to find her standing mere paces away. He hadn't heard her footsteps when she walked to him; such things slipped his notice easily. He had become prone to brooding. Yet there she was, as though she had materialised from the fabric of the world, as though her short legs hadn't carried her there, and she was un-human.

Trees and Birds and Ships and Shadows

Mmakoma (or Gloria, as she was called by the white people) had long found that the trouble with raising another woman's children was that you couldn't do it properly.

She had tried it for too many years, see. Although, truth be told, she should have known the whole thing would unravel when she realised that the father of the children believed in nothing and the mother had been severed from her people even before she was born. At least with white-white children, the parents believed in the Bible-god, who had to be appeased every week on a specific day. The things Mmakoma saw in white people's houses, ah, they were unbelievable. But she supposed that even a Bible-god was something, he was better than nothing.

The trouble, as she reverted to her dilemma, was in the raising of children you didn't carry or birth or name. For example, when Dido and Emilia were born there was no ceremony to tell their Ancestors of this blessing, not even the burning of incense in the colour of the homestead, or the building of a small shrine somewhere in the yard, or the burying of their womb-cords in sacred ways. Nothing was done, eh.

The children were simply born, given names that might as well have been plucked from passing rain, names not tied to a fate, and then thrust into the world unguarded. Mmakoma had kept quiet. There was nothing she could do except discreetly burn incense in her own quarters.

Otherwise, the children lived just like that, like *marula* hanging from a tree. At any moment anything could yank them off and sever them from the tree before they were ready to be themselves. If not yanked, they might fall with rot. The branches were weak, eh, nothing was tethering those children to life. All the while Mmakoma kept quiet and watched.

It is a heavy thing, though, to watch children wander in the world like lost spirits. It's not a thing that can be easily done; it weighs on your heart and makes you swallow a part of yourself. But what can you do when the mother and father pay you a fee for the raising of those children, heh? You keep quiet and do your job. Even if you're older than them, even though time touched you first, you shake your head with disbelief, keep quiet, and at the end of the month you go to the post office and wire the money you were paid to your own mother.

Of course, staying out of other people's matters will save you some trouble, but you must know that the Ancestors will haunt you with dreams. "Help the children," they say. "Tether the

68

children to life," they say. "Eh, you who is sleeping and burning small incense and keeping quiet, help those children you are supposed to be raising," they say. "Do you see that you are not raising children? Do you see that you are raising ghosts? Why are you wasting your time with ghosts, heh?"

Ah, the Ancestors will haunt you. Isn't it they have time, too much time, in fact. Meanwhile, they can waste yours with trees and birds and ships and shadows and other symbols you have to sit down and think about. Then, having finished all the maize kernels you were casually throwing into your mouth to chew, you dust off your hands, fold your arms, bite your lips, and think, *But couldn't they just tell me these troubles simply? Why send the vision of a snaking shadow smothering a child in her bed? Ah, these people!*

Your dreams can become enemies, eh. The Ancestors don't understand that this is not an easy world anymore. They don't care that it's not enough to simply be touched by time first, to be an elder. Now there are things like money and skin and education, and somehow men are becoming more important than women, even in her own tribe, where it is taboo to have a king, and the highest thing a man can be is a regent or an *ntuna*, or chief, as the white people say. Who had decided this sudden importance of men, she didn't know. No one knows. That is just the way things are going these days.

Of course, Mmakoma was sent to the missionary schools as a child and the nuns said she was cleverer than the boys. Overall, however, she was Black, poor, female, and by the time she walked to the secondary school in Mašupini to seek admission, it was to find that they had reached their quota for female students. That was how she ended up here, where she couldn't go around just like that saying things to people who were not Black or poor or female or uneducated, people who were higher than her.

The Ancestors didn't care about any of this. Isn't it they have time to pester you even with mundane things sometimes, or things that are still years and years away? Isn't it sometimes you can interpret the symbols incorrectly? Because sometimes the Ancestors become so bored with all that time they have, they start to throw strange symbols into your dreams. They can show you a child being smothered by a shadow-snake or a shadow-hand when the prophecy has nothing to with snakes or hands. Now you have to be sitting there telling people, "There is a prophecy, but I must tell you, eh, it might turn out that the prophecy is not what I will tell you."

Ah, people didn't like to be frightened with things like that. They wanted to be told things that made sense. They don't want to have their time wasted with ramblings and suggestions and things like, "But sometimes a shadow is a good thing. Sometimes it can mean that your Ancestors are calling you to a talent you have ignored. Shadows that are smothering *might* be a good thing because they are trying to take a deep poison out of you. But a shadow can be a bad thing. Sometimes it can mean fire and death. Also, I don't want to frighten you but isn't it you have children? But I'm not sure that the dreams are about *your* children, specifically." Then you shrug your shoulders with uncertainty. What must happen after that? Mmakoma kept quiet. She wanted to be sure.

She shook her head with disbelief and kept quiet until one day the younger child was carried off into her mother's tragedy. That sweet, sweet Miss Alisa, who had travelled the world in all its bigness to look for something to tether her to life, something to explain why she danced so easily between her moods. Ah, this "something" she wanted eluded her until one day she danced and slipped into a deed that couldn't be undone.

Mmakoma had no choice but to intervene at that point. The *baas* was overtaken by his grief, there was no one left to absorb the living child's. So Mmakoma did as she was taught by the elder women of her clan. She went to the sleeping child, who lay fighting for her life, and whispered to her, "Your mother has died. Your sister has died." Then she rubbed her hands with rock salt. The child might never be at peace with the deaths, but her spirit had to be eased to the news; it, at least, must find peace. The child had groaned in her sleep, a tear had fallen and trekked its way into the pillow, and at last, the Ancestors were somewhat appeased.

Mmakoma's duty wasn't done, however. The spirits of the mother and the dead child needed to find peace too. They couldn't be left to wander the spirit realm as aimlessly as they had done the realm of the living. Mmakoma had to intervene again. She had to cast away the rules of this new world that changed and changed and changed even as the Ancestors pestered her.

She threw more maize into her mouth and thought to herself, chewing, *The elders have taught me how these things should be done. I must start at the beginning. The* baas *needs to be lulled into accepting his reality. He needs to be eased the same way a child's spirit is told in a dream that its mother has died. I must be patient with the* baas. *After all, he has buried a wife and child before time had a chance to erode his face with its mark. I must be patient with him.*

Mmakoma knew it wouldn't be easy; he was a man who believed in nothing, who hated easily. But above all, he was a white man who, at the end of the month, must pay her fee for her care of his children. Ah, but the world was morphing into strangeness now. It was no longer enough to simply shake her head with disbelief, burn small incense, and keep quiet.

She saw him there, wallowing in his loneliness, watching the sunset in all its futility, guarding his daughter while he, himself, was unguarded.

She had to speak now. She had to help him.

Fields for Maize and Cows and a Way of Life

She stood against the looming dusk, ethereal. The sinking sun shone behind her like a herald of divinity. Abram was briefly blinded by it, and looked away. "I tell you," she continued, apparently oblivious to the effect of her arrival, "the years will clean your heart. The bitterness will fade. Where darkness now lives, will be joy again."

She was a kind woman, Gloria. Her words were kindly spoken. Abram didn't want to shock her by expressing his true feelings on the matter. He might dance on Alisa's grave if the priest suggested it as a funeral rite. Yet, as things stood, he didn't want to further upset Dido and so restrained himself, simply saying: "I only hope for peace for Emilia's soul." When the silence that stretched grew too heavy for comfort, he added: "And for my wife's, of course."

"It will be hard for Dido," said Gloria. She seemed so calm to

Abram, not a woman who might ever be moved by the winds. "But time will take her pain."

Abram looked at Dido. She sat under the willow tree and wrote in a journal. Every so often she closed her eyes, stretched her legs, and rested her head against the trunk as though in prayer. Moments later she raised her hand to her head and patted the leaves that had settled there. She smiled strangely, fleetingly, and sadly, and closed her eyes.

Just yesterday he found her running to and from the eastern wing as if chasing Emilia, as though she was not now a child alone, deserted by her beloved companion. Oblivious to his presence, she had stopped in the ruins and cried into her hands. When he told her it was going to be all right, she nodded and asked to return to her game. He had tried to sway her into playing with him, but all she said was, "Can we do it another time?"

Abram had relented and watched as she receded towards the vineyard.

"May I sit with you, *Meneer*?" Gloria asked.

"Yes, please." Abram patted the bench in welcome. "We have many things to discuss. If only the world stopped for a while and allowed me time for this healing you speak of, I might fare better. That isn't the way it's gone, however."

Gloria assumed the seat and settled into welcome silence. They watched Dido in her tranquillity. The breeze caused the falling leaves to dance around her in a soft flurry; every so often, like before, she opened her eyes to smile at the sight. The breeze turned into light wind and the black ash of the ruins mingled with the willow leaves. When she saw the ashes, Dido's smile vanished, and she promptly went back to writing.

"Leaving this place will break the girl's heart," said Gloria. "I know it is not my place to speak, but her mother's bones rest here. And although it was not her place to do so, Miss Alisa chose this place as the grave of her daughter's bones. To separate them now is a great calamity. This is her home, the only one she knows. You hate it now, but it is yours as well."

Abram first arranged his thoughts in what he hoped was coherence. When he spoke, it was measuredly, with care taken not to provoke further questions. He was a man weary. He was steadily nearing the end of his patience. "You know, I first came here as a child," he began. "It was a wondrous place, I thought. I once visited a museum in London, where the head of some famed king was displayed in what I thought was honour. I asked my father: 'Where did the king come from?' He said, 'Egypt.' I then asked, 'Where is Egypt?' And simply, my father said: 'Africa.' When I met Alisa, I told her about the museum. I said to her: 'I've loved Africa since I was a child.'"

"Alisa laughed. She thought I was naïve. When all was said and done, I thought she was bitter and poisoned in her opinion. My understanding of her was incomplete, perhaps as incomplete as the belief that heaven is a paradise meant for all righteous souls departed from the world. I cursed her resentment. I thought it poorly informed. After all, when we met she hadn't been to Africa. She hadn't fallen in love with it yet," he scoffed.

"It's taken me too much time . . . it's taken the passing of a law and the death of a child to help me realise it: in her bitterness, her poison, Alisa was right. There's nothing left to love here. This is not my Africa. This is not my home, nor is it Dido's. I understand the need for belonging, Gloria. I must admit that it's an irony, and worse, it was given to me by Alisa's cowardice. But in its profoundness—it's an unambiguous prophecy of foreboding, it is an irony I must heed. It isn't wise to keep my daughter where she isn't wanted. We don't belong here anymore. We can't.

"How can I belong to a place where my daughter cannot? I think it best to keep her loved. That is my right as her father, and I will see to it thoroughly, always, until I die. I must take her away from this place." He felt that that should suffice. He nodded to himself and waited for Gloria's rebuttal.

She smiled. "I'm a simple woman," she said. "But like you, *Meneer*, I have stories about Africa. I've been thinking about things, and I think that it's necessary for me to tell you one of those stories now."

Abram nodded.

"See," she started, "my elder cousin, who was the daughter of my mother's eldest sister, and given the name of Nnadi by our then dying grandfather, is the dearest friend of a woman she calls Mantšha. They are people from the north, where the bones of my Ancestors lie."

She allowed him time to fix the cast of her tale in his mind, after which she promptly resumed: "I must first tell you about Mantšha's beauty to make you understand the odd trail of her tragedy. To hear Nnadi say it, a man once killed another for that beauty. Both loved her, it was said, and each was too cowardly to live unloved by her. She was a woman touched by strange troubles, see.

"When Mantšha declared, upon being employed on a farm in Kroonstad, that she had started a love affair with her married *baas*, it came as no surprise to Nnadi. But see, that was also when Mantšha's imprisoned beloved, he who once killed another, returned to reclaim her. Like before, two men fought, and in the end one of them lay dead in payment for Mantšha's beauty.

"The *baas*-man, who was the victor of this new tragedy, was asked questions by the police, such questions about lost treasures from his home. In answer, the *baas*-man pointed to Mantŝha and said: 'This woman seduced me and conspired with her felon-lover to steal from me. This is the reason I shot him dead.' Please bear that I speak with respect, *Meneer*, but that is how a man black as me came to be blamed for his own death. And that is how Mantŝha came to be prosecuted for first being Black, and then for loving a man not of her race. Do you see my point?"

"I think I do."

Gloria nodded. "See, I don't pretend to understand the freedoms meant to be taken from my people with this law. But this I know: although insulting, this law is unneeded. My people are wise enough to realise these things on their own. The law can only be another curse for us. You have been kind to me, but you are a white man, and such things must be respected. But you are leaving now, and so I can easily say these things to you.

"I can easily tell you that my clan came from a place where a father and his son walked from their hut and to a field, a field that didn't end, *Meneer*, where a man worked from sunrise and he stood and put his hands on his hips, and he spit into the distance and wiped his forehead with the back of one hand, and he flicked the sweat into the wind, and he said, 'Ah, but this land is hard work,' and his son dreamt that one day, one day he will wake before the sun has risen to work the field, that he will put his hands on his hips and spit into the distance and say, 'Ah, but the crops will be good this year. All we need is rain.'

"A field, *Meneer*, a field that carried maize, that carried cows, that carried weeds, even. That field was a thing he could own. But I, myself, will not birth such a clan. There are no fields anymore.

There was a man who came and told us we could not farm beyond our yard; that that place didn't belong to us. Some unluckier
branch of the clan was taken from the field they'd looked at since
old and old forefathers lived there. They were taken from there
to a barren place, a barren place that had too many clans in one
place.

"Us, we had a field suddenly meant only for looking. Cows, we
couldn't keep there. Maize, we couldn't plant. Cows need to graze.
If there is no field, where will they graze? So my mother looked
around and said, 'My child, your brother must leave the mission school. We must send him to the mines, to Johannesburg.'"
Gloria paused to laugh. "Ah, my mother never learnt English, not
Afrikaans either," she continued. "When she says Johannesburg,
Meneer, you will laugh. Ah, but that time I didn't laugh because
men who go to the mines, they don't come back. But my mother
wanted to send my brother there.

"You can ask why my mother might do this thing. And the
answer is that the clan needed feeding, too, like the cows. But
there was no maize because the field was only for looking now.
There was a fence now around the field, and a man with a gun
to watch it. I don't know if this is true, but it was what my
mother told me: she saw a man who came back from the Great
War without a leg because of guns. She told us not to go to the
field, and we didn't.

"So only the very young children of the clan she sent to a mission school. One brother she sent to the mines. One brother she
sent to a farm that yields mangoes. One sister went on her own to
Johannesburg, too, but not to the mines. She went to a place like
here, like me. She looks after the children of a kind *baas*-man. But
back home, the cows began to die. These were my grandfather's

cows; we buried him in a hide from one of those cows when he died. We slaughtered it for the Ancestors. But now the cows die on their own.

"It was a small thing, *Meneer*. It was a small thing that started with fields, fields—fields for maize and cows and a way of life. Fields meant only to be looked at, but never ploughed or grazed or carried into a child's history. Fields that once belonged to a people, then didn't. Fields, *Meneer*, fields that carried a clan. And only when I came here I finally knew the name of the thing that scattered the clan. The Natives Land Act, they call it. Like a loved child, this thing has a name. But to go back to my point, I don't pretend to understand the freedoms meant to be taken from my people with this new law.

"But this I know: if a man comes to tell us that a thing is forbidden to us, we start to die. Our ways die. I'm telling you these long stories because I want you to understand Africa; Africa, at least, as *I* have lived in it. This place has been this way for a long time now; but these strange troubles didn't touch you until now, so you loved Africa incompletely, in the same way a child can love the warmth of a winter's fire without knowing or understanding how the fire itself came about, or that it can turn foe and burn you. Now that the fire has burnt you, you think there's nothing left to love about it, so you want to run away. But you're running from the wrong thing. If you must run, please do it properly."

Abram considered what she had said in silence. Then, "Africa is a complicated place."

"Africa is Africa, *Meneer*."

The silence grew longer. They sat admiring the splendour born from the timid mingling of night and day. It gave a golden light to the world and painted the shades and shadows long and bold. The silence having ripened, Gloria, for the first time since they knew each other, looked at him as a mother would at a child. The familiar submissiveness was gone from her face, as was the pity of days past. Her eyes, crinkled by age at the edges and made wise by a lifetime of hardships, were filled with an authority that unsettled him, for it was as foreign as the certainty in her voice.

She said, "Miss Alisa did a terrible thing, but it is unwise to refuse to mourn the passing of her spirit. My own knowledge of Africa has taught me that ghosts, when fed by hatred and other far-reaching things of this world, roam; and when left to roam, they haunt, *Meneer.* Hauntings are never easy to lift. You need to be cleansed to drive your wife's ghost to her Ancestors. Miss Alisa was of my people; her passing must be marked in this way.

"As someone who loves you and your kin, I beg that we do this thing for the child. We must cleanse her of the touch of death with time still on our side. We must lift the omens following her. I can help you with this. It is a small thing. It is a small, small thing." Seeming to regret her outburst, she retreated further into the bench and folded her hands on her lap. "It is only that I'm worried, *Meneer,*" she offered. "These things must be done properly."

Over by the weeping willow, Dido was weaving its golden stems into what Abram assumed was a basket. Often when he looked at her, he searched for signs of himself in her face; to see whether her eyes were his, her cheeks, or the way she extended her syllables when she wasn't supposed to. Had he given her these things, had Alisa, or were they simply the symptoms of childhood?

People liked to say Abram believed in nothing but that wasn't entirely true. Yes, he believed life to be precisely what it was, with nothing before, after, or beyond what he saw and touched and knew. He believed that once he fled South Africa, the troubles of here couldn't touch Dido through some mystical hand of fate or inevitability. And he believed, whole-heartedly, that any calamity that befell them henceforth wouldn't be a result of his reluctance to forgive Alisa.

But now, over by the weeping willow, Dido looked too much like her mother. And if Abram could pass on something as inherent as a habit of speech, couldn't Alisa pass on her legacy of wandering and melancholy? Not in the supernatural way, of course, but simply because Alisa was her mother, couldn't Dido, too, be restless with the world, couldn't she grow just as disillusioned with it? Couldn't she, one day, repeat a past she had so narrowly escaped?

People said he believed in nothing, but that wasn't true. He believed in the need for people to belong; to a place, a people, a power they didn't or couldn't understand, anything, so long as they belonged. He would uproot his daughter from her home in pursuit of that very thing. He would surrender everything familiar to her, every hiding place she shared with her sister, every adventure and memory and dream they had. He would renounce these things for her to belong somewhere, anywhere. Hadn't he tried to do the same for Alisa? But hadn't he failed? Could this last thing, this last small thing offered by Gloria, succeed? Finally, he asked, "What will you do?"

She said, "If history had opened itself differently, I would call the names of Miss Alisa's forebears to guard the child, lest their spirits turn foe and lead her astray. But Miss Alisa never knew her people, neither tribe nor clan name, so I will call your people and mine. The child must belong somewhere, *Meneer*, lest she wander the world like her mother. If, in her womanhood, she chooses her own path, away from you and her mother's fate, she needn't be lost."

"I daresay my ancestors forsook me the day I married Alisa," said Abram. "And yours, Gloria, though of this place, are not Alisa's. Also, Emilia was tainted with my blood. Will your ancestors freely welcome *her* soul?"

"Miss Alisa was an orphan woman. I will beg for this last refuge for her. My forebears will take her, I know. They were an orphan people too—expelled from their lands to some barren valley. They know the plight of wandering. I promise they will take her and the children. They will not care about skin. They will guard them until their spirits find the spirits of Miss Alisa's people. They might even find the spirits of the departed kin who never forsook you."

Abram nodded. He figured that the plan would require nothing from him, and even if Gloria turned out to be a charlatan, Dido would walk away with the belief that she belonged to something, to a people, even if he, himself, didn't understand it.

He couldn't say Emilia's name without yielding to tears, so he said what was left swiftly, before the tears spilled and he was reduced to a weeping fool. "Will my daughter's spirit truly find refuge?"

Gloria answered simply, with confidence: "She will, *Meneer*. I promise she will."

"It's all right then. Do what you need to do." He rose from his seat, gathered his clothes about him, and tipped his hat to Gloria. She mirrored him, then retreated to the kitchen wing to start preparing their evening meal.

Abram remained standing for a while, basking in the coolness of the breeze and savouring the sunset hues ablaze in the western sky—they scattered and remerged rather splendidly. Then the sun gave a last bright jab and descended unceremoniously. The colours congealed into a sombre shade of blue that rapidly turned into darkness.

That was when Abram settled the hat atop his head and went to his daughter.

Ghost of Verlatenbosch

When Dido opened her eyes, she saw her father sitting on an armchair near the bed. The chair was low, much lower than the bed, so Dido found herself looking at the top of her father's bowed head. "Papa," she said. Her throat was coarse and dry. She coughed and cleared it, and her father roused.

"Hello, Dido," he said, yawning, parting his face with a faint smile and sitting straighter. He had taken to watching her while she slept. Even by the dim light of the lantern, Dido saw tiredness in his eyes.

"Hello," she said, rising from her bed and jumping to the floor. She walked into her father's hug. "It's still night, isn't it?" she asked.

Her father stood, the better to place her back on the bed. "Yes," he said. He still wore his suit, and his hat was on her bed. It was likely he'd come back from the city only minutes before. He had taken to frequenting the auction house. "I didn't wake you, did I?" he asked.

Dido shook her head. "No," she said.

He tucked her beneath the blanket and sat back on the arm-chair. "Did you eat?"

"Yes. Nanny Gloria sat with me. She told me a story."

Looking at her father, Dido felt a flush of sadness. The small smile he had given her moments before was still on his face. He looked at her the way her mother had done on the night of the fire. It was as though he wanted to tell her something but hadn't yet decided whether it was a thing worth telling.

She had heard Nanny Gloria and the maids whispering to each other. She already knew that he planned to leave South Africa. She knew that he was surrendering the farm and homestead and ev-erything else either to the Provincial Council or to a man named Alfred Aaron de Pass. She felt that she should tell her father about these things—that he didn't need to worry about her. "Papa," she said, "is it true we're leaving?"

Her father didn't seem surprised that she already knew. In fact, he looked somewhat pleased; his smile got wider. "Yes," he said. Then his face became unreadable. "Would that make you sad?"

Dido wasn't sure how to answer. She looked away from her father, away from his sad eyes, and looked instead at the contents of the room. She had once shared it with Emilia. It felt strange to think of it as hers and hers alone. For example, the bassinet in the corner was made for Dido, but it was used for Emilia too. The teak drawer next to it was filled with china dolls that belonged to both Emilia and Dido. They had shared the bed too.

Once, when Emilia was frightened by one of their mother's stories, she had begged to sleep on the left side, away from the door, because she had convinced herself that the Ghost of Verlatenbosch had left the mountain slopes to haunt her. Even after Emilia died, Dido never slept on the left side. That was Emilia's side. Dido herself belonged on the right, closer to the door and any intruders, where, as the elder sister, she could better protect Emilia.

If her father left the estate to someone else, these things wouldn't belong to Dido and Emilia anymore. They would belong to memories. And what would happen with Emilia's and Mother's graves? Would her father carry those with him? Or would he leave them where they were, on the hillside in the vineyards? Would Mother and Emilia truly rest in peace (as suggested by the inscriptions on the graves) if their souls knew that Dido wouldn't visit them again?

"Dido," said her father, interrupting her thoughts, "would it make you sad to leave?"

Feeling that she had no escape, Dido finally nodded. She wanted to speak, but she was afraid that if she did she would cry. So she wove her fingers together and hoped her father wouldn't notice the tears in her eyes.

"It will make me sad too," he said. "But we can't stay, darling."

"Why not?" said Dido, feeling that she could risk uttering two words.

Her father disentangled her fingers and just as swiftly weaved his own fingers into hers. He sighed deeply. "Because I love you, Dido," he said. "Because if we stay, we may be taken away from one another. And because . . ." He sighed again. "Because . . . I want an adventure with you."

Dido nodded. "Okay."

"I'm sorry, my love. You know, I have news that will make you feel better."

Dido sat up.

"Would you like to be a part of Nanny Gloria's clan?" he said.

"Like the red young men?" said Dido, clearing her voice.

"Well, somewhat like that. A red young woman, you would be."

"Really?"

"Oh yes. Nanny Gloria says so."

"And you? Can you be a part of Nanny Gloria's clan too?"

A flash of sadness returned to his eyes. He shrugged. "We'll see," he said. "Emilia will be part of the clan as well. And your mother. Well, their souls, as far as Gloria says."

Dido felt suddenly uplifted. "I wish they were here." Her own words made her feel suddenly sad again. Her voice was lowered and the mirth gone from it when she said, "That way they would know it. Emilia would be happy to belong to a clan. Mother too, I think."

"Yes," said her father. "Yes."

"When will Nanny Gloria do it?"

"In the coming week."

"Will it hurt to do it? I only mean . . . will it change me?"

Her father shook his head. "It won't hurt you. It won't change you. It will only make you Gloria's kin."

At that, Dido found herself burdened with a new worry. "But, Papa," she said, "you and I are a clan, aren't we?"

"In a way, yes."

"If I become of Gloria's clan, can I still be of your clan too?"

"You can."

"Are you sure?"

"Of course I am. Our love binds us. You and I will always be a clan."

"That's good," said Dido. Her father nodded his agreement.

They were silent for a while. In the quiet, her father leaned into his chair, crossed his legs at the ankles, and folded his arms behind his head. This, too, was reminiscent of the day of the fire. While Dido and Emilia had played at the edge of the vines, their mother had fleetingly existed in the sort of eerie joy now planted on her father's face. Dido didn't know when the silence ended; without intending to do so, she had fallen asleep. When next she woke up, it was morning.

. . . . . .

Nanny Gloria vigilantly supervised the carrying of the clay pot from the wagon to the weeping willow. Dido suspected that she wanted to carry it herself. But alas, she didn't have the strength and so unwillingly surrendered the task to the men.

The pot was larger than any other Dido had ever seen, nearly perfectly spherical, burnt in places, and smooth all around. From simply looking at it, she thought it was the strongest pot that ever existed. But from the way Nanny Gloria scolded the men for turning too close to the cellar walls, or for relaxing too much in their shoulders and therefore in their duty, Dido started to believe it was, in fact, the weakest. "All the way to the tree," said Nanny Gloria. "Put it near the grey stone. Gentle now, do it gently." Although they shook their heads in what Dido assumed was annoyance, the men obeyed. "I see you, Khaled," she added. "You don't carry your share of the weight."

Her father watched with something like happiness on his face.

He tried hiding his smile with his hand; Nanny Gloria saw none-theless, and she was quick to shake her head and quickly return to her task of overseeing. Dido thought that if they hadn't been tired, the men might have found the whole thing funny as well. They straightened their backs, stretched their arms, and said farewell to her father with slight nods and smiles. Her father and Nanny Gloria both said: "Thank you."

Once she looked at the pot more closely, Dido found that she was even more curious. "It has a small opening," she said. "How can you cook in it?"

"It's not for cooking," said Nanny Gloria. "In my language we don't call it a pot. That is a word used by Westerners for their own convenience. This is for keeping water. It makes it cool in sum-mer. It gives it taste too. Sometimes when there is a celebration, we keep beer in it."

"How does it give water taste?"

At that, Nanny Gloria shrugged nonchalantly, a smile on her face. "That is a mystery." She turned to Father: "Can we start, *Meneer*?"

Father nodded, and they stood around the pot and linked their hands together, with Dido's right firmly held in her father's and her left in Nanny Gloria's.

Nanny Gloria leaned over the pot, and in a language Dido knew to be her native tongue, she called to her Ancestors. As she had earlier explained to Dido, she resounded their names and praise names to bring them forth, to beg their attention. Those names, sacred as they were, trailed the tales of a people's exile from an old chiefdom in the north. They told of Mmaselekwane, their queen; and of the warthog clans that tamed rivers and ruled new chiefdoms of their own.

She called to bring them from graves near and far, from here and there, even those who were scattered in the south—down, down where Mmaselekwane stretched the roots of her legacy. Nanny Gloria called them faithfully, and when she knew they were at last assembled, she began her plea.

"It is I, Mmakoma," said Nanny Gloria, "the eldest daughter of Khelelo and Matome, the seeds of Mokope and Moselana, of the Great Leopard of the Mmamolapi rivers. I beg you to heed me, for I have come to beg the gift of bonds for these orphan people. I give them to you. Please hear their names, mark their blood, and keep them safe."

She signalled for Father to proceed as she had instructed. He leaned over the pot's opening. "I was named Abram van Zijl by my father," he said, in Afrikaans. "My people came from Holland and England, across the western seas. It is there my roots lie. I bring my daughter to you, whose mother, named Alisa Miller by *her* father, was of this land in some ways. But her clan and tribe she didn't know, nor the names of her forebears. This child I bring to you, I beg that you keep her as your kin, as blood of yours. I beg that you keep her safe. I . . . I thank you."

He looked at Nanny Gloria, who nodded to signal he had done his part well. Father sighed with relief and leaned away from the pot.

When it came Dido's turn, she went as close to the mouth of the pot as possible. Her voice, quivery with emotion she didn't know how to explain, was close to Nanny Gloria's in its loudness and boldness, or so she hoped.

From what she'd been told, she understood that she and her father were cleansing themselves of any ill-luck that might result from Emilia's and Mother's deaths. Dido wasn't sure she understood everything there was, but she knew about her father's worry for her, and about Nanny Gloria's faith in omens. She supposed that since the secrets she'd learnt about her mother worried her, that maybe the ritual *was* needed. And as her father had said, she would belong to Nanny Gloria's clan.

She cleared her throat and stayed her tears from falling. Again, she began her call, also in Afrikaans: "I was given the name of Alisa Dido van Zijl by my mother and father. I have come to seek refuge. I was given the name of Khelelo by Nanny . . . by Mmakoma." Her voice dropped to a whisper. She was afraid that if she raised it she would surely cry and muck it all up. And so a whisper it remained. "I am Khelelo. Please hear me," she finished.

She thought she heard the words echo. Or maybe it was a dream. But she felt them transcend the wind now blowing from False Bay. Loudly at first, then the call settled into a soft rhythm that carried the many voices that called her into the sky. The language sounded foreign to her, but she knew she'd heard the songs they sang, the secrets they held.

The song carried her name through the wind, through time and time and time and all the echoes of the people that bound her where she stood. That call lulled her. It wove her into its endless ribbons of foreign faces and strange names and shadow memories. It pulled her gently, and then strongly into the pot, where the faces and names and memories told her stories that sheltered her soul.

Her heart lifted in relief. She closed her eyes and followed the path of the echoes. As they receded into the cradle that bore them, as the song died and the web released her, as the convened scattered, they said goodbye. Dido said to them: "Please find my people . . . protect me." The faces, the many eyes that looked from the realm beyond—she knew they saw her. It was to her that they called, not the wind. In time they would hear her.

But it was all a dream, thought Dido. If she said what she'd just seen and heard to Nanny Gloria and her father, they would surely laugh at her. So she smiled and tried to wipe the tears pooling in her eyes before either of them could see.

Her father draped his arm around her. "I am here with you."

"You have done well," said Nanny Gloria. "Now I need to send off their souls."

For this, Nanny Gloria took two offshoots from a branch of the weeping willow tree and went to the east wing of the manor. She knelt down and spoke to the departed souls. She told them that they were now dead, that they didn't belong to the realm of the living anymore. Then she asked them to be patient, to be calm, and not to worry, because she would help to guide them to their graves. Still calmly, she told them that their graves were the gate-way to the afterlife, where the Ancestors were waiting. She said all this with a broken sort of English speckled with Afrikaans. When she was done calming the spirits, Nanny Gloria took the willow offshoots to the hill in the vineyards, where she buried them beside the graves.

"Now we must burn the clothes," she said when she returned.

Dido and her father brought the clothes they had worn on the night of the fire. They were to be burnt to ashes, then bur-ied beneath the weeping willow; and thus reduced to nothing that could follow them where they went. Nanny Gloria said in ordinary circumstances Dido and her father would be the ones to cast the clothes into flames. But the circumstances were not ordinary—Dido didn't like being close to fire—so they only built the small wooden pyre where Nanny Gloria would set the fire.

Once done, Dido and her father left for the safety of the manor. With her father then occupied with the papers on his desk, Dido stole away from the house and hid near the corner of the cellar, the better to watch what happened under the willow tree.

Nanny Gloria wasted no time. Already, smoke was rising into the sky, polluting it slightly with its smell and its shadowy blackness. The flames below wrecked everything they touched. It seemed a simple thing, if in fact true, that to shed the clothes and feed them to the thing that had stolen her sister would also lift any curses following them. But that was the very thing promised by Nanny Gloria, and Dido hoped with all her heart it was true.

How the Milky Way Came to Be in the Sky

Dido sat behind the kanferboom and imagined her mother keeping her vigil under the weeping willow. But it was no fun without Emilia constantly pestering her. There was a quietness to her days that made her want to cry.

She tried to invent new games that wouldn't need Emilia. When she ran through the vines, she felt an emptiness behind her. It felt unnatural. That was the space where Emilia would have run, with her hair waving wildly behind her and her laughter interrupting the eeriness of the fields. It felt unnatural for Emilia to suddenly be gone, leaving Dido all alone. It made her sad, and sometimes when she thought about it too long, she couldn't stop crying.

It helped to sit under her mother's willow and write everything she remembered about Emilia. That way she wouldn't forget anything, not even the time she and Emilia tried to find fireflies in the vineyards but instead found moths and their larvae. Emilia was convinced they were butterflies, so naturally, a debate on the differences between moths and butterflies ensued.

There was also the time they found a starfish lingering just at the edge of the beach. Emilia tried to feed it a small piece of her apple, but to no avail. Dido remembered it all and wrote it down. And when she visited the graves, she read the stories to Emilia.

Gloria said the afterlife was a better place than the here-world. Dido was glad that was so: her mother would be happy there. But Dido didn't want Emilia to be lost in the joys of the hereafter and forget her, so she told the stories as faithfully as she could, hoping that her voice could reach that far and unknown place.

She would soon leave the Cape, crossing the Transvaal, the border into Rhodesia, and maybe the sea. She wouldn't belong to the Cape anymore. With that in mind, Dido made sure to finish her tutorials quickly, because she wanted to spend every other second noting down everything she could in her journal. When she was done she played the games she once shared with Emilia. It was the last time she would do so—that she would run between the vines in breathless futility. These were the last moments she would belong to that place she loved so much. She wanted to make the most of it, to say goodbye to it, and to her adventures with her sister.

And so she ran in a near-dance, as she had once done with Emilia. She veered left and right, swiftly, nimbly lifting her legs and stealing a gaze at the emptiness behind her, imagining Emilia's hand missing her skirt by a heartbeat—spiralling her way down the vineyard path, around and around, every time returning to the burnt east wing. Soot layered the once whitewashed walls, so they looked to be hidden in shadow. But in places to the west, the walls remained blazingly white and clashed rather violently with the shadow-cast ruin.

A dust devil scooped ash from the ruins and spiralled up, up, and up until it stood as tall as the burnt walls. The ash danced in the dust. It speckled the brown with its blackness so deeply, the dust devil turned black as night. The gust spun away from Dido; down, down all the way to the red alder.

She threw her shoes down and followed the path eroded by the gust. As the manor receded from her sight, the devil steadily weakened until, at last, all that remained were the remains that had migrated with it. Dido followed the path of debris all the way past the gulley of botanic disarray, to the vineyard.

Upon seeing her, the workers raised their hands in greeting. "Good day, Miss Dido," they called. She raised her hand and repeated the greeting. They smiled, adjusted their sunhats, and swiftly returned to their work.

The ground prickled her feet. Feeling the need for her shoes, she returned to the burnt walls to retrieve them. The sun was getting hotter, so she discarded her coat and stockings. Tariq or some other field worker had swept up the debris when Dido returned to the tree, so she didn't follow the debris path. She ran instead, along the path of the trees. She stretched her arms out as if flying. "I'm a crane," she said to the wind. And the wind called back. The voice was soft, and the words soothing in their faintness.

The voices of the workers, too, rose and receded in rhythm; they erupted into laughter, inflections of shock, a hubbub of secrets and other things lingering on her periphery. Sometimes it sounded like a song or the buzzing of bees; other times, like Dido's name being called and echoed through the wind.

It lulled her, rooted her, pulled her into the sky that sheltered Emilia's and her mother's souls. She closed her eyes and followed the path of her memory.

Once upon a time, Nanny Gloria told Dido about her own people. They came from the Transvaal, she said, and each of them was as short as she was. She spoke about the birth of the ploughing months, when the seven stars of Khelemela rose in the dim light of dawn to call the sowers from their rest. It was then that time began. The things of summer were born. Girls were sent to the hut to become women, the plains thrived with life, children grew fat from joy. Dido pointed at Khelemela and said to Emilia: "See the herald for summer, right there in the sky? And see the Three Zebras as they flee the hunter? Do you see the things of summer?"

Emilia shook her head. She knew other names for the stars—names such as the Pleiades and Orion's Belt. "That is how the star game was born," said Dido to the wind. "We charted the sky with the names given by Gloria's people. But we knew, too, the names from the West."

Suddenly, Dido's mother was there too. She said: "I will carry whoever recognises the most stars on my back as I run through this field to tame the wind." And just as suddenly, in the way of dreams, Emilia won the game. She shouted in glee as she flew on Mother's back. Dido sat on a grey stone beneath the willow tree. Nanny Gloria's arm was around her shoulders. Together, they watched the blur of her mother and sister as they cut through the wind like birds.

"Did Mother always know the names of the things of summer?" Dido asked the wind. "Did she know about the things of the sky?"

"Her bones have learnt," said Nanny Gloria, her voice more distinct and livelier than that of the dream. Dido's eyes flew open from the sudden fear she felt. Her heart beat faster and her blood felt too hot. She listened. The voice of the wind was now silent, departed, as though it had never called her name at all.

She looked around to see if Nanny Gloria hid somewhere in the thickets. She found nothing. Nanny Gloria's voice, in its eeriness, had gone too. The workers raised their hands to her again. "Is all well, Miss Dido?" they asked.

"Yes, thank you. Is all well with you?"

"Oh yes, Miss Dido," they said. And like before, they smiled, adjusted their sunhats, and returned to their work.

With a whirl very sudden and strong, a second dust devil rose where Dido stood. It lifted fallen leaves from the ground and spiralled up, up, and up until together they stood taller than the willow tree. The dancing leaves speckled the brown with the hue of their passing, as golden as her mother's crown. The gust spun away; up, up, up all the way to the burnt manor wall. Dido quickly followed, and as she reached the wall, the dust devil weakened until all that remained were the remains that had migrated with it.

Dido stood in silence, in attentiveness. She knew that if she closed her eyes for even a heartbeat, she'd open them to find the debris gone from the yard. When her eyes finally protested with tears pooling at the corners, she reluctantly closed them, yet quickly opened them again. It was then that Nanny Gloria emerged from behind the kitchen. "What game are you playing today?" she asked Dido, in Afrikaans.

"The star game," said Dido, as always when she spoke to Nanny Gloria, in a rapid and seamless mingling of English, Dutch, and

Afrikaans. "Were you in the fields just now? Did you call my name?"

"I wasn't in the field. I came outside to take your things inside. Why are you asking?"

"I thought I heard your voice. You told me stories. It felt . . . it felt like a dream, like a memory that lasted for forever, but a second . . . like you were the wind and you called my name. My mother and Emilia were there too."

"Were you afraid?" said Nanny Gloria.

Dido wondered whether what she had felt was fear, or if her initial feeling of relief was more apt. "I don't know but I think so."

"Do you remember the story of how the Milky Way came to be in the sky?" asked Nanny Gloria.

Dido nodded. "It was when time began and the world was young. A girl threw embers and ash into the sky. The girl was blessed by the Gods. The ash she flung glowed and shone a path for those who were lost."

"Good," said Nanny Gloria, a smile on her face. "Come," she ushered. "You must eat your lunch. I've made all the vegetables you love."

Dido gladly took the elder woman's hand and together they abandoned the burnt wall.

The Photographer's
Lifeless Product

S ister Alice came by the estate every two days if she could, but sometimes only once a week. It was to see that Dido's mind didn't rot away with idleness, she said. She brought books with her; she sat with Dido in the library to read and do sums. It was simple enough. Sister Alice was much younger than Sister Elizabeth, not much older than twenty, which seemed to make Dido feel easier about her lessons.

Sometimes, hours after Sister Alice had gone, Dido was still fascinated by a sum that had been tricky to start with but, when she looked at it, wasn't difficult at all. Abram listened and nodded. When she was done, though, he saw that a shadow of sadness passed over her face again, so he asked her about what they'd been reading. "We finished the Oliver Twist story," she said. Then she became enthralled with narrating the details to him, which lifted the shadow from her eyes and replaced it with concentration. For this, Abram would forever be grateful to the nuns.

On the last Thursday of May, however, which was just over a month after the funeral, Sister Alice didn't bring books or lessons. Dido was off in the vineyards, helping to prune the vines to prepare for winter. She wasn't likely to be of any help, but chores, like her lessons, kept the shadow of sadness away from her face. She was likely a hindrance—asking questions, distracting Farouk and his people, slowly becoming so bold that she took shears and cut stems on her own, doing damage. For this, Abram would forever be grateful to the workers.

When Sister Alice called, right around noon, her voice was first heard by Tariq, who was sorting the grain for feeding the ducks. Tariq was a soft-spoken boy who, unlike Hafsah, could be counted on to waste his time with flowers and the like.

That day he wasted time with pointing to a small tawny duck and saying, "Her name's Willow, like the tree. She doesn't like grain. I grind it and feed her there." He pointed to a bright red bush near the cellar house.

It turned out that Sister Alice was also the kind to waste her time with ducks, or she was painfully polite, and this was perhaps the reason Dido was so fond of her. Or, and this was more likely given the Sister's character, she wasted time for the simple sake of doing so, for she dreaded the task she had been set. In any case, she asked Tariq to tell her how he knew that Willow didn't like coarse grain, and he gladly obliged with the details.

Their voices were heard by Elina, who was herself a timid girl who, while mourning Alisa's and Emilia's deaths, had decided she was in love with Tariq. She watched him and the nun from a distance. When she heard the sound of laughter, she decided that enough time had been wasted. At once she ran to call Gloria, who was helping Abram to pack Alisa's books into crates, all of them to be shipped to England, to her parents. "The teacher nun is here," said Elina, her head bowed and voice quivering, almost like a soft whistle in the wind, her uncertainty turning her announcement into a question. Then a strange detail occurred to her, and more to herself than anyone else, she whispered this: "But she got no books."

Both Abram and Gloria were tired, and gladly took the chance to leave the mustiness of the library. Abram was forced to return to it rather soon, though, because as soon as she saw him, Sister Alice, contrary to the established order, did not waste time in remembering that she had an urgent issue to alert him to. "Sister Elizabeth sent me, sir," she said. "She's been watching how things have been going with Parliament, I'm sure you'll know. But she's been watching other things, too, sir."

Abram was suddenly panicked. "What does she know?" he asked.

"Well." Sister Alice looked around the library. Seeing the empty shelves, the general mess, she nodded. "Well, she'll be happy to know that you're preparing to leave. Do you trust your workers, sir?"

"What do you mean?"

"How many of them know you're leaving?"

"My daughter's nanny knows the details. Everyone else knows the estate is changing hands. I couldn't simply leave. These people loved my children," he said. With reluctance, he added, "They loved my wife."

"Do they know precisely *when* you're leaving?"

"Yes. Sister Alice, what is this concerning?"

Where Sister Elizabeth was precise, Sister Alice was fretful. She now sat on a chair, right where Daniel Ross once stood and upturned Abram's life. She clasped her hands and smiled, or rather grimaced. "Two men came to the school on Monday. They came again yesterday. They were ordinary to look at. If what they said can be believed, they were looking for a school for their daughters.

"But they asked . . . strange questions. Whether we taught mulatto children at the school. And more precisely, how long ago the living Van Zijl girl was at the school. Sister Elizabeth also remembered that she knew one of the men. Might be five years ago or so, when she helped Father Benedict in doing the last rites for prisoners, she saw one of these men. He was a guard at the Island. Sister Elizabeth thinks he became a policeman. She isn't entirely sure. And of course, each of these things wouldn't be alarming on its own. But given the circumstances, one has to consider the sum of the whole, the entirety of it all. It would seem you need to leave as soon as possible."

Abram slumped into his chair. "My business isn't done here," he said to himself, to add to his tally of failures. "My daughter isn't ready. We need time . . . she needs time."

Sister Alice didn't immediately offer her thoughts. She looked around the room, everywhere save at him, as though she knew the answer to the very meaning of his life, but by some rule of providence couldn't tell him. He had to untangle the dilemma on his own.

He needed time. He needed time. "But I suppose it can't be helped," he concluded.

. . . .

Abram swiftly gathered the things of his life away; he was heading north at last. There wasn't time to gather them with gentleness. There wasn't much to gather, nor much to leave behind: beneath the meagre suits and papers of passage chosen for the journey, he stowed a portrait that illustrated him, Alisa, and their daughters. They each stared at the invisible photographer with stoicism. The thing had been produced a year before, and Emilia's attempt at earnestness was tinged by a smile playing at the corners of her lips.

The photograph was taken in front of the manor house. Alisa had been told to sit on a wooden stool with her hands on her knees. Emilia stood to Alisa's left, and Dido to her right. Abram stood behind them like a looming shadow, a pale man whose devotion to the two girls couldn't be deciphered from the photographer's lifeless product.

Looking at Emilia then, frozen in her doubt, Abram wished she could have defied the photographer's instructions and smiled fully. But the time for that had passed, and he couldn't stow her liveliness—absent from the portrait—beneath the meagre treasures and requirements he'd chosen for his departure.

Together with Dido, he took the winding path that led to the hillside where Alisa and Emilia were buried. It was near midnight, dark, and their memory of the place led them more faithfully than their eyes. Abram carried a lamp that lit only a step or two ahead of them. They must have looked like a strange firefly, small, alone, and gliding along with a dull red glow until at last their pilgrimage ended.

Abram's eyes rested on the smaller of the graves, Emilia's. "We must leave, my love," he said to her, to the hard stone. He wanted to tell her he loved her, to help her linger in this world. But he, too, was departing from that place that was once his home. "We must leave," he said, again.

Dido placed flowers on the grave. "Goodbye," was all she said.

Abram blinked his eyes to keep the salt from them, to keep away his unfallen tears. Then, swiftly gathering the things of his life onto his back, he climbed back down the hill.

. . .

At the same time that Abram reached the foot of the hill, as he pulled a hood over Dido's head, a dog barked outside the hostel where the madman John Ashby slept.

It was a stray dog, a rabid thing that once bit the magistrate's son. The magistrate wanted it dead but no one could catch it; it slunk away to the docks and no one saw it for a week or so. Then that day it came out and barked and howled, and woke John Ashby from a frightful dream. He might have gone back to sleep if the dog didn't go on yapping until other strays were compelled to challenge it.

John Ashby couldn't sleep with all that noise. Besides, the more he thought on the dream, the more fretful he was. There was a man in the dream. John knew the man. The man was called Abram van Zijl. The man called Abram van Zijl was doing something he wasn't supposed to be doing, that's what the other man said, the other man who was called Daniel Ross.

He trusted John, Mr. Ross. He didn't call him mad. He listened. He believed. He said to John, "Tell me when Abram van Zijl comes to the auction house. Tell me what he buys. Tell me what he sells. Tell me whom he meets . . . tell me things. Tell him things."

Abram van Zijl wasn't going to the auction house in the dream. He was standing under a tree. He was standing under a fat tree. It was a fat tree that had thin hungry branches clawing at the sky like clawy claws. But not claws; the branches actually looked like roots. It was an upside-down tree. Yes, it was an upside-down tree. It was a fat upside-down tree that a train rode through.

There was a train, yes. There shouldn't be a train and a fat upside-down tree, only the auction house. Mr. Ross had to be told. Yes, the man named Daniel Ross had to be told that the man named Abram van Zijl was in a strange world with strange things.

Of course, he wouldn't say the part about the dream when he told Mr. Ross about Mr. Van Zijl. He wasn't mad. He'd say that he saw Mr. Van Zijl sneaking to the station. He trusted John, Mr. Ross. He didn't call him mad. But like most men John knew, Mr. Ross wanted the coincidences of life to lock into each other, to lock into each other perfectly. He trusted John, Mr. Ross. But he didn't understand that sometimes life happened without a reason. Mr. Ross had to be told, though. He had to be told. John climbed out of his bed to get dressed.

. . .

Abram's car reached the train station. The journey had started in silence, and in silence it ended.

Each person knew what part to play in the saga. Farouk parked the car near the cargo depot. The city's bustle had died sharply after dusk. Now it slumbered in silence at the mountain foot, and the mountain itself loomed like a shadow in the sky, like a ghost, a sentry spirit that lulled the city into dreams. But the trains and their platforms were not born with this old city, they were a newly adopted child, eager to be loved. As the city slept, they toiled on. And so, when Abram's car got there, it was to find the station in a bustle of its own.

There were lampposts of Victorian design all along the platform, coach attendants and other workers preparing for departure, crates with mail freshly arrived from the docks, wine from the valleys, and other cargo. Most alluring, though, was the train itself. It was a blue locomotive named the Union Express. It glittered like a sapphire, like the dreams it promised—not sapphires, but the gold and diamond fields in the north, or in Abram and Dido's case, escape.

While Farouk unloaded the suitcases from the car, Sister Alice found the ticket man. He was a short man from the Natal Province. Sister Alice knew him by way of Sister Elizabeth, who knew him by way of the Great War: in the dying days of the war, the man, whose name was David, had promised what years he had pending to God; that is, if God thought it prudent to save that very life now promised. God had seemingly obliged, thus David owed a debt he now paid by his devotion to two entities—Sister Elizabeth and the Catholic Church.

David and Sister Alice whispered and pointed and nodded and she promptly returned. "Don't leave your coach if you don't need to, sir," she whispered. "The coach attendant will attend to your needs. He won't be any trouble; you're a white man. Keep Dido hidden nonetheless." What she didn't say, maybe as a tenet of her devoutness, was: *If asked who Dido is to you, lie.* Abram nodded at both the spoken and unspoken counsel.

So finally came Abram and Dido's part in the saga. Dido, who had been carrying herself determinedly, didn't look quite as brave anymore. Her lips trembled, her eyes watered, and to Farouk she said: "I'm going to miss you, Uncle Farouk. Please tell Nanny Gloria to look after the tree I planted. If it doesn't grow, please ask her to plant another one. Please tell her that I love her. I don't know if she knows." There, as a tear escaped her left eye, Dido stopped and bowed her head.

Farouk wiped the tear and hugged her. "I'll do like you say, Little Dido. Don't stop being a good child, okay. Don't stop being clever." Dido nodded. He turned to Abram and smiled a sad half-smile that brightened only half his face. He wasn't a man of many words, Farouk. It was thus shocking to find that he was a man who shed his tears rather freely. "All will be well, *Meneer*," he said, sniffling. "God has willed it." Abram nodded and hugged Farouk.

Sister Alice's farewell was more subdued. She told Dido to read and keep up with her sums. Then she urged Abram to be careful, wished him luck, and tersely shook his hand. Having completed their parts, Farouk and Sister Alice retreated into the general slumber, and the darkness of the city quickly welcomed them back, swallowing them completely.

Abram and Dido, renouncing that sleeping city, now had to toil away from it with other things that didn't belong.

When the train at last burrowed out and on towards De Aar and Klerksdorp and then Pretoria, it left the city waking into its bustle.

. . .

Cape Town was an entity of habit; it always woke up early. The fog was clawed away like a blanket no longer needed.

On the farm, Mmakoma woke up with it, as she had done for eleven years. She boiled water at the servants' hearth for her bath.

By then a rooster had announced the sun's coming several times, but the sun was an unwilling servant that day.

The morning slowly surrendered the chill that was born sometime near dawn. The sun finally conceded, at first peeping over hills and mountains and buildings and then, finding that the city's residents had woken without its go-ahead, lazily stretched out to fill the eastern horizon.

Leisurely, the city came alive. The churches with their Gothic, stoic faces; the market halls and hotels and other places humming with commerce, resplendent in their mimicking of Victorian London; the Docks' Clock Tower counting the hours off in the harbour—they all came alive, every one of them trying to best its neighbour, to praise his own builder, to say, *I'm a better mirror of the Old World than you.*

Once done with her bath, Mmakoma walked to the manor kitchen for breakfast. She passed the cellar, the pond and its ducks, the pathway leading to the fields and graves, and finally, the burnt, crumbling pillars.

She stopped there for a while, to think, to calm herself, to ease her heart to the changing world. Her breath came too quickly when she remembered that Miss Alisa and Emilia were now graves. It came quicker still when she remembered that deep in the night, *Meneer* Van Zijl and Dido had melted away as swiftly as the fog. They were gone. Where they went, she wouldn't know. She'd never know. So she stood there. She stood there. She cried.

PART THREE

To Teach a Monkey to Climb

Flutter and Frolic
of Other Insects

The train arrived in Pretoria some forty hours after its departure. It was daytime; Abram and Dido were greeted by a busy city. Here, the architecture assumed a Dutch identity, but with flecks of something foreign in the buildings, as though the architects had created rebellious children that couldn't help but resemble their parents in a general sort of way, in the high gables and whitewashed shutters.

Abram had hoped to find a few odd jacaranda trees that might have bloomed early, or carried their flowers longer than autumn allowed. He had hoped for Dido to see their splendid purple flurry. Sadly, the trees were bare of their flowers.

The sun set much sooner and far too quickly in the north. It wasn't too long after Abram found the driver Sister Elizabeth had called ahead for that darkness shrouded them. It could have been his eyes failing him, but it seemed to Abram that once it cloaked the world, the darkness of the north was deeper. The sense of urgency that had expelled him from Cape Town had accelerated tenfold. There was something about being in any of the Union's capitals that greatly unsettled him. They were both very tired and needed to rest, but the sooner he and Dido got out of there, the better.

The road still stretched very far ahead of them. To make matters worse, they were headed to a place where they weren't expected. Would they be welcomed? That was a problem he'd face when he got there. For now, he gathered Dido into his arms and drifted into a deep sleep.

. . .

Because Johannes Joubert couldn't be counted on to avoid needless tragedy of his own making, his farm was nestled at the very edge of a tropical belt. It was like a poor relative that lived on the outskirts of its family's mercy, the haggard sapling that cowered in the shadow of a better loved, better nourished sibling. Struggling to nourish itself with the leftover rains that sometimes wandered over, Johannes's farm looked on to the tropical valleys with envy; and as though ashamed, its offspring of trees and maize and other plants hanged their canopies with defeat. Why Johannes hadn't extended all the way into the lush belt for his exile, Abram didn't ask. His former friend was prickly in the best of times. In the worst, he was downright spiteful.

He had apparently spent the better part of his adulthood trying, yet failing, to understand how such a promising young man as Abram had fallen prey to the more avoidable temptations offered by their continent. He'd said as much to Abram, who at the time was bewitched beyond sense by his wife.

But whatever else could be said of Johannes, it couldn't be said that he was inconsistent in his convictions. He practised them without the slightest deviation. So when he said, in his rough voice and with his tobacco pipe clouding the air between them, that Dido wasn't welcome in the house for the duration of her visit, Abram knew that his mind couldn't be changed. He casually rested his arms on his lap, leaned forwards, and rebutted with as much conviction as he could muster. "I will sleep in the servants' quarters as well," he said.

The smoke from Johannes's pipe swirled in a hesitant dance, and the men's eyes followed its fickle rise. Just when it threatened to disappear into nothing, Johannes decided to point out Abram's fallacy. "See here, Bram," he said, "I won't have it said I condemned you to a servant's place. Not here. Not while I still live."

"How else can you condemn me, if not as a living man?" retorted Abram.

Johannes remained silent and proceeded to seethe, huff, and threaten unkindness with his eyes. Abram realised that he and Johannes had descended into a well of redundant chatter. The intricacies of politeness were delicate: each man knew what he must say and what he must not, and in the things unsaid, much was said too. That was the way these things were done. In their eloquence, the Basotho termed such a predicament "to teach a monkey to climb." Abram recognised it immediately, for he had practised it numerous times with traveling Europeans who occasionally sought refuge on his estate. In teaching a monkey to climb, a man could say what was known and, in that way, lessen the effect of his discourtesy.

"If anyone asks, John, tell them I've gone as mad as the rumours have been saying these past years." Abram had taken to calling Johannes John as a joke in their youth. But Johannes had, strangely, liked that name, and so it had stuck. "Tell them you insisted most profusely and I refused to see reason. Surely that will render the whole thing understandable, old friend," he added as an afterthought.

"Where will my servants sleep?" said Johannes.

Abram knew Johannes enough to realise he believed himself to have found a moral standing on which they agreed. He asked, "Are they all African?"

"Do you think my farm is like yours?" asked Johannes, restraining his annoyance. He allowed his pipe smoke to cloud the air again. "Of course, they are natives. So I ask again, my dear man: where will they sleep?"

Abram recognised that he and Johannes had progressed to teaching the monkey more things he already knew. He submitted himself to the futility of the exercise, for what else was there to do? He needed John's help. He needed somewhere to hide while his estate was sold, funds transferred, and Alisa's books shipped to England, and while Gloria and Sister Elizabeth tried to help him in forging papers to cross the border; in short, while he sorted out such essential things for his and Dido's survival. Abram needed this man who now taunted him, and the man who taunted him knew it as well.

"Surely the quarters are not so small that the addition of two individuals will cause a catastrophe, as you suggest, John. The girl will sleep with the women and I with the men."

"You presume to inform me of my own property," said Johannes. "You assume too much of our friendship."

"Forgive me. I didn't mean to be insolent," said Abram.

"I don't say these things for the sake of being a difficult man. You know that you've brought me trouble, Bram. The mere presence of that girl here can cost me my vote. You know this . . . you have always known." Johannes paused dramatically to draw on his pipe—being, as Abram knew, a theatrical sort of man. He waved his hand at nothing in particular. "But I suppose we can make do."

Not for the first time, Abram noted that when Johannes spoke, spittle escaped his mouth, and occasionally, he coughed into the brief silences between his words. His breath seemed to escape his lungs reluctantly, but he seemed unconcerned by the labour. He was, as a whole, an imperfect model of humanity. Although taller than most people, there was nothing domineering in his presence. The whites of his eyes were ever speckled by redness and lingering tears. The blue of his irises was not as arresting as it might have been on a handsome face. There was also his jaw to be mourned: maybe that more than anything, for it was square, heavy, and dimpled beneath his thin and pallid lips. And the brown wisps of his hair receded to the very top of his head, and his nose was nearly as broad as the jaw.

The years and the heat of the Transvaal had taken their toll on Johannes. But more than that, his own bitterness had, by the looks of it, poured from his heart and seeped into his skin, reddened it, and polished it to an unnatural shine. It wasn't easy to do, but Abram felt that he should pity his old friend. And if he could not, then he needed to repent for the part he'd played in exiling Johannes to the north.

Despite their parent nations' converging interests in Africa, the South African descendants of Europe had found themselves disillusioned with one another. Most recently, their enmity was compounded by the Second Boer War. After a spectacular show of jingoism and death by forces on both sides, Johannes had felt that further loyalty could be shown and, being a Dutch descendant, had chosen to migrate from the British-governed Cape of Good Hope to the Boer-controlled Transvaal. Such was his diligence in these matters. In that regard, and perhaps ironically, he was a lot like Alisa. They both considered matters of patriotism to be profoundly personal, and as absolutely essential to a person's existence.

Abram and Johannes's friendship had ended there. For, although his name suggested an allegiance to Holland, Abram hadn't renounced the English part of himself. Johannes had taken it as a slight. And of course, it didn't help that Abram had fallen in love with Alisa, a woman who was both Black and English. If pestered, Johannes might have forgiven one of those transgressions, but not all three.

Presently Johannes stood up and walked to the window. He tucked his left hand in his trouser pocket, looked outside, and tapped the pane with his pipe. Even in half-darkness, there was nothing elegant about his former friend. He didn't look like he belonged in the nobly furnished library. It was as though he, too, were a traveller in need of rest.

"It's quite a thing, isn't it?" asked Johannes. "Some ten years ago you stood in this room and renounced me with such finality, I felt foolish in trying to save you. Today you sit here with the hope that I can save you." He turned his back to the window and faced the man he taunted. The lantern's light touched his face at an unfortunate angle, and the tears lingering in his eyes seemed to sparkle more than usual. "Don't mistake me for a man who dances on the grave of a fallen foe," he continued. "But these are strange times. I won't have it said that I've been fornicating with natives and spawning mulatto children. I won't have my name stained, Bram. You know how these sort of rumours can ruin a man. They've ruined *you*, haven't they?"

Abram folded his hands together. When he spoke, it was with a deliberate softness to his voice. He didn't want to reveal the anger rising within him. He said, "You forget that I haven't been fornicating, that I'm not ashamed of my daughter."

He rose from his chair and walked to the window. He wanted to face Johannes but decided he preferred the scene outside. The darkness was disturbed by nothing save the wind that had blown through the day. He imagined that it rose and swirled as if born from some unseen god's pipe, dancing between words spoken by the god and his opponent, then disappearing into nothing, leaving only the words and darkness.

It was an ordinary summer evening. Time was narrated by the chirping of crickets and the flutter and frolic of other insects colliding with the window in their effort to reach the bleak light of the lantern. The few that found cracks in the window frame swirled around the light, then dove to their deaths and clouded the lantern glass, further dimming the light.

"I'm desperate, John," said Abram, taking care not to face his opponent. "You once loved me. You know I loved you. I haven't come with pride or . . . or . . . I have nowhere left to run, John. We'll be here for a little while, only a little while. In that time, please don't hate my daughter. Please don't show her . . . She's very clever and brave, but she's wounded and homeless, and she's very precious to me. This is the last thing I'll ever ask from you. Then we'll both go away and leave you in peace. Please."

Johannes submitted himself to a bout of coughing, which he abandoned with a heavy sigh. He walked to his desk and rang a bell. Minutes after the third toll an elderly, especially dark, African woman entered the study and stood by the door. Abram judged her to be close to his own height, which was a rare thing for a Southern African woman.

She was scraggy, for her dress hung loosely about her body; and too tall, for such clothes were usually seamed for shorter women whose hips had widened with childbearing, age, or gluttony. Her face seemed on the verge of breaking into a smile, but didn't. She half-glanced at Johannes and nodded to convey her understanding.

"Josephina, Mr. Van Zijl and the girl will be living here for a week or two," said Johannes in Afrikaans. "Prepare two rooms in the east quarters."

Josephina nodded and exited the room.

Johannes returned his attention to Abram. "Our time together must end," he said, returning to English. "It's late and I need to sleep. You can wait here until Josephina is done with your rooms. I do hope you enjoy my hospitality. Good night, Bram."

"Good night, John," said Abram. "And thank you."

"Yes, yes," dismissed Johannes.

Abram returned to his seat. He watched the futility repeated by the insects in their pursuit of light. They seemed hopeful, certain that they would achieve a victory that, although it eluded their cronies, would surely be theirs. He smiled sadly, and shook his head in frustration.

The hour was late, approaching the familiar coldness of dawn.

Rhodesia's Night Sky

Dido knew she wasn't welcome in the house of the big man with brown hair and blue eyes. Miss Josephina called him *Baas* Joubert; her father called him an old friend who would help them cross into Rhodesia. Dido herself hadn't yet decided what to call him.

Her father told her to be on her best behaviour. So, although she sat on a hard chair and the room was chilly, she didn't complain. Not once. She also missed her journal, but it was packed at the very bottom of her suitcase. She didn't say a word about that, either, since it might annoy Miss Josephina. She drank the orange juice Miss Josephina had given her, also without complaint. "It's delicious," she said.

Miss Josephina nodded and smiled a toothless smile. "Eat," she said, pointing to the boiled chicken on Dido's plate.

Dido shook her head. "I don't eat meat," she said. "Thank you," she added with a smile, hoping she looked repentant.

Once, she had gone hunting with her father and her uncle Yuri who wasn't really her uncle, and who liked to visit from the Transvaal because, he said, the Cape winter rains reminded him of Leningrad (which he still called Saint Petersburg). Father had complained that Uncle Yuri was fairly useless with a gun, a point that was proven when Uncle Yuri shot an eland and the animal didn't die immediately.

It bled while bleating a terrible sound that was too much like crying. Before her father shot it between the eyes and completed its death, it had looked at Dido as though begging her to save its life. Dido had cried while her father held her and scolded Uncle Yuri. She hadn't meant to cry. Even at seven years old, she understood that her father was generous in taking a daughter hunting. She was proud in being the near-boy he taught how to hunt. But in the end she cried, and she couldn't eat the meat from the eland, nor another piece of meat after that.

She wasn't sure how to say all of that to Miss Josephina, whom she'd met only hours before. Instead she said, "I'm sorry."

"Oh," exclaimed Miss Josephina. "Vegetables?"

Dido nodded. The woman went to the oven and filled a plate as promised. "Carrots and potatoes," said Miss Josephina, placing the plate on the table.

"I can speak Afrikaans," said Dido, in Afrikaans. "Well, only a little," she added, returning to English. "My father prefers English. And my mother never liked Afrikaans at all. But my nanny taught me a little . . . a little. I understand it, though."

"Can you speak the other languages," asked Miss Josephina, "the languages of our people?"

Dido was used to questions like that. Nearly everyone she met assumed she was African and only that. No one ever asked if the man who doted on her like a father was, in fact, her father. She knew it was because of how she looked. She had skin darker than her father's and eyes as brown as her mother's. And although her hair was long and loosely curled, she realised that people assumed this was a result of some unspeakable, secret tragedy.

People tended to greet her with friendliness, but following her inarticulacy with native languages, they quickly returned to their submissiveness. She didn't quite understand, but guessed they perceived snobbery in her. Once that happened, it was difficult to make friends. "No," she said to Miss Josephina. "I can't."

To Dido's surprise, the woman showed no signs of disappointment. Instead she smiled her toothless smile and said, in fluent Afrikaans, "I will teach you. That way we will have something to do while you are here." Then, seeming to doubt her words, she shook her head. "Will your father allow it?"

Dido didn't know. However, she figured it wouldn't do harm to give an answer. "I think so. Which language do you speak?"

"Sesotho. From the north. A small tribe we are; the Balobedu."

"That's curious. Nanny Gloria spoke the same language. I hadn't met anyone else who spoke it. Now I know you as well as Nanny Gloria."

"That *is* curious," agreed Miss Josephina.

Just then, one of the bells on the wall rang and Miss Josephina rose to her feet. "*Baas* Joubert needs me," she announced. "You must eat," she said, pointing to the food.

"Thank you for the food," said Dido, and Miss Josephina nodded and left the kitchen.

To soothe her sudden loneliness, Dido contemplated all the stars that would be visible in Rhodesia's night sky. Her father had agreed they might be different from those in the Cape, which was all the way in the southernmost corner of Africa.

Once she found Orion she could easily find all the others. Her journal would be filled before the year ended. When that was done, maybe she and her father would go farther north, far enough to see Polaris, the North Star. She hoped it would be just as bright as her textbook said it was, just as useful. They could follow Polaris and never be lost.

As though bidden by her thoughts, her father entered the kitchen. "Hello, Dido," he said. "Would you mind if I shared your food?"

"I don't mind," she said. "Miss Josephina gave me my favourite." She smiled, for her father looked sad, and she knew that if she smiled he'd do so too.

He sat beside her and pulled the plate of chicken to himself. "I have good news," he said. "We will be resting here awhile, after all."

"Can I please learn Miss Josephina's language?" said Dido. "She won't mind teaching me. She suggested it. And speaking her language will be like carrying Nanny Gloria with us. And I would so love to learn it, Papa—"

"Of course, dear," said her father. "But you need to speak more slowly. I missed nearly half of what you said." He laughed.

She smiled. "Thank you. If I do well I will teach you. Imagine the fun!"

Her father laughed even louder. "That would be something." Then a look of confusion passed over his face. "You said her language is the same as Nanny Gloria's?"

"Yes. It's curious, don't you think? You and your old friend both made friends with the same kind of women."

"It is," he said. "It is." Although he nodded, he also looked troubled by the coincidence.

"How long will we stay here?" said Dido.

Her father swallowed the bite he'd been chewing and said, softly, "I haven't decided." He cut another bit of chicken, chewed and swallowed. "I have to ask a great favour of you, Dido. You know we have to be as discreet as possible, right?"

Dido nodded. A familiar flash of sadness had passed over her father's face. "No one must know you're my daughter," he said. "Do you remember when I told you we would be taken away from each other?" Dido nodded again and her father continued. "Right now those people are looking for a white man and his young daughter. I know it might not work, but it might be better if, from a distance, you seem like a boy. Or at the very least, you don't seem . . ." He swallowed. He didn't finish his thoughts.

Dido knew what he meant. This had happened on the train. There, she was less to her father than a daughter. Yet he still felt he needed to elaborate: "You know it's for your safety, right?" he said, and she nodded again. "One more thing, my angel," he added gravely, wrapping her shoulders with his free arm, "we have to shave your hair—"

"No, Papa, please don't make me," she begged.

Her father sighed, as though defeated by some enemy she couldn't see. "We have to, Dido," he said. "In Cape Town you had Nanny Gloria and Farouk and all the others to protect you. Here you have only me. No one here owes me loyalty. Do you understand?"

"Do we have to cut all of it?"

"It will grow back, my love."

As always, Dido didn't mean to cry. It was only that her father didn't understand about her hair. His eyes were green and his skin pale. People only had to look at him to know who he was. But the same couldn't be said about her. "It takes long to grow," she said.

"It will all be back by your next birthday."

He looked tired. And even though he didn't understand the reason she had to keep at least a portion of her hair, Dido decided it was better if she wasn't another burden for him. "You promise?" she asked.

Her father hesitated a bit. Finally, he placed the cutlery on the table, removed his arm from her shoulders, and held her hands in his. "I promise."

The tears rushed more heavily from her eyes. They eroded her face with their salt, tainting her, causing her breath to come laboured from her lungs. Whatever else her father might be able to achieve, he couldn't grow her hair as quickly as he promised. So she leaned into his chest and cried to her heart's fill.

Scatterlings

Johannes watched the girl with great curiosity. She studied his books with the flippant interest of a bored child, briskly hopping from shelf to shelf, moving deftly. It was as though she had challenged herself to examine every title by a set time.

"Have you found one you like?" he asked, startling her out of her busy oblivion. She turned to face him, and she looked as frightened as he had expected. It seemed that she wanted to flee from her task.

"My grandfather started the collection, my parents continued it, and I've added choice selections of my own," he said. "I daresay my grandfather would weep at the staggering fictional additions of recent years."

He sauntered to the armchair by the window. That way, as soon as he sat and stretched out his legs, she would be trapped between him and the bookshelf.

"He was not an imaginative man, you see," he continued. "He preferred historical works—my grandfather. My mother once confessed she doubted his understanding of the collection he claimed to cherish so dearly. She even wondered if he was literate at all." Realising that she was trapped, the girl made a motion to free herself. "Do you read?" he asked.

"My father gave me a copy of *Grimm's Fairy Tales* as a birthday gift," she answered. Johannes noted that when she spoke, every word was like a syllable of a single, long word, such that her sentences flowed uninterrupted into each other. Her voice was small and held a steady quiver. In another time, when he wasn't exasperated that she dared invade such a sacred place to him, he might have admired that she spoke with a perfect English inflection that even her father couldn't boast. She must have learnt it from her mother.

"My grandfather hated the Germans," he said. "He hated their legacies as well. I inherited his bias." He studied the girl's face, trying to detect traces of her mother besides her golden complexion and the brown of her eyes. There were none. The girl was Bram's daughter through and through.

She had inherited his saucer eyes and the distinctly pointed nose. Her mouth was wide, though not too much for her heart-shaped face. And her forehead was large and open, just like Bram's. Had she inherited the green eyes too, looking at her would be the same as looking at a younger, faintly darker Bram. The likeness was emphasised by her shaven head.

"I must confess, though opposed to the people, I remain curious as to whether their literature is any better than their wine," he continued. "Is it?"

"I've never tasted their wine," said the girl, backing towards the shelf.

"I don't imagine you have. How did you get in here?"

She seemed to be brewing a deception in her head, or at least trying. Failing, she arrived at a truth he had known even before asking the question. Well, a half-truth. "I was helping Miss Josephina with her cleaning and I suppose she just sort of forgot I was here—" He interrupted by raising his brow, challenging her to at least be more inventive. "Miss Josephina didn't know I was here," she went on. "I didn't mean to make trouble for her."

"You know whom you remind me of?"

The girl went quiet.

"Frederick Courteney Selous. Do you know of him?"

"The hunter?" she said excitedly. "He wrote the—"

"I never liked Selous," he interrupted.

"Oh," she exclaimed, apparently saddened.

"Don't you want to know how you remind me of him?"

She pondered awhile. Her forehead creased and her eyes wandered all around the room, to the floor and ceiling, searching for answers she probably guessed didn't exist. "I don't suppose it will make a difference," she concluded. "Will it?"

"You're light on your feet and quick with your hands, the way I imagine a hunter would be. And your eyes." He searched her eyes again, deciding whether the brown of their shade was lovely or repugnant. "I don't think I trust your eyes."

"Oh," she exclaimed, seeming closer to tears.

"You also remind me of your father. You look too much like him, too much like a boy," he said. "It must be the hair," he said to himself.

The girl gave a tentative smile, strangely revelling in his words. She seemed completely oblivious to the fact that he had meant to insult her. Then the moment passed as she remembered she had just been caught where she shouldn't be.

"I have one quarrel with Selous," said Johannes. "Just one. I've thought long on the matter, and it's the same I have with all men like him and your father. Can you guess what it is?"

It didn't seem that the wheels in her golden head were turning. Perhaps it was the insult he'd hurled about her father that irked her so. He found himself more intrigued than annoyed, and so asked: "Do you like hunting, little girl?"

"Who wouldn't?" she mumbled.

Johannes smiled at the notion of a girl-child idolising the sport of hunting and those who practised it. Even as a man, he couldn't appreciate the allure of firing a gun and cheering as an animal bled to its death.

He found himself curious what she might think if he revealed his aversion to meat. Naturally, he immediately decided against it. What purpose would it serve to share his eccentricities with a child? "I don't suppose it matters," he concluded aloud.

"You don't suppose it matters why you hate a man?" she asked, then instantly covered her mouth with her hands.

"Why should it?"

"Well, it's just that Nanny Gloria once asked why I loved lemons and not oranges. 'They are almost the same,' she said. They aren't, you see. But I couldn't explain it and I think she thought I was a little mad . . ." Her voice trailed away. Perhaps she regretted volunteering too much about herself.

"You never figured it out?" he asked. The girl stepped onto her left foot with her right, folded her hands behind her, and looked at the ceiling with a contorted face. She unfolded her hands and allowed them to flick in small gestures to indicate the weight of her words.

"Well," she started, "it must be because oranges are sweet. I don't think I've ever liked sweet things. Emilia was the one who liked sweets and orange juice . . ." She folded her hands again and shyly looked at the floor, and swapped the position of her feet.

"That doesn't seem like something difficult to decide."

"But . . . but . . . it doesn't matter."

"What?" he cajoled.

"Everyone likes oranges." She said it as though confirming the colour of the sky, or the brilliance of the sun—as though he was a fool to miss it.

"And you thought you'd be different?"

"I know you think it's childish. You don't have to mock me."

"I'm not mocking you. Why would I mock you?"

"My mother didn't understand . . . I think," she said, her voice returning to its small, quivery state. "Anyway, why do you hate Selous?" she asked, her voice rising an octave and her eyes searching his for answers he might try to deny her. "I thought everyone liked him."

"That's because you are your father's daughter, and your father is quite an accomplished Englishman," he said. The girl didn't seem to understand, so he obliged her by elaborating: "Do you know what Africa's greatest treasure is?" he asked, hoping she would give a frivolous answer, so he might mock her.

"Everything," she declared. She grinned foolishly and almost bounced on her feet. Pride, he thought, she felt pride in that moment. "I think it's everything, but my mother said I was too young to understand the way of the world. When I told my father my answer he smiled and rubbed my hair." She looked sad then and, apparently deciding silence was a wise friend, resumed looking at the floor with her hands folded behind her back.

"I'm glad to inform you that your mother was wrong, as she was with everything else."

"You knew my mother?"

"Yes, briefly."

"Well, she didn't like Selous, same as you. It was always my father who talked about Selous. But not anymore. Do you know why?"

"I can't presume to understand your father's peculiarities," said Johannes. "But see here, men like him have but one goal. They pursue the creation of a new Europe, a home away from home, as it were. I concede that it is a noble goal, but often executed clumsily; for men like your father think it right to freely mix the principles of colliding worlds.

"I'll also concede that lesser races can be lifted, but it is a process that needs be monitored, closely, constantly. To neglect these regulations can only create a second race so elevated above its natural state, its people might revolt against its liberators. This race, newly literate and civilised, could not be controlled, and might fancy freedoms best left denied. Tell me, little girl, what would be the point of two Europes in the world? What would be the use of an Africa depleted of its unique curiosities?"

As Johannes had expected, the girl didn't answer. She looked dazed and unsure. He tried again: "I've confused your little brain, haven't I? Let's see . . . let me try putting it this way, I once visited a village in the north. There, I sat with a man who had lived a hundred and two years, or something close to it. No one knew his true age. His people marked years in great calamities and blessings, in droughts and floods, and in bountiful harvests.

"All he knew about his birth was that it was in the first year of an eight-summer drought, and they called him wise for it. Maybe he *was* wise. After all, he was a chief, and chiefs and queens are made wise by some default of fate. I therefore considered his words as a sacred sort of wisdom." He paused, wishing he had his pipe with him, then continued: "Do you know what he told me?"

The girl shook her head. At least she was still able to accomplish that much. Johannes feared he might have paralysed her with his ramblings. "You see"—he cleared his throat—"the chief told me about the abduction of his only daughter. It was in a year of winter rains. The abductors came from a village ruled by a witch woman who was called the Rain Queen for her gift of commanding the heavens to give her people rain. Her mother, her mother's mother, and all the women of her lineage had been gifted with this magic by the gods of that place."

He paused to clear his throat again. The girl leaned forward and tilted her right ear towards Johannes. He surmised it was in effort to trap any words that might try to escape her curious mind. Strangely, he found himself pleased by that.

"The queen's people didn't know about drought and famine," he continued. "But now, she held a great secret." Johannes imagined he could see the girl's heart beating faster at hearing those words. He smiled. "The queen was childless. A vision showed her that the line of queens was at an end. But there was a girl who, when shown the way of the gods, could be the new rain-giver. Are you still with me, little girl?"

The girl nodded vigorously.

"Good. On seeing the vision, the queen assembled her strongest warriors and blessed them with her magic. The warriors couldn't be followed by any living man. Their footsteps were washed away by rain. When they spoke, their voices couldn't be heard, for they were followed by thunder. Their faces couldn't be seen, for a bright light shone upon them. They travelled hidden—"

"Is their realm in the Basotho Lands?" asked the girl.

It was Johannes's turn to be curious. "If you already know the story, then I shouldn't waste my time," he said.

"I'm sorry. It's only that I've been trying to remember if the Balobedu tribes were the ones ruled by a rain queen. Miss Josephina has been teaching me."

"They are. May I continue?"

The girl nodded doubtfully.

"Thus the queen's warriors abducted the chief's daughter," said Johannes. "When he told me his tale, three decades, or something close, had passed since he last saw his daughter. He heard from passing tales and gossiping wives that his daughter had a great many wives, and that she had raised sons and daughters of her own, and brave and beautiful they were. The chief's daughter was a wise rain-giver, whispered the rumours.

"The chief told me, with his hands holding a cane between his knees, that the seers of his grandfather's time foresaw his descendants living in greatness, in the songs of all who followed, and forever on the tongues of gossiping wives. He said it with pride, you see, with contentment, without worry for his lost kin. Have you heard everything?"

The girl nodded again.

"The chief told me of his daughter's efficient rule. He said to me, 'My good man, the cattle in her lands are fat and the grass is greenest of all valleys.' He smiled, nodded to himself, and stamped the wooden cane in his frail hands.

"I asked why she didn't give rains to her father's lands. After all, the chief's people were plagued by a drought of four years or so." Johannes stopped to guffaw, without mirth. "Do you know what he told me?" he asked, earnestly hoping the girl would give the same answer as the chief. If she did, maybe there was sense in the madness he had witnessed.

Alas, the girl only shook her head—though she looked as disappointed as he felt.

"He said to me . . ." Then he stopped again, hoping she'd come upon an epiphany. Seeing that she hadn't, he continued: "He said: 'The gods' gift cannot follow her here. And it will not exist away from her. That is how we find ourselves in this divine quagmire.' Then he laughed, coughed, and retreated to his hut, because he was nearing his end. Do you understand now?"

The girl nodded thoughtfully, as though the chief's response made sense to her. She opened her mouth, but apparently decided her thoughts might not be sufficiently insightful. "That's the reason you hate Selous and my father?" she asked eventually.

"I don't hate your father. He's my oldest friend."

"But you said—"

"Then you misunderstood. You're too young to understand. This was a waste of time."

"I'm also very clever. I can tell the difference between the Southern Cross and the False Cross. I know all the seas on the moon, and all the Galilean moons of Jupiter—"

"Yes, yes"—he waved—"and the names of hunters, apparently; which only magnifies your ignorance. I don't mean to mock you—"

"I'm not crying."

"I didn't say you were." He felt the need for his pipe grow with every second, so he spewed his words more swiftly. Maybe her tears would subside and the discomfort he felt would do so as well. "See here," he said, "I don't think Selous and your father would understand the chief's story. Do you know why?"

"No," she said, shaking her head, seemingly shunning him and all his philosophies.

"Come now. It's no fun if you don't try, dear girl."

"Well, if I had to guess . . ." She looked at the ceiling and then the floor. Finally, she looked at him and repeated the folding game with her hands. "I'd say you aren't an ordinary man. I mean, well I suppose . . . you don't even like Selous, who was the bravest hunter that ever lived. He killed scores and scores of lions, buffalo, and rhinos. There's never been anyone like him—"

"And there should never be!" he shouted. The girl flinched. He had conducted himself calmly. But as often happened with such matters, Johannes was unable to continue with civility. He still tried. He figured that if he could teach the half-Black girl anything, it was that vagabonds like Selous shouldn't be revered.

"See now," he cajoled, "these people who, by the joke of some bored god, have the fortune of being white . . . these people find it perfectly acceptable to polish their rifles and shoot scores of lions. For what? So they might drag a lion's mane back to England, or a buffalo's horns to display at a private library? Do you know what happens when an old friend of this hunter sees the buffalo horns, and the lion's mane on that wall?

"This friend decides he, too, is brave. He empties his sundries account, boards a ship, and before anyone can warn the lions and the buffalo, we have a new hunter in the savannah. Just as we have a new hunter, we have a dead lion. Like that it continues. They only take from this wild land of ours—each exotic thing they see, they take from our plains with impunity.

"They go back to their home. But we, the children of this land we love so dearly, are left behind with angry animals that seek revenge—elephants that remember, that seek their slaughtered young; dwindling herds of rhinos that fear their own kind; elusive leopards that grow ever more distrustful of us. Do you understand what I am telling you, girl?"

"I don't think so," she mumbled, almost close to tears. She now looked absolutely frightened by him.

"I should be explicit then. What I mean to tell you is that we freely submit our treasures to them. Them." He stretched his hand to retrieve the tobacco pipe from the drawer. It was difficult to quit the thing. It made him cough and his eyes often stung, yet an hour without it made his chest burn with longing and his hands itch for the familiar smoothness of the wood.

Josephina had already loaded the tobacco. He found a box of matches, struck one, and lit his pipe. The first puff was the most divine. He inhaled deeply, allowing the smoke to fill his lungs. Once satisfied, he exhaled slowly, savouring the taste, briefly closing his eyes to appreciate the beauty of such a simple thing. "We Africans are a meek people," he said, grinding his teeth in frustration at his short-lived pleasure. "It's an easy thing to be meek and cowardly."

"But you are a Boer—European," she informed him. "You can't also be African."

He laughed, puffing out more smoke. "What robs me of my African identity? Your mother was Black, yet she imagined herself English. Do you imagine that she—"

"There you are, Dido!" announced Bram, entering the library with relief on his face.

The girl sprinted from the shelf, jumped over Johannes's legs without a thought, and completed her sprint to her father. When she reached him she jumped into his arms, holding him around the neck.

Bram smiled. "Josephina was sure you went to the river with the other children," he said. "Yet here you are."

The girl looked at the floor, for her father had just revealed her lie.

"She found my library more interesting," said Johannes.

"I'm sorry if she was any trouble, John," said Abram. "I told her not to set foot in here."

"There lies your first fault," said Johannes, "you told her not to do it. So of course, she had to do it." They laughed. Even the girl, who was crouched to the size of a rodent in her father's arms, gave a giggle. "You will take her to the river?" asked Johannes.

"She has to keep up with her lessons. As soon as we leave your library, we will be entwined with subjects she complains are boring. I do apologise for the trouble, John, most sincerely," said Bram, a look of sadness on his face. At that, Johannes felt uneasiness bubble within him.

Fortunately, the girl saved them from further discomfort by asking Johannes: "Do you know more stories about the Rain People?"

"A million more," he answered. And at that, Bram briskly turned to leave, as though impatient to remove the girl from

Johannes's presence. It was well enough, he thought; inane chatter with the girl was sufficiently amusing to pass a few minutes, but there were other ways to waste away an afternoon.

Tentatively waving her farewell to Johannes, the girl grinned and chatted happily to her father. She spoke in a way Johannes now deduced was her nature—with everything as a single, long word, as though nothing existed independently.

As he closed the door to drown her voice and giggles, Johannes frowned at himself. He'd forgotten to ask the girl who had shorn her hair. But alas, she was gone. So he puffed his pipe and allowed the smoke, the questions, and solitude to hug him tightly.

A Traveling Man

Miss Josephina said the northern tribes were Sun people. They told time by the sun, planted their seeds by it, and counted their years in summers and other sun things.

Dido asked her: "Have you ever been to the south?"

"No," said Miss Josephina, chuckling. "But my husband has visited many times with *Baas* Joubert. He buys nice things there, my husband."

"Oh. Mr. Joubert has been there?"

"Oh yes. He came from there. He is a southern person," Miss Josephina said, smiling. "*Baas* is a traveling man, you see."

"Is that how he met the chief?"

"The chief?"

"He said he went north and met a chief whose daughter was stolen by the Rain People."

"My Julius . . . my husband has not spoken of a chief," said Miss

Josephina. She walked around Mr. Joubert's bed, neatly tucking in the sheets. Then she rested her hands on her hips and heaved. "Maybe there *is* a chief and *Baas* met him."

"Mr. Julius will know, won't he?"

Miss Josephina laughed until her merriment was interrupted by a soft cough. "My husband will know, maybe. But many things my husband knows and does not say."

Dido was not sure she understood. She smiled anyhow, and shrugged, in case Miss Josephina thought it was strange that she didn't find Mr. Julius's secrecy amusing.

"Please hand me the pillows," said Miss Josephina.

Dido did as she was told. "Has Mr. Joubert told you the chief's story?"

"*Baas* tells many stories. But I am an old woman and sometimes I do not remember." She spoke distractedly, her attention on the pillows. "Come, we are finished here. We must pack your things now."

Dido followed Miss Josephina. She checked around corners and over her shoulder to make sure that no one was around to see her leaving Mr. Joubert's room. Since their meeting in his library, she had successfully avoided him and the scolding she had been dreading.

"Do you think there will be people like me in Rhodesia?" she asked Miss Josephina, taking care to keep her voice soft.

Miss Josephina didn't answer immediately. She opened each door and closed it, steadily marched on, then opened and closed another, until they reached Dido and her father's quarters. Just when Dido lost hope of an answer, Miss Josephina sighed. "I knew a man who went to Uganda. He promised to come back to tell me of his adventures. But time is short. I don't believe he has finished the adventures."

"He was also Black and white at the same time, like me?"

"He was Indian."

"Oh," said Dido, feeling disappointment wash over her. "When did he go?"

Miss Josephina sighed again. "It was long ago," she said. "I had all my teeth."

"Did the man have a daughter too?"

"He did not. But like your father, he was a fugitive of his past."

Dido was not sure she understood that either, but she nodded. "I think *Baas* Joubert will give better answers than these," said Miss Josephina. "You must ask him."

"No, thank you," Dido whispered to herself. "Where is his wife? Does he have one?"

Josephina was then carrying Dido's suitcase, which she almost dropped onto her feet. But she steadied herself by balancing against the wardrobe and then slowly heaving the suitcase onto the bed. "Shame on you, young girl," she said, smiling. "You are making the old woman do the work." Dido didn't miss that Miss Josephina looked unsettled.

"My father had a wife," said Dido, "my mother. But she died in April. I think she loved me . . . sometimes I miss her." Dido knew she would cry in only moments. She shrugged and said, "Now I just have my father . . . Sometimes I think he misses her too."

Miss Josephina hugged her. And for a moment, Dido felt as though she was sheltered in Nanny Gloria's arms and Emilia was flying on their mother's back somewhere close by, laughing at the top of her lungs.

"My friend who went to Uganda, he knew many things," said Miss Josephina. "It may be that he passed the home of this chief."

"Maybe," whispered Dido.

"You know, my mother was a *ngaka*—a traditional healer. She knew many things, even unknown things, things that are years away and beyond this world. Her gift was strong. But I never had it myself. I miss her. Many people miss her. But I think they miss her gift more."

"Could she do magic like Nanny Gloria and the Rain Queen?"

Miss Josephina laughed. "We do not call it magic."

"Oh."

Miss Josephina emptied the suitcase on the mattress and signalled for Dido to climb up onto the bed. "*Baas* Joubert has told me there will be new clothes coming for you. But even the sun cannot be relied on sometimes. In case they do not come in time, you must show me which clothes you want to use when you travel. They must be packed at the top."

Dido chose her favourite dress, the yellow frock with a ribbon around the waist. She owned another in moss green, and one in dull brown. She liked those too, but not as much as the yellow. Emilia had owned one similar to it and worn it whenever she could, which was every time she begged Nanny Gloria for permission.

"I love the colours," said Miss Josephina. "But I was told you must choose boys' clothes."

"I know, but just in case, you know. I have matching socks," said Dido. She dug through the pile to find them. "My sister had the same. Did you ever have a sister, Miss Josephina?"

"I was the only child born to my mother."

"Couldn't your mother do magic . . . I mean, she was a witch doctor, couldn't she make sisters and brothers for you?"

"Being a *ngaka* is not the same as being a witch. And it is not the same as having magic."

"Oh, I see. Then why couldn't you be a *ngaka*? If it's not the same as magic, couldn't you just choose to be one?"

"Because my Ancestors never sent me the call," she said. She set the chosen dresses and trousers aside and walked to the wardrobe to fetch the iron. "I will have to fetch embers from the oven for this. Will you come with me?"

"Will there be fire there?"

"Only embers now. The fire has died, I think."

"Okay," said Dido, hopping off the bed. "How did your mother die?"

"It was the coughing disease of nearly ten years ago, and her age. She left me the bones of her talent and two huts by the river. But not the Ancestors' call. That is the reason I am not a *ngaka*. I do not think the calling will come for me now. I am too old for the initiation."

"My mother didn't leave anything for me," whispered Dido.

"The dead always leave something," said Miss Josephina, "even when they do not intend it. How else would they haunt us?"

They walked past Mr. Joubert's library and Dido felt her cheeks burn with worry. She smelled the smoke from his pipe and feared that her feet weren't carrying her away quickly enough. So she stepped lightly, and prayed that Miss Josephina would remain silent as well, so they could pass without his notice. But he coughed, thus helping to mask the sound of their footsteps.

"Do you think my mother will haunt me? And my sister?" she asked, as soon as they entered the kitchen. She wanted to ask about the eland as well, but she was afraid Miss Josephina wouldn't understand. So she left it at just her mother and sister.

"No. I do not think your mother and sister will haunt you," said Miss Josephina.

"What if they do?"

"Tell them you are a child. Children should not be haunted."

"Will they return when I am older?"

Miss Josephina answered after a long moment of silence: "It is not easy for me to tell you."

"But there is something for you to say, right?"

Miss Josephina nodded. "But it frightens me because you are a child."

"Miss Josephina," said Dido, "I have watched my mother and sister die. Sometimes I've watched my father become as sad as my mother was. He tries to hide it because I'm a child. But he doesn't hide well and I see. Nanny Gloria tried to shield me too. Emilia never saw these things. She was a child, but *I* see. I have always seen."

"You have the heart of a child," said Miss Josephina, "the fears of a child, even the eyes of one. You see these things simply. There is beauty in that kind of simplicity."

"There is also ignorance."

"And the peace of innocence."

"The peace of fools."

Miss Josephina laughed. "You are too clever," she said. "Too clever for this old woman."

Dido was forced to yield a smile. "So will you tell me?" she said.

"I must start from the beginning for you to understand. And to start from the beginning will make it a long story."

"I love stories," said Dido. "My mother told them when she wasn't overcome with her sadness. Emilia loved them too, especially the one about the Swan Princess and her adventures across the Heaven Lands. My mother wrote that one, and she named the heroes after me and Emilia. It made us happy."

"My father did not like stories," said Miss Josephina. "He did not find them useful."

"Sometimes I think my father is the same."

"This makes you sad, I see."

"One day I want to be a storyteller. I like to listen when people tell stories. I want to learn. I want to be as good as my mother. But I think it will make my father sad."

"I see."

"So will you tell me?"

"It is your time you choose to waste," said Miss Josephina, shrugging. "This is the way it went: my father was simple; this, he gave to me. He worked as a farmhand. For his service he received fresh milk, shillings, and old things his *baas* no longer wanted. When the people of my village looked at my father they said: 'There goes Ntlhabeni. He is rich, you know. In the winter he buys blankets and shoes for his family, and bread and jam. He sleeps on a bed that was gifted to him by his *baas*. What a blessed man Ntlhabeni is.'

"My father carried these epithets with pride. And when the people of my village looked at me and said, 'There goes Možaži, she is the only child of Ntlhabeni,' I smiled and shared in my father's pride." Miss Josephina paused and sighed, it seemed to Dido, to gather her thoughts.

"Your people call you Možaži?" asked Dido, her accent somewhat bending the name.

"Yes. That is the name my father gave me."

"Why don't the people here call you that?"

"Josephina is simpler for *Baas*. That is how these things are done."

"I suppose that's the reason Nanny Gloria didn't call herself Mmakoma. I thought she liked to be known as Gloria, but I suppose . . . I suppose I was wrong."

"And now you know the true reason."

"How do your Ancestors find you? Have you told them about the name of Josephina?"

"They find the blood of my veins, and the spirit of my people. This way I cannot be lost."

Dido silently pondered that. "I never knew my people," she whispered. "My Ancestors were never told I was born . . . Nanny Gloria fixed it, I think. She gave me the name of Khelelo, with the praise name of Mmamolapi, and the clan name . . . I forgot the clan name. I wrote it in my journal, though."

"Those are good names. Strong names," nodded Miss Josephina.

"Nanny Gloria told me so. Khelelo was her mother's name, I think. Do you think the Ancestors will find me if I am lost, even in Rhodesia and wherever else my father and I go?"

"That is the way it goes."

"Are you sure?"

"Oh yes," said Miss Josephina. "My Julius has lived many years in foolishness. Yet no calamity has befallen him. He has travelled to Rhodesia and beyond, on boats and camels and other things my eyes have not seen. Through that, the Ancestors have watched him, and returned him to me well." She smiled and shook her head, and continued, "If such a fool they guard, then a child like you will live to be older even than me."

That lifted Dido's spirit. "What happened to your father?"

"See," said Miss Josephina, "the fights between the Dutch and English masters confuse me. If one master has roots in one country and not another, it makes no difference to me, the same way it made no difference to my father. 'Your father works for a white farmer,' said my mother to me. And this I knew to be true until the day my father did not work for that farmer.

"My father's farmer, who was English, abandoned the farm, see, it fell into disrepair. Slowly, my shoes became too old and small. The blankets became thin and the bread, rare. And so, near the end of his life my father's face became strange to me. He was a man who inherited his fortunes and misfortunes from another. When it could not be said he was a blessed man, I saw his spirit break.

"He walked for many hours searching for new work. He failed. Then he was bitten by a snake and died in pain. In his shame, he wept. I was a child, so I asked him the reason he felt ashamed. Do you know what he said?"

Miss Josephina looked at Dido. Dido didn't know the answer, just as she hadn't known what the chief told Mr. Joubert. But she wanted to say something. Miss Josephina looked sad and Dido wanted to make her smile. In the end all that she did was shake her head, hug Miss Josephina, and say: "I'm sorry."

"There is nothing to regret," said Miss Josephina. She hugged Dido tightly and then released her. "This is an old tale and the pain is almost gone now. Shall I continue?"

Dido nodded.

"My father asked for my forgiveness. 'Možaži, my child, remember me kindly,' he begged. I believed . . . I believed that if I remembered him weeping, shameful, or wallowing in the stench of his failures, he would haunt me. His ghost would hate me and turn his memories bitter. I lied to him. 'I will remember you kindly,' I said. He smiled and left the world content. When I slept I dreamt of him. He wept and asked, 'Do you remember me?' I told him I did not remember him unkindly, and woke from the dream unburdened." Miss Josephina paused again to shake her head. "These things, Dido," she said, "they are difficult. Old tales of an old woman . . . What business have I, telling a child? But if that child asks of the things of hauntings, she must know them.

"He was my father. He gave me my name, my nose, my eyes, and all the things my mother did not. He loved me. If I walk among my people they will say, 'There goes Možaži. She is the only daughter of Ntlhabeni. How her father would smile with pride if he saw her now, blessed as she is.' So, I ask myself: What does it mean to be haunted by such a man? Is he a ghost; a memory; my life-giver; or just a man who, given his common deeds, will be lost in time?

"I cannot know these things. I have not travelled like my husband. I cannot read or write in the sophisticated way you can, and I do not have my mother's gift. I only know that I wasted many years trying to forget my father. If he was cruel it would be wiser to forget him. But he was not. I do not think his ghost would be cruel. His memory, now fading with my age, is pale. When I could still remember him I tried to forget him. And now that I try to remember him, I cannot. I have even forgotten his voice. That is the way it went." And so Miss Josephina's story ended.

Silence stretched between them, as Miss Josephina wiped her tears and Dido thought about the story. Her own memory had not yet been changed by time, but by the smoke that had filled her eyes and lungs. But from what she remembered, she hadn't made a promise to her mother, nor to Emilia. In fact, she didn't remember the last words she had said to her sister.

"This was a sad story," decided Dido. "When did your father die?"

"Nearly fifty-eight summers now," said Miss Josephina.

Dido thought about the meaning of that. She said at last: "It still makes you sad, even after all that time. Does it mean the night of the fire will make me sad until I am older even than you?"

"It means you will remember those you loved for as long as you live."

"But I'm not sure I want to always remember Emilia and my mother. My mother was sad and Emilia's face frightened me that night. My father says I was a good daughter and sister, that they will never haunt me. But what if they change their minds and think I wasn't a good sister or daughter? What if they do haunt me, like true ghosts, like the tall man whose face can't be seen? What if death makes them forget I loved them and that it broke my heart when they died . . . ?"

Her speech became too broken by sobs for Dido to carry on. She folded her body so her head touched her knees. She wanted to stop the tears, like she always did. Yet they teemed from her eyes and she was afraid they'd never stop. All she felt, beyond her growing shame, were Miss Josephina's hands as they lifted her from the bed and into warm arms. "There now, my child," said Miss Josephina. "Let the pain leave your soul. Let the tears fall. This way it will leave you."

"I'm . . . so . . . sorry," said Dido, between sobs.

"There is nothing to regret. Even I, old as I am, find reason to shed tears from time to time. There is no shame in it."

Assured by Miss Josephina's words, Dido cried freely, copiously, until she felt the beating of her heart slow down. Miss Josephina's hand continued to softly rub her back, and her voice whispered, "Let the tears fall, sweet child. Let them fall," again and again, until Dido's eyes grew tired from crying and closed themselves to rest.

A Weightless Cloak
of Blindness

Dido woke up to find herself in darkness. The sun had set and the stars risen. Her hiccoughs had gone, as had her short breath and tears. When she rose from the bed she heard her father move in the armchair. "You're finally awake," he said.

"I didn't mean to sleep. Miss Josephina and I were packing and—" She searched for a word, a simple word that wouldn't make her father sad. Before she could find it, he lit the candles and joined her on the bed.

"Josephina told me," he said, indicating for her to sit on his lap. "You cried in your sleep," he whispered, too softly; if he wasn't so close, she wouldn't have heard him.

Afraid she would cry again, Dido swallowed and blinked repeatedly. She wondered if there was ever anyone who cried until their tears couldn't fall anymore. It seemed, in that moment, she was such a person. Even the breeze wafting through the window couldn't provoke a single teardrop. "I was tired," she whispered to her father.

"Do you remember everything from the night of the fire?" he said. Dido shook her head. She added, "Sometimes it feels like a dream. I forget most dreams . . . but not the fire. That's how I know the fire wasn't a dream. It makes me sad, Papa. I miss Mama and Emilia. Sometimes it feels like my heart will never stop breaking. The pain frightens me."

Her father nodded and took her hand in his. "I miss them too," he said.

"Even Mama?"

To answer, her father looked at the window and sighed deeply. Then he said: "The first time I saw her I lost my breath. For a heartbeat, my heart stilled in my chest. I loved your mother, Dido, from that moment until her last breath. But it was never the same with her. You're a child, her child. I don't expect you to understand what it means to be shunned by her until all the love is consumed by bitterness. Do you know that she tried to kill you? Do you know that?

"That is what she did. She took my heart and returned it ruined. Then she burnt herself from this world. She stole your sister and would have stolen you too. For that, I cannot forgive her. Her love I could live without. I accepted my fate with her, but what she did to you, what she did to your sister, it was unforgivable . . ." Her father's voice trailed off. It sounded to Dido like he was trying to catch his breath. She hugged him tightly. His heart beat fast and strong against hers. "I'm sorry, Papa," she said. "I didn't mean to make you sad."

"I'm not sad," he said. "I am tired. Come, you must eat." He stood up, placing her on her feet. "Josephina saved your meal—"

"Papa?" she interrupted. She figured that if she wasn't brave in that moment, the chance might slip away and never come again.

"Yes?"

"I have a secret, you see," she started. "I know the reason Mama started the fire. She wasn't trying to steal me and Emilia from you. I think she was trying to save us. She said she poisoned our skin so she had to take us to the stars—" Dido stopped to swallow.

Her father knelt in front of her and looked at her with concern. "Is this another dream, Dido?"

She shook her head. "No. Nanny Gloria gave me one of Mama's journals. She found it in the ruins. Parts of it burnt away, but some of it survived." She stopped to swallow again. "That's how I know she loved you, Papa."

Her father still looked at her strangely, but his concern was replaced with what looked like confusion. "You have your mother's journal?"

"Yes," said Dido. "She wrote about her fathers and Ireland and the West Indies. She wrote about her dreams, about her journey to Africa. She wrote about you. She tried to stay alive, Papa."

Her father seemed numb with confusion. "Gloria found it in the ruins?"

"Yes," said Dido. "After the fire died. But she only found one of them. I tried to look for the others but I didn't find them. Are you angry with me?"

He shook his head. He reclaimed his seat on the bed and looked at nothing in particular. Dido wasn't sure what to say. The silence unsettled her. She tried to find shapes in the dancing shadows born from the candlelight, to construct them with her mind so she could say to her father, "Doesn't that look like a rat gnawing where he isn't supposed to, or a cat chasing a rat, or a dog chasing a cat?" But the shadows only resembled, vaguely, the rise and fall of sea waves. They danced on the walls ordinarily, imperfectly casting their feeble darkness. They fascinated her only in the way they seemed to want victory over their dancing fellows, as though their rise and fall was some struggle for supremacy. It was futile, she decided. Every shadow fell as easily as his neighbour rose, and he too fell as soon as he rose, yielding to a new victor born from a rival candle. She looked at her father, who seemed to be as fascinated by the shadows as she was.

"Have I been failing you since that cursed night?" he asked, suddenly.

"No," said Dido, quickly.

"Would you tell the truth if I were?"

"I would, Papa. I promise I would."

"Then tell me, Dido: have I done my duty with you? Have you felt loved?"

"I know you love me, Papa."

"But you need more from me. More than the duty of a mother, or the companionship Emilia gave you. More than my protection—you need more, don't you?"

Dido wasn't sure she understood. She looked at her father's face to measure his feelings beyond what he said. "I don't understand."

"Do you need anything else from me?"

She shook her head.

"Dido, it pains me to tell you: I'm your only family, and you are mine. I realise I . . . I have neglected the sentimental aspects of my duty. I assumed that my love for was you enough to keep you happy. It pains me to vilify your mother, but I think I'm the better parent. It seems, however, that I've been failing you. To correct these faults, you must always tell me the truth. It won't do us any good to deceive each other. So I'll ask you again: do you need anything else from me?"

"You won't be angry with me?"

He slowly shook his head, held her face in his hands, and said, "I promise."

"Okay," nodded Dido. She left the bed to retrieve her mother's journal from the suitcase. She handed it to her father. "Most of the stories Mama wrote were burnt by the fire," she said. "I've finished the ones she read to me and Emilia from my memory, the one about the Children of the Sky God, and the one about the Ghost of Verlatenbosch. But she never read most of them and I don't know how to finish them, especially the last one. Can you please read the journal to see if you can help me with the unfin-ished ones?"

"That's what you want?"

Dido nodded. "For now I think . . . I think that will be all. Are you sure you're not angry with me?"

"I'm sure, my love." He smiled and rubbed her head. "I'll help where I can."

"Thank you, Papa," she said, hugging him.

He gently rested his chin on her head. "You must eat now," he said. "Come."

Dido took her father's hand and followed him outside. The night draped them like a weightless cloak of blindness. The moon, a crescent rising leisurely in a corner of the western sky, only served to signal the end of the month, the start of another; and maybe, Dido hoped, an easier path. She smiled, willing her thoughts to turn true and the truth to remain true. Maybe that was it—the promise of the moon.

"We have cursed you," she thought she heard her father say, softly, too softly—like the whisper of the wind that once called her name. She couldn't be sure. She carried on walking beside him in her doubt and silence.

PART FOUR

To Africa

A Small Black Book
with a Burnt Spine

Alisa's journal was a small black book with a burnt spine. Parts of it were burnt completely, others were water-damaged; in some places, the original writing was still legible, or Dido had traced over the faint letters. Most of it, though, was ruined and couldn't be salvaged. There were missing pages too. At best, the thing was a fractured story Abram had no desire to read at all. At worst, it was Alisa's excuse for her crime, and Abram had no desire to forgive her.

But he had to read it, didn't he? For his daughter's sake, he had to endure Alisa only a little while longer. Finally, carefully, he opened it.

Miss Alisa Miller's
Journal: 1912

Monday, 1 January

My biggest fear is that I won't be able to hold on forever, that one day I will give in and end my own life. It's a very complicated predicament to find oneself in; even I don't understand it. As I've reached a milestone of sorts today, my thirtieth birthday, I've decided that it is, perhaps, time that I started to at least *try* to understand. Surely, I owe it to myself.

I should start by saying I'm not suicidal. In fact, I'm not inclined to any form of murder at all. I do think, however, that when I was eleven years old and ground up glass so I could put it in my tea, I was surely trying to kill myself.

I understand that these are contradictions. I'm supposed to

know the specific reason for seemingly wanting to kill myself, that if asked, I should recite such tragedies as: my father was born a slave, I never knew my mother, and so forth. I feel that if I told anyone about my predicament, they'd surely want a pathology, a tangible thing that can easily be cited; but the truth is neither my birth father's slavery nor my mother's death, nor any aspect of my life for that matter, has left me so completely without hope.

A natural question to ask is: *How can you not know? How can you not understand? This is about you, after all. It has to be something.*

Of course it's something. That's what frustrates me—it has to be something. But like love or joy or even hatred, I can't quantify it, nor explain it. For me it's like a child suckling its mother's breast simply because it knows to do so. Or that same child saying "Mama" as its first word. Or that same child falling in love thirteen years later, simply because it can't help it.

I can't measure my melancholy when I sink into it. I can't dissect it. The best I can do is this: sometimes, when I think about the burden of breathing and living and carrying on for the sake of carrying on, I feel helpless. It frightens me, this state of living for the sake of living. And the more I think about it the harder it is to breathe. If you've never had the feeling that you've died, been buried, then abruptly resurrected, it's not something you can easily understand. (Although to be honest, sometimes I think my mind concocts these stories as an excuse.)

My dreams are surreal. I remember one in which I couldn't breathe; then a hand made of shadows dragged me into a deep and dark nothingness where I was suspended like a marionette held up by countless shadow hands, and all the while I still couldn't breathe. When I awoke I was paralysed in my bed, unable to move or scream or cry, and I was cold, so cold and stifled, as though I had come out of a grave.

It's as though I'm less alive, as though my life has been siphoned off into the nothingness I dreamt, siphoned off to birth the shadow hands that press down, press down to siphon out more of my life. They take their life from me, my dreams. I dread having to sleep. That kind of fear is so simple, so rudimentary, but with time it webs itself so intricately, so deeply, that it starts to web itself around your mind and heart and everything you see. It crouches at the base of your being, and no matter what you do you know it's always there, waiting.

It's the waiting that frightens me, because waiting ends, and then it must unfold into something new. By then, that web of fear and poison and malice will be old and familiar, so much like a comfort, like an enemy I can't recognise. It will be a long-forgotten friend I must embrace, and that's when I'll give in. It's like I'm falling into a hole that never ends, a hole I can't quite see, but I know it's there, gaping, swallowing me, and there's nothing I can do about it. *This* is my biggest fear: I don't know if I'll be able to hold on forever.

I don't want to be this way: curled in my bed and crying over an emptiness I don't understand. I want what my mother wants for me: a smile, a clear head, lightheartedness, freedom from these chains I can't even touch or feel or smell, these chains that exist only in my mind. Freedom. Freedom.

More and more, I know I must go to Africa. I think that's the best chance I have of understanding whatever it is that's ailing me. In the same way I can't explain the contradiction of my attitude to life, I can't explain why I'm so pulled to Africa; well, not beyond the obvious reasons. Something not quite of this world has been calling me there. I need to go. I need to understand the shadow hands I've been dreaming since my childhood.

I must convince my mother to let me go.

Tuesday, 2 January

Africa is far. It is large too, with its coastlines claiming camaraderie with the Atlantic and Indian Oceans. On each side, the shores surrender the continent's people with abandon, while occasionally receiving prisoners from Europe and slaves from the south of Asia.

Cape Town, being among the oldest of Europe's bastard cities in the New World, and by consequence, among the most obligated to soothe its wayward children's homesickness, was designed to closely resemble the Old World.

Having proven itself a waystation worthy of further transformation, this Tavern of the Seas was soon injected with slaves from the East Indies—whose people are now called the Cape Malay. In this way too, the city was designed to echo the imperial success of the Old World, relying on the enslavement of one race for the betterment of another. In Cape Town, Europe could perfect its past, it could do so carefully.

It is, I have concluded, an apt place to begin my exploration of the place that supposedly birthed me. It will be familiar, I think. "From Cape to Cairo," as Cecil John Rhodes put it in his assessment of his own capabilities.

And so, through the city of the sea, to Africa it is!

[Missing Journal
Entry Text]

[Exact date unknown]

While gathering my things for the pending voyage, I found a scrap on which I once scribbled the beginnings of an adventure story. I started the thing by recalling my childhood. But for one reason or another, I can't remember the reason I began the story, nor why I abandoned it. Quite annoying, I must say. Yet here I am, starting again.

When I was seven years old and the so-called Russian flu swept across the world, my father, having been caught by the tragedy, called me to his side and said, "I never told you the story of the Sky God Children, did I?"

He spoke with the kind of rhythm that blended the words into each other, erasing punctuation and other formalities. He swallowed the soft consonants almost completely; I had to dig them out of my memory, out of my own familiarity with the words. He sounded like a song.

To his question, I shook my head, and at this my father's memory retuned to him. "No, I never did," he concluded. "The Children of the Sky God were three, you know. One was the sun. One was Night. One was the moon. You can't trust Night and you can't make the sun do what you please. You can't make him change. But the moon never changes, my Lissy. She never changes." As he said this, the moon glowed not fully but as a faint, shy crescent that hid itself behind gliding clouds. The scene belied my father's words. The moon changed even as he spoke— shying away in one moment, then boasting its glow in the next.

"Come winter or come summer, the moon never changes," he went on. He coughed, for the wind suddenly blew more strongly, reminding my father of his ailment, and so reminding him to shiver and cough and wipe his mouth with the back of his hand. "I see it changing now," I said, looking at the sky. "It's full one day and gone the next, and sometimes it's only half of itself." I tried to copy my father's rhythm of speaking, but I never could, not quite. I always broke my rhythm where I shouldn't, where my father wouldn't.

"Oh yeah. The night eats the moon away," said my father, nodding. "It eats and eats and the moon becomes a crescent that shines only so-so. Darkness is greedy so Night eats some more till the moon goes away from the sky and you don't see it anymore. But time is kind, you see. When the moon comes back it comes back whole and shines same as old times." Another gust of wind assaulted us, and my father, deciding he could endure no more, beckoned for me to follow him into the darkness of our hovel.

There was still a bit of light outside, a bit of sun to warm away the chill of the wind. I was reluctant to leave it. But my father couldn't sit too long in the sun either; it burnt his skin. The cold of our hovel made him shiver too, but he could abide it. He said, grimly, that "his bones were kindred to the evenness of it." He wasn't cold one moment and hot the next. He just was. There, I sat on the wooden chair that shivered and creaked when I shifted my weight, and he on the bed that was too short to carry his feet.

He narrated, in a voice made hoarse by his constant coughing: "The moon had secrets you see. Night was jealous because the moon told her secrets only to winds and sands and dead things. Night thought, *If I eat the moon it will be the same as me swallowing her secrets. If I swallow her secrets it will be the same as me getting her beauty. If I get her beauty it will be the same as the winds and seas and dead things worshipping me.*"

"Night wanted beauty?" I asked. "But he's got the stars for his beauty. He wants more?"

"Yeah, Lissy," he said, nodding, clasping his hands in his lap and nodding some more. "That's what Night thought to himself. And he sat and he made a plan in his head. And he went and he told the world: 'See here, World, if you let me eat the moon and her secrets and beauty then I'll never come back to haunt you. I'll let you live all your days in the light of the sun. There won't be night anymore. But I want the moon and her secrets and you need to help me get them.'"

"But the world needs the moon's light," I said. "The world can't give the moon's secrets away. That would be bad!"

"Ah! The world didn't want night anymore," said my father. "He didn't want darkness. So he told Night: 'I'll call the moon over to this side and you can take her secrets. Then be gone, Night! Go on and leave us be! I don't want darkness no more.'

"That's what the world told Night. But the sun heard their whisperings, see. He heard and he didn't like the whisperings. The sun knows that if Night is gone, he'll be in the sky all the hours of the day. The sun doesn't want that. It's too much work for him to shine and shine and never be gone from the sky. To shine and shine for all time. The world called the moon over to his side and the moon came over. So the sun said his own whisperings to the moon.

"The sun gave the moon his shine and told her: 'Night wants to rob you. He wants to steal your secrets and beauty. The world is helping him because he doesn't want darkness anymore. This shine that I'm giving you isn't a gift, now. This is my magic. It will protect you from Night and the world. But now you'll share the sky with me for all time. When I rest you go up and shine. And sometimes I'll get lonely even in the day and you'll come up and shine with me.'

"That's how the moon got its shine to this day. But she's still sad that the world turned on her, so she turned on the world too. That's why any time the moon is up in the sky, you look up and see that she only shows one side of her face. She keeps all her secrets on the other side, where the world and Night can't see them. And when Night eats her she poisons his insides and he spits her back to the sky. That's the way it is. The moon never changes. It's only our seeing of things that makes us think it isn't so. It's the coming and going of the night, see," he concluded.

"Why doesn't Night stop eating the moon, if she poisons him?" I asked, leaning forwards, the better to seize the words that drifted into the emptiness between us. "Why doesn't he ask for her secrets? Why doesn't he share her beauty, same as the sun shared his shine with the moon?"

"It was greed, my Lissy," he said. "It was greed and hope that made him do it. And he does it some more and some more and time comes and goes but Night keeps hoping and hoping the moon will run out of her poison. But that isn't so. She keeps on. She keeps on."

"She keeps on forever?"

He nodded again. "One day you and me will be gone from the world, but the moon will be in the sky poisoning Night and hiding her secrets. Come winter or come summer, she won't change. That's the way it is."

I mirrored him, nodding my understanding. Seeing that his words were etched, somewhat, into my heart, he said: "I need my sleep now. Wake me when the sun is gone from the sky. I'll need the outside air when that is so. I'll need to tell you another story. Wake me before I forget, my Lissy."

The Russian flu was merciless. In the night, in silence, my father died. I woke up in the morning to find that despite my best efforts, I couldn't call him out of his sleep. The vicar, who was sent to complete the last rites, told me I needn't worry, since my father now basked in the glory of God. "He sings with the angels," he said.

He was a simple man, my father. Death, like a hooligan, caught him unawares: he had miscalculated his own mortality, and his own death shocked him. When the end came, he mourned it in fear and bitterness.

Upon that fateful unravelling, he was awakened by a simple epiphany: he was the sort of man who measured his wealth by the hours he worked and the food on our table. There was nothing else he owned, nothing else to give. Except for my name and my skin, there was nothing to leave to me on his passing.

Thus, he called me to his side and for the first time told me stories his people had carried across the seas. But the salt of the sea, the farness of Africa—these things had changed those stories. His wealth, in its entirety, was a broken tale that had spoiled with time, and the promise to tell another.

That story was a gift of sorts. Through my childhood I watched as the moon was born and departed, in and out of the sky. Then I closed my eyes to imagine that my father sat not far from me, on a creaking bed that couldn't carry his long legs. There, he coughed violently into the space between us; he blinked away the tears gathering in his eyes; he cleared his throat, and patiently sang songs and myths he had nearly forgotten.

I miss him, I think. I don't remember enough about him to say this with certainty, but I think I miss him. It seems right that I start the unfinished tale of adventure with this memory. Perhaps it's fateful that I found it now. Given my pending voyage, it seems right that I once more become enamoured with the details of my origins.

Also, I feel that I need to know and understand precisely when and why I started having the dreams with hands and snakes made of shadows.

Tuesday, 23 January

You see, although it came about as a result of numerous, profound tragedies, I have had the fortune of having two fathers in the same lifetime. And two mothers too, but that's a more contestable fact, as I hardly remember the woman who brought me into the world.

But returning to the matter at hand: once, after my nineteenth birthday, I asked my second father the reason he chose me as his daughter. It was a simple answer he gave, a noble one. This was the way it went: he was acquainted with a man who owned a sugar plantation in Jamaica. Through this man, he met a second man who was born on that same plantation as a slave.

The second man, the slave, was my father. His name was Twentyfive because he was born in 1825. His mother had been separated from three of her eldest children before she had my father. She'd given them grand names. She didn't want to lose my father. And at the time there was a myth-rumour, twisted out of African beliefs, that if a child were given a bad name, the Ancestors wouldn't covet that child, and so the child lived long. My grandmother, desperate enough to at least suspect that slave owners and African Ancestors might have similar outlooks on *some* things, gave my father the callous name. It worked. They lived on the same plantation until she died.

Anyhow, my father liked to tell stories while working in the fields. Sometimes he told the stories to the house slaves (legally called apprentices after Abolition). The house slaves repeated the stories to each other. One day they repeated them in my (second) father's hearing, and liking what he heard, he wanted to meet the man who first told the stories. From that day the two men, my fathers, became acquaintances of sorts. They were as friendly as a white man and a slave could be without completely flouting societal convention.

I don't know what my second father saw on the plantation; he has never said, but I know he knows something he hasn't yet told me. In any case, a tragedy transpired sometime between then and the year I was born. Whatever this thing was, it was so profound that by the time my natural father died and it became apparent that there was no one left to inherit me, my second father, without hesitation, nominated himself for the role. Money might have changed hands, I don't know, I honestly don't want to know. He loves me.

It's also apparent that shortly after my first father died, the Russian flu caught me as well. It's not something I remember. In fact, the details of my origins are rife with fractured facts. But my father has recounted that the disease riddled my body with weakness, bouts of retching, high fevers, and other horrors since buried in my mind.

"You were a small thing," said my father. "The vicar placed you at the orphanage for a time. The nuns feared you were no longer of this world. You called to your father, reaching out your hand as though you could touch him." He shook his head as though the memory of the episode still pained him. Then he sighed and went on: "Sister Mary sent for me. She sent for the vicar too. I think she feared for your soul." He laughed, his head thrown back and his hand wiping a tear streak that had sprung from his eye.

"I rushed to you and wouldn't you know it, I said my prayers and the life was breathed back into you," he continued. "It was a strange time." He reclined in his armchair and linked his fingers on his lap, and the merriment that had been brought on by Sister

Mary's piety was suddenly gone from his face. "For the first time, I understood the transience of life," he finished.

I want to remember the details for myself. I now believe that I, too, having witnessed my father's death, and having nearly been taken by the same culprit, must have understood the transience of life. Maybe I even understood the meaning of it, if fleetingly. But the moment is gone, my epiphany lost, and the message wasted.

Soon after my convalescence, my father and I sailed from the Caribbean to England; I, on a maiden voyage, and he, returning home. Here, where few welcomed and none loved me, was where he met and fell madly in love with the daughter of an impoverished farmer. She was the first of my father's peers to wonder, loudly, whether he loved me as a pet, servant, or daughter.

Sister Mary liked to declare my father a charitable soul. She liked to say: "He hasn't met a creature he can't love, and not one who can't love him in return."

After my father married the farmer's daughter and then carted her around the world to see every wonder she desired, it was Sister Mary who divulged to me, during our rest in the Indies, that perhaps my father was too kind. "There isn't a drop of good breeding in that woman," she said. She sighed to herself, seemingly mourning some tragedy that plagued her. "Love is a silly thing, I tell you, a silly, silly thing."

Though I failed to understand much of what she opined, I didn't miss that "that woman" was meant to be my new mother. I was a child; the implications of my new father's low class were not yet apparent to me. To me, he was a wealthy man who had shown me the greatest kindness that could be shown to an orphaned child.

He had not told me of his roots as a grocer's son, and of the stink that came with earning his fortune in a rather common way—as a merchant. All that I heard from him were chants of the fruits of hard work, ready to be plucked by anyone who didn't mind a bit of sweat. With the teacup delicately held in her hand, Sister Mary whispered these troubles to her heart's content. "Does she treat you well?" she asked, when her well of woes was depleted.

"Yes," I said, understanding that we were still on the subject of my mother.

"Does she love you?" she asked. Her prodding eyes were enough to shame me into silence. I cowered longer than necessary, perhaps. That may be the reason she rescued me in the end. "It makes no matter. If it came to it, Mr. Miller would be wise in his choice."

In honesty, I didn't understand Sister Mary's meaning. But as was becoming my habit, I silently noted three things at once. Firstly, Sister Mary never referred to my father as my father, but always as Mr. Miller. Secondly, we never spoke about anything other than my father (or things immediately relating to him). And lastly, she liked to remind me of my great fortune in having attained Mr. Miller as a father.

"Do you think *he* loves me?" I asked her.

For a moment, Sister Mary looked insulted. Then, recovering herself, she said, "Yes, yes. Of course he loves you." She flicked her hand to illustrate the obviousness of her answer. "But what does that have to do with anything? I've overseen the adoption of many orphans. Believe me when I say you are among the lucky. No better father than Mr. Miller could you find; *that* I assure you." She sipped her tea, crossed her legs at her ankles, and extensively praised my improved diction.

"Mr. Miller has bettered himself too. Oh yes, he had to," she said, wagging her finger for effect. "There were snobs all around," she gestured that bit with her hand. "He easily slips into old habits when he doesn't watch himself, but he has raised himself quite high. His speech is quite improved, his manners too. To look at him now, one couldn't guess his humble roots. Oh yes, he has become quite the respectable gentleman."

Shaking her head thoughtfully, she concluded her tale: "Drink your tea, dear girl. Drink before it gets cold."

I silently drank my tea and played the audience she relished entertaining. When all the tea was finished and her tales completed, she returned me to my parents.

Thursday, 25 January

Given Sister Mary's revelations, my journey back to England was filled with melancholic curiosity. Although I was a child, I realised that the composition of my family inspired a curiosity of its own in those who observed us. People liked to point at us and whisper amongst themselves. And so, I can't say, without irony or deceit, that England has been my home. I have felt as I imagine a visitor would—that my time here will end and I will travel home.

My father and I once travelled to Japan. I consumed its beauty in great gulps, with greed, because I knew that my time there would soon end. And when I thought of home, it was of some yet unformed place still budding in my mind.

For twenty-two years, I have felt in England as I did in Japan. This place is not my home. It can never be so. This is what I tell my mother when she asks the reason for my unnatural obsession with the world. She said to me, only today, "How can you feel at home when you are never here? You haven't allowed yourself to be at home."

You see, my mother doesn't want me to go to Africa. According to her, I have seen enough of the world. France, Spain, Italy, the Americas, much of Asia, the Caribbean islands, and our little piece of *this* island—this is my mother's idea of the world. Having braved only the Anglophone of these, she has concluded the rest too foreign for her interest. "I terribly miss you when you are gone," she said. "Please reconsider."

We sat in the drawing room side by side, watching the damage of winter. The windows spied onto the frigid grounds, which were cloaked in barrenness. The roses and lilies of summer had wilted, submitting to the season; the lake, where I had learnt to swim as a child, had quieted into a still, cold sheet, and the willow tree, under which my mother liked to sketch her dismal landscapes, was bare of leaves and fruit and birds. Watching the scene, I was reminded of how deeply I have grown to detest the coldness of this place. The sun likes to hide and the sky likes to brood; and in the cold, my mood is that of gloom.

"I'm not happy here," I said to my mother.

She looked as though I had stabbed her heart then danced on her grave. She held her right hand to her chest and, as softly as the wind, a small gasp escaped her lips. I darted my eyes away from hers. "I don't mean to break your heart, Mother," I said. "But I need to go." I chanced another look at her.

She shook her head, then lowered it. "You know," she said, "sometimes I do think you do these things to break my heart. What has been my crime, that you wish so desperately to always escape me? Have I not been a good mother to you?"

I looked at her. I waited until I was sure my tears wouldn't fall. Finally feeling calm, I said: "I know you've loved me." I pondered my next words for a long while. I wanted them to be as follows: *But sometimes it hasn't been enough*. Yet this I knew I couldn't say. It would be cruel. It *would* break her heart. So silently I formed an argument she could appreciate for its sentimentality, for what she would call the fruit of my poet-soul.

"Sometimes I remember the house where I lived with my father," I started. "But sometimes I don't. In these times I wonder whether the memories I do have are true, or whether I have imagined them over the years. This is the reason I've returned to the Caribbean so many times. I've needed to build my own realities, to confirm them, to know that although I belong with you, I also belonged with him in his small and broken shack.

"You've allowed me passage to the rest of the world, to places wholly unconnected to me, places that birthed nothing in me, and gave me nothing. If my world . . . my world in my mind and heart . . . if that is to be complete, I must begin where it began. And it began in Africa. How can you allow me everywhere else but not Africa?"

My mother shook her head and I saw tears fall from her eyes and onto her clasped hands. "I haven't denied you Africa," she said, "just as everywhere else you have gone was never mine to give. I never consented to this madness. It was your father who did that. You've always done as you wanted—traipsing off without so much as a chaperone, ignoring all the dangers . . . a young woman alone in the world. You never asked before. Why ask now?"

The answer was simple for me. And I gave it quickly. "Because this time I need your blessing," I said. "I don't want my journey to be tainted with your heartache. And I feel that in going there, I am betraying you and Father. This time I do need you to give me your blessing."

"If I don't allow it, you won't go?" she said.

"I will not," I said.

"You mean that?"

"Yes."

"Really?"

"Yes."

"But why go at all? You may not feel that this place is your home, but I'm your mother. Surely you've never doubted *that*."

I went silent. In the time since she became my mother, I had doubted that fact many times. Sister Mary, perhaps unintentionally, had planted the seed, and strangers with their pointing fingers and whispered voices had watered it. Or perhaps the circumstances of our family were the actual culprit, or my natural propensity for melancholy, or, as my mother so rightly assessed, I hadn't allowed myself to accept my home as home. Any of these could be the reason, or none of them. In the end, however, it didn't matter. The seed was planted and nothing could be done to stop its bloom.

I was silent, because, as our uneasiness progressed, I wondered if she ever wanted children of her own womb, who belonged to her since their births, whose blood were hers—whose hair and eyes and skin were hers.

But again, these things I couldn't ask. They were cruel. Even in my desperation I couldn't invoke her barrenness for my own gain. She is a kind woman, my mother, and gentle too. She will never say, and I can never ask these things. So we tenderly danced a dance of deception, unfailingly speaking only words of kindness, of untruth—slowly knitting some corrupted, half-finished, elaborate thread of love.

"I've never doubted your devotion to me," I finally said.

I saw longing in her eyes. And when she spoke, I imagined that I heard it in her voice too. "Please promise me you will come back, Alisa."

"I will," I said. "I promise to come back."

In silence, we carried on watching the barrenness outside.

To tell the truth, I don't know if I'm happy that she's letting me go. But finally, *The Black Swan* is sailing me to Africa. I'm going to Africa. I'm going to Africa!

Wednesday, 31 January

I believe I've dedicated enough time to the mystery of the scrap on which I once scribbled the beginnings of an adventure tale; I believe I've solved it.

I think this must have been the reason I started the story: I wanted to narrate the misfortunes of a mythical princess who, as a sickly child living in her father's care, learns of an ancient enmity between Night and the moon. Her discovery prompts her to sail to the moon, as she believes that there, in the secrets entombed on its dark side, she can unearth the cure for her illness. By some benevolent magic, this princess, whom I will name Emilia, becomes acquainted with ancient tribes that live there.

On the other hand, I might yield to vanity and name her Alisa (since no one will ever read these stories). I might even blacken her skin and make her language foreign. Who would care? Who would not? In any case, I've concluded that this was the reason.

If my father had told me more stories, I could have recorded them as well. But alas, he bequeathed only this one. I will preserve it.

Miss Alisa Miller's Journal:
[Most Likely 1912]

[Missing Journal Entry Text]
[Exact date unknown]

I saw a very beautiful thing today. We've been sailing very close to the northern coast of French West Africa. Suddenly, there was a hubbub as someone, I don't know who, spotted a dolphin swimming beside us and quickly called for everyone to come and admire the sight.

It turned out there was a whole school of the dolphins, about six or seven in total, and they swam as though chasing the ship. Some flipped fleetingly into the air, then quickly dove back into the safety of the sea. This caused another hubbub of excited chatter among us. We clapped and cheered and called more people. All in all, it was a very beautiful thing.

Then, around noon, someone else saw a splash in the distance. I think by then we were all rather desperate to see something else that would excite us. Maybe too hopefully, Mr. Brown suggested that the splash was made by a whale. He would bet his life on it, he said. In fact, he was ready to do just that when his wife stopped him. Logic suggested that the splash wasn't made by a whale. Firstly, it was too small. Secondly, are whales known for splashing around the same way dolphins do? Can they carry their own weight that efficiently? I suppose Mr. Brown, like the rest of us, was at that point, eager to be further enthralled by the wonders of the sea.

I think we've been on this voyage for too long. I know this because Mrs. Brown's intervention wasn't enough to save us from a debate about the dolphin that might or might not have been a dolphin. Mr. Brown quickly reminded everyone that he was a learned man. When no one either supported or denounced this, he quickly added that he was inaugurated into Charles Darwin's closest circle by the man himself. Nature is as familiar to him as holy scriptures are to a monk, he says. No one had the heart to compete with that sort of confidence.

I must admit that I wish Mr. Brown was right. Maybe if I saw a whale I'd enjoy my self-assigned duty as chronicler. However, before the dolphins found us, we had settled into a humdrum sort of dullness, the sort of dullness that does little to inspire poetry. I've concluded that my mother might be right after all. With the exception of a dolphin school or some rare fish I didn't already know, there's nothing new for me to discover on these voyages.

I've been traveling for too long, for most of my life. On this voyage alone I've noted the turn of every tide, every wind's route, every storm and change in the ship's course, and every star that patterns the sky as we sail south. If the lantern light flickered in the slightest, or the drops of some torrent fell slanted (faintly) left or right, rest assured I recorded that as well. I've become disillusioned with the novelties of travel.

If I gazed on the horizon and sang that no greater beauty existed, then a falser ode could not be sung. In all its glory, the sea no longer impresses me, and I find the beauty of the horizon as common as that of any shore or peacock or forest I've ever seen. I've turned my attention to frivolities such as lamenting a fellow traveller's unfortunate dress, or a frayed suit that doesn't quite match its wearer's complexion. The first tragedy is Mrs. Brown's. The poor woman has long been trying her hand at fashion. This is tragic enough on its own, but she's been ambitious enough to inflict the same fate on her husband.

I heard that for last night's dinner she chose a red gown that, regrettably, strongly matched her complexion. If the tragedy was nearly as catastrophic as the plum atrocity she paraded last Sunday, maybe it was best I didn't witness this last episode. I might have forgotten my manners and laughed. Such is the pointlessness of my life—I've descended into pettiness.

To interrupt the humdrum, I might fling myself into the sea. My rescue (or demise, depending on fate) might give my fellow travellers some reprieve. I daresay the scandal of a near-drowning might be the thing to catalyse my belated presentation to society. But I wonder, in the event of my rescue, who would be the fool to play my hero? Who would risk his own death to save me? And would such a hero, undeniably foolish, inspire his own saviour to sustain that perpetual progression of foolishness?

I'm tempted to consider the plan seriously, if only to know the outcome more precisely. Even though the episode might end in tragedy, it might also earn me a friend—a kind soul to tender his pity.

I'd laugh if it wasn't so heavy on my soul. You see, my fellow travellers have chosen to forget that I'm on this ship with them. And I must say, if the ship didn't belong to my father, their pretence wouldn't be necessary. I doubt they would have let me board it to begin with—such is the profoundness of the ironies that plague me. I really ought to be used to this sort of thing by now. For one reason or another, it's painful every time it happens. Strangely, sometimes it still shocks because I never quite expect it. What can I say? I'm a hopeful soul.

Therefore, and returning to the matter at hand, I must also say that the monotony of the sea isn't the only source of my misery. That would be a tale half told. Like a comet bound to the sun, it seems I've once again found myself in a tragedy of my own making. The blueness of the sea, or its sheer vastness, has likely kept me sane.

[Reminder to self, annotation made on 27 March. This is something I need to reflect on in a later entry.] I haven't had shadow dreams since I started the journey.

Tuesday, 26 March

The dawn of a new day has somewhat lifted my listlessness, my sadness. I'm glad to write, with renewed passion, about the splendour of the vast, blue sea, and about any slanted torrent or faintly flickering light. You see, last fortnight I staged a rebellion against my shunning.

Around dinnertime I got dressed as a lady does for dinner and presented myself at the table. I did this with hope. I did this in futility. When I entered the room it got, suddenly, rather quiet. I don't know how else to explain it except to say that I saw rejection on every face around the table. I felt like an exotic animal that had escaped its cage to mingle with its keepers.

The zookeepers, finding that they preferred the exoticness of an animal when that animal was safely away from them, where they could prod and marvel and deride it without any danger of being tainted by it, by its wildness, were quick to restore balance. The first to do so was Mr. Brown, who wore an ill-fitting suit that greatly exaggerated his scragginess. "How . . . how curious it is to see you here, Miss Miller," he said, hesitation halting his speech.

"And what a pleasure it is," I said.

Perhaps afraid that Mr. Brown would fail in explicitly outlining that I wasn't welcome in such polite company, Mrs. Windsor was quick in taking over. She was kind enough to remind me of other facts I might have forgotten. "Oh dear," she said, "I don't believe enough places have been set."

To rescind any offer I might believe extended to me in the future, she went on to remind me that my relation to my father lacked the bond of blood. What could I say after that? What she said was true. There was nothing else to be said. I went back to my cabin.

In times such as these, I find the power of the sea, the finality it offers, very attractive. I wish there was a spell or a prayer I could say to wash the darkness of my skin away. If I wasn't who I am, black as I am, no one could assume my history. No one could, by simply looking at me, assume that my family had been stitched from the symptoms of a plague, the remnants of slavery, or, quite simply, the transience of life.

If I wasn't who I am, they couldn't so easily see evidence of tragedies I inherited from my ancestors. But I am Black and this history is etched in my blood. It marks my skin. I'm a descendent of slaves and retired slaves, a slave child, saved from slavery by chance and the transience of life.

And it *is* such a brief history, one that starts right in the middle of itself, as though a people's history can start without a proper beginning, without a place of origin. People like to ignore inconvenient nuances, though.

In the same way, the British Empire doesn't like to speak about its role in the proliferation of the slave trade. It does, however, like to remind of the role it played in its ending. Such is the way things go—some stories start in the middle because no one wants to hear the beginning. They can be told quickly because no one wants to know the details. Sometimes all that matters is the conclusion.

How to free a people, or, *Why all people deserve the dignity of freedom*, a story can start like that, without first telling why the people needed freeing. Ah, but every child inherits its parents' history. It inherits the history of the world in its entirety. We're all burdened with what came before us. Everything that has happened has shaped the world in one way or another. We're all tethered to the larger world, to the past and its consequences. That's what the world is—a series of lives slowly decaying into history. We can't escape it.

My history started before it started, but today Mrs. Windsor and her cronies narrated only the past they know. They did so with a level of intimacy they shouldn't be allowed. Although they don't know me, it's also true that they do. They can say: "Alisa Miller isn't her father's daughter. From pity, he saved her from some Caribbean tragedy. What a kind man he is." All they have to do is look at me and see I'm a carrier of slave blood, not a daughter or a woman.

It's true. These things they see, I am. And if I stood behind a curtain and recited, as fluently as my governess taught me, every lament ever sung by Keats and Shakespeare, these peers of mine might sing praises. If I spoke of the universe, as it was untangled by Copernicus and Kepler and Galileo, they might praise that too. But if the curtain should fall and my skin be revealed, will they praise, or renounce these treasures as tainted because someone like me dared to touch them?

I admit that these frivolities I often indulge in feed my melancholy. But as we get closer to Africa, it has become necessary to consider the possibility of another failure in my pursuit of a home. I must ask myself these questions: Who waits for me on the African shores? Will I find the half-devil, half-child beasts lamented by Rudyard Kipling? Or will I find people like my father, people who count their fortunes in what they give to the soil and what the soil can feed them?

I don't want to be defeated again. I don't want to fail. I've decided that for that to be the case, I must first conclude that

Rudyard Kipling was wrong. To do otherwise is to admit defeat before the die is cast and my fate revealed. I have to believe that my ancestors lived as entities more sentient than slaves, as beings included in Darwin's proposal of common origins that diverged as a result of need, or survival, and that alone. I have to believe this.

The gift of my skin is precisely that—a gift. I cannot shed it. I cannot return it to whatever deity created me. And as I am learning, I cannot hate it. The world does that well enough.

For this simple reason, my sadness and listlessness has somewhat lifted away from me. I'm glad to write again about the splendour of the vast, blue sea, and about any slanted torrent or faintly flickering light.

Thursday, 28 March

Following my recent musings, and given all my past experiences both in England and everywhere I have travelled, I've come upon a rather peculiar conclusion. Well, I say "peculiar" when really the more peculiar thing is that I didn't arrive at the conclusion sooner. Firstly, and most importantly: I believe that my fellow travellers think I'm less English than they are. This is true; they aren't wrong. After all, I've never felt at home in England. But although that's the case, it's worth noting that these people don't know this fact about me. On what basis do they decide the matter of my identity?

Idle as I've been, I immediately decided this was a most profound crisis, and I needed to attend to it as quickly and thoroughly as possible. It's all done and dusted and I'm sad to say this will not be an exciting report. It's been rather disappointing to discover that the analysis was, in fact, wholly unnecessary, since the sequence of events that led me here is so very obvious. All I needed to do was follow the proverbial breadcrumbs, and they are thus:

Yesterday I found myself rather fascinated by an oddly shaped cloud, such is the scope of my loneliness. (Although, I shouldn't overstate things. It might be worth saying that my loneliness hasn't been complete since, out of loyalty to my father, Captain Anders maintains an acquaintanceship of sorts with me. He speaks happily about his mother and modestly about his father. As an added credit to him, he hasn't yet found it necessary to remind me of my race. I must be fair to him, but it is worth saying that his companionship is limited. He doesn't dare inflict me on the rest of the ship. His gallantry doesn't extend to such simple things as insisting that I dine with my peers. But I digress.)

Anyhow, it was a dull morning and I took a walk along the deck. I had stopped for a moment to inspect the cloud, when I suddenly found myself un-alone. "May I join you, madam?" said a man. I thought that he was addressing someone else, so I looked around me. I saw confusion in his eyes. Later, he said he found it strange that I questioned his interest in talking to me.

"Aren't you afraid of my leprosy?" I asked. The confusion in his eyes intensified. So I went on: "Everyone on the ship has been warned of my illness. You see, they maintain their distance to preserve their health." I grinned, I think, and he did as well. "You're welcome to join me, Mr.—" I said, extending my hand.

"Mr. Yuri Ivanov," he said, taking my hand in his and shaking it. "You are Miss Alisa Miller?"

"If not leprosy, what illness am I rumoured to spread?"

"Only your . . . eh . . . uniqueness." He cleared his throat in discomfort.

"I suppose you've come to see the oddity for yourself," I said, apparently stunning him for a third time.

When he was recovered he removed his hat, held it to his chest, and began anew. "I did not mean to offend," he said. "I only meant . . . eh . . . how does one say?" Seemingly frustrated by his own ineloquence, he delved into some dialect of the Russian Empire, and into French. Once he found the word that had eluded him, he said: "You are much . . . eh . . . discussed, yet hard to find. But now I see word of the leprosy was eh . . . overstated. It is the fire from your mouth we must fear." He said the last part with a tentative grin.

My smile got wider. "What frightens you more—the leprosy or the fire?"

"The fire," he said, simply.

"Then I will be tame."

After we exhausted the expected pleasantries, we sat on a bench and spoke briefly and candidly, keenly touching on polite and familiar subjects. Like the captain, Mr. Ivanov spoke happily of his mother and father—who, I learnt, still lived in the Russian Empire with the firmest degree of patriotism. The dullness of the morning quickly melted away.

As Mr. Ivanov and I carried on into further politeness, I noted some things about him. Firstly, his speech is strongly peppered with the accent of his natural tongue. Secondly, he needs clarification for most words in every sentence. But even so, I think he is considered more English than I am. What's the difference between me and him?

I asked him: "How long have you been English?"

He admired the waves until I believed he wouldn't answer. Then briefly, he said: "Not long. But too long." He left it at that, and I thought it impolite to prod further.

Despite the several other curiosities I have about him, I've decided that he's a kind man. He is pleasant. My parents would no doubt find some fault to be corrected; not the obvious accent or his impoverished family, but something beyond that, such as his outlandish politics. When I met him in the evening he spoke at length about the advantages of an independent Ireland, and of a Russia not governed by a monarchy. Granted, the better part of the conversation was stolen by his struggle with the English language. "How does one say this?" he asked, often.

I'll try the Russian language and see if the pace doesn't improve. It might be the case that his politics aren't so outlandish after all. One can hope.

He laughed when I told him the purpose of my journey.

"You . . . eh . . . want to understand your roots in a place your parents never saw?"

And so, I once again found myself narrating the need for my voyages. "Yes, I was born in the West Indies," I said, "but it was never home. I was a child when I left. Although I was English from that moment, I was aware enough of my origins to think of England as a foreign place: it was never home either. I think in the end I loved the Caribbean simply because I was born there, and my parents were born and buried there. But I also resented it since, by the rules of colonialism, Jamaica is an extension of the British Empire. It was under the Empire that my parents were born as slaves and died in squalor. Also, my experience of England was never pleasant. I couldn't love it." I laughed with nervousness. "I sound foolish, don't I?"

Mr. Ivanov didn't immediately answer, but instead asked a question of his own. "Have you gone to the Indies since you . . . became English?"

"Yes," I said. "Many times. I've been to every island in the Caribbean, mostly Jamaica."

Mr. Ivanov nodded. "What did you want to gain in going there?"

As he elaborated, a doctor may butcher a patient not from malice but to rid the man of disease viler than the doctor's own action. What then, he repeated, was the purpose of my actions? What fundamental result did I hope to achieve in returning to Jamaica, and did I hope to achieve the same goal with my passage to Africa?

I answered as I'd done with my parents. "I don't know," I said. "Maybe when I achieve that goal I'll know. I gained nothing from my visits to the Indies, but Africa—a cradle of sorts for someone like me, is a reasonable contingency. I think that in Africa I will finally understand whatever there is to understand. My eloquence is failing me right now but I feel that I'm close to the end. I've come too far to fail." I looked at him with a nervous smile. I searched his eyes in hope, and at last asked him, again: "You think I'm a fool, don't you?"

Mr. Ivanov didn't laugh, as I'd expected. Instead he called me brave, then smiled and finally called me foolish. "But foolishness and bravery, they are the same, I'm told," he said, his face kindly.

"I believe they are," I said.

To that, he nodded, and we delved once more into the politeness of things spoken easily—of the tides that carry us south, of the beauty of music, the mystery of death and other things unknown, and finally, about the lure of Africa. He spoke somewhat eloquently about his exploits as a naturalist. And an hour later, I'd forgotten my desire to fling myself into the sea.

[Missing Journal
Entry Text]

[Exact date unknown]

The wind has picked up. The sails have been fully hoisted and our pace has improved. To my pleasant surprise, the same can be said of Mr. Ivanov's grasp of the English language. Our conversations have swung from politeness and into stranger tides. He hesitates less with his speech, and emphasises his outlandish philosophies without ambiguity.

I've since learnt that it's not only his politics that produces raised eyebrows and a cacophony of scoffs. His opinion of the origins of our species are far more interesting. As he puts it, the African apes are more likely to give insight into the Eden-years of humanity. The proposed alternative of French or Asian apes is absurd. He stomped his cane and pointed southeast, where lay the western coast of Africa. "That is where the world began," he said. "Even Darwin said so."

"It's Africa, then, where the world began, not Eden?" I asked.

"Eden is in Africa."

"What do your colleagues think about that? Your priest, your beloved parents—what do they think of an African Adam, an African Eve?"

He countered that, as neither his parents nor priest had examined the bones of the extinct apes, they couldn't be trusted to give an accurate analysis. In a sense, he said, this was a journey home for all of us, because we all scattered from Africa to fill the world.

Besides, he said, the general public's opinion as a whole didn't matter on this issue. The truth didn't need to be proven. It was the truth. Yes, some people could and would contest it. A person was allowed to reject a philosophy, but that didn't nullify the philosophy, it only meant our understanding of the world is as different as the many parts and people and ideas that form the world. For centuries humanity believed that Earth was at the centre of our galaxy, not the sun. That didn't change the facts, it just meant we needed someone like Copernicus to come along and enlighten us. The truth came easily to some, not so to others. *That* was another truth, he said.

He pointed at the growing audience of people who went about gawking at us. No doubt, they mourned the fall into scandal of such a promising, if peculiar man as Mr. Yuri Ivanov. Take these people, he said, they've no doubt formed stories about us; among those stories might be something close the truth, which is this—that we are two lonely travellers who were drawn to one another. But everything else will be far from that. It won't matter what we say. And for the rest of time, they'll never know they were wrong.

They might say sinister things about us, they might not. They might believe those things, those things might haunt us forever. On the other hand, they might say kind things.

It made me happy to hear him say what he did about Africa. I don't think I agree with everything he says (my understanding on the subject is so limited), but his ideas are strangely fascinating. Wouldn't it be something to find that all of humanity did, in fact, scatter out of Africa? Oh, but why did we leave? What exiled us from there? Why did we need refuge *away* from Africa?

Oh, this really is fascinating!

[Missing Journal Entry Text]

the Bible my mother gave me.

On a completely unrelated note, I must remember to thank a man named Abram van Zijl for his kindness. It is he, this Dutchman, who adopted Mr. Ivanov as a student of sorts. He's the tutor responsible for Mr. Ivanov's improving diction.

He's another strange one, Abram van Zijl. When he speaks of South Africa, of this voyage, he speaks of "a journey home." By my understanding of the African identity, I'm not sure I can call him African. He was born in Amsterdam. His father is Dutch and his mother English. But he has lived his whole adulthood in the Cape of Good Hope, where he makes and trades wine. He holds South African citizenship. Thus, despite his name and country of birth, he *is* South African. As Mr. Ivanov would say, Mr. Van Zijl is a brave fool.

Mr. Van Zijl only smiles when asked about the muddled mess of his identity. "I belong to the world," he says. Presently, a rather splendid sunset blazed in the western sky and we were obligated to admire it. "See there," said Mr. Van Zijl, removing his hat and pointing at the sky, "it's amazing how the golden flecks ebb softly in places, heavily in others, and the setting orb brightens it all." Even I had to admit that this analysis of a sunset was surely excessive and unnecessary.

Luckily, and as I've noted, there are other aspects that, for someone like me, render him an incredibly interesting person. Put simply, I envy Mr. Van Zijl. He can explain the details of his heritage with intimate knowledge. I, on the other hand, can't say my people came from this place or that one. I only know that they likely descended from West Africa. But West Africa is massive; so massive, in fact, that when European nations met in Berlin to divide its resources, over a dozen new countries were cut into its face.

My parents are English so I can say with some sense of loyalty to them, if I'm forced, that I'm English. As I derive this half-identity from my parents, can I then claim, as a subject of the British Empire, the territories of Nigeria, the Ellice Islands, New South Wales, and all the places only familiar to me from the pages of books?

These sorts of things don't trouble Mr. Van Zijl. To belong to the world seems simple to him, something he chooses for himself. I wonder: Are his freedoms afforded to him by his skin, that skin having been denied to me by the circumstances of my ancestry? If so, are the same freedoms, as an extension of my birth, denied to me? But if they're afforded simply by his state of mind, then it's something I can achieve, and should pursue.

Presently, Mr. Ivanov saved us from further poetry about the sunset. "The South African School of Mines and Technology has a resident naturalist, no?" he said. He is headed there. He hopes there's an open position for a naturalist.

I don't know why, but in that moment I realised something about Mr. Ivanov. He volunteers very little about the details of his life. He always speaks carefully. I thought this was a result of his ineloquence, but I now see that he's simply a careful man. It's possible that before, he didn't only stumble with his diction because of the linguistic restraints. It's possible that he says only what he wants to say, that he deliberately hides the rest.

He might have a wife and children he left behind and I wouldn't know it. I don't suppose it matters either way, but I've somewhat started to think of him as a friend. He showed me kindness when no one else would. For that, I will forever be grateful to him. I know this is a fickle and unimportant thing, but I was sad to hear that he is going to the Transvaal and not the Cape Province, where Mr. Van Zijl and I are headed.

[Missing Journal
Entry Text]

[Exact date unknown]

My acquaintanceship (or friendship) with misters Ivanov and Van Zijl has taken me back to rather unpleasant memories. Firstly, I must say, without self-indulgence or hyperbole, that I've never been in love. Secondly, as far as I can tell, my parents have been in a sort of denial about my prospects as a potential bride. They love me, I know this. Everyone else has regarded me with a cold sort of indifference. My parents know this. Yet somehow, I think they thought my race would be immaterial once I became a woman and had to get married.

I can't blame them for their naivety. After all, they liked to tell me stories about people like Gustavus Vassa, Frederick Douglass, and Harriet Tubman—people who not only broke free from slavery but also went on to apply their ideas to moulding the world. These people didn't only inherit what came before them, they also gave something to history. When I was a child, I didn't understand why my parents told me those stories. It felt like a such a burden, like they expected me not only to be myself but to exceed the confines of my origins, to justify my freedom. I now realise that they likely wanted to show me the possibilities available to me.

The Vassas and Douglasses and Tubmans of the world went a step further—they seemed to have seamlessly assimilated into polite society. They were married and had children. When I entered my womanhood it suddenly dawned on me that I had to live up to one more thing, one more thing beyond simply being myself, one more thing beyond leaving the world as a better place than I found it, one more thing.

At the same time, it dawned on my parents that few men would find me to be a suitable wife. I, myself, had realised this years before. I didn't know many Black people. Only once in a while did I see a Black man in the city, as someone's coachman or driver, or as a retired soldier. But the coaches and cars drove away, and the soldiers likely drifted off to fishing towns.

The next time I saw another Black man I couldn't be sure he was the same one I saw the time before. Here, again, I must concede that my mother was right. If I'd stayed in England long enough at a time, I might have made friends with some of the Black men and women who peppered the city with their hushed presence. Maybe I should have given that a chance. Maybe that would have better rooted me to England. I may never know. I don't think it matters now.

My point is that my parents hadn't prepared for the possibility that I might not be as desirable a bride as *they* imagined. That's when I realised that it's a curse to love a person; you become blind to their shortcomings. That's the only way I can explain my parents' naivety. I, myself, had long prepared for the disappointment by curing myself of a desire to, firstly, find a man who was willing to marry me and, secondly, have children. I have to admit that I don't find this stance entirely tragic. If I don't have children then I can't pass on my skin to them. It's a faultless solution to an otherwise impossible problem.

I knew my place in the world. But as it turned out, my parents didn't. My father tried to negotiate a contract with a barrister's son in London. He offered half the rights to his business to the barrister in exchange. He even added a house in the West Indies for me and my new husband. The end result was this: my father knew without a doubt that no dowry, however staggering, was attractive with me as the bride. It broke my mother's heart beyond belief.

As the years went on, I travelled less with my father. He no longer had the bones for it, he said. To shield myself from the scandal of being a spinster who travelled alone, I concocted a rumour. I whispered to a maid that I once married a tobacco merchant in the West Indies and watched him die of consumption. The world receives me much better as a widow; although I have to say, widowhood is terribly burdensome. Sometimes, if I meet someone particularly sentimental, I'm forced to endure excessive pity, at which point *I* have to perform excessive sentimentalities of my own. It's a ridiculous chore.

But returning to the fickle and unimportant things that have changed—these fickle things that, like a chameleon tasting new colours into its skin, have evolved into what they shouldn't be.

There are moments when I look at Mr. Van Zijl and think: Why does he fascinate me so? How can he be so unburdened by everything, by his muddled identity?

Sometimes I think that what I feel for him is close to love, or at least close to the beginning of love. I breathe easier when I'm around him. He makes me forget the world. Sometimes he makes me want to love it too; for in these moments, he makes me believe that I belong here, because *he* does, and so effortlessly. He makes me want to love myself. I only wish I knew how to fall out of love with him. That is, if this is in fact love.

It's a curse, to love another person. It's a burden, and I already carry so much confusion with me. Confusion about my birth parents and their significance in my life. Confusion about my adoptive parents and whether I truly belong with them. Confusion about my place in the world. Confusion about the history that birthed me. Confusion about my responsibility to retired slaves who, unlike me, live in squalor, at the fringes of society. Confusion about this journey, confusion about everything. I carry too much. It would be wildly reckless to add to this heap of confusion a man who is, himself, riddled with paradox.

Ah, what a bother this is!

Truth be told, I've wallowed alone in my own thoughts for too long. I've started to think in redundant patterns. This isn't love. This can't be love. It's a simple fascination, but I've wallowed in it for too long and thus convinced myself that it must be more profound than it truly is. I must take a break from my journal, enjoy the remainder of this voyage with my strange friends.

I must forget this nonsense.

Wednesday, 10 April

It's possible that if I saw another oddly shaped cloud and sang its praises, Mr. Van Zijl would continue to be as enthusiastic in noting every aspect of that cloud's wonder. "How fascinating! How very fascinating," he would say.

"Indeed," I would say.

"Look there," he would chime, pointing, "look there, look how it glides into that other cloud and creates something completely new. Truly, how fascinating!" Thusly, the inanity would carry on. But fortunately for me, there was no such cloud in the sky that day. He looked longingly into the distance, as though retrieving a memory from his mind, or from the blue endlessness of sea and sky. He sighed and said: "You haven't been writing in your journal. You don't watch the sea anymore. It's grown tiresome, hasn't it—our confinement to this vessel?"

It turned out that before Mr. Van Zijl was acquainted with me, he liked to watch as I walked the decks and noted down some of the wonders we passed. So when that wasn't the case anymore, he took notice and wondered, rather politely I must say, if anything was amiss.

I had been standing at the stern, gazing to the horizon, where we had passed. We trampled the water to near flatness—bent it to the will of the ship, though only for a moment, for the sea soon reformed its might and waved its waves back into the fold. Lamenting this fleeting bending of the will, some seabird breed wailed in the distance, and the wind blew cold.

"These things of nature," I said to Mr. Van Zijl, "they repeat themselves through time. The sea has always been here, the sun has always risen, and every flower—pretty or not—has bloomed since time began. In a time and place not now and here, another woman, foolish and idle too, stood against some other precipice and admired, then chronicled, futilely, the *rareness* of these things. Yes"—I nodded—"our confinement to this vessel grows tiresome."

Mr. Van Zijl stood beside me to gaze as I did, futilely, where the ship beat against the water. "I've never told you about my first journey to Africa, have I?" he said, unceremoniously interrupting the silence between us.

I shook my head. "Is it a happy story?"

"It's a necessary story."

"I'm intrigued, Mr. Van Zijl. No tale, new or old, was ever narrated to me as *necessary*."

He laughed. "I was still a child," he said. Clearing his throat and sliding his hands into his pockets, he continued. "Do you remember what I told you when we first met?"

Like him, I gazed wistfully into the distance to retrieve the memory. I nodded. "You called yourself an Englishman, a Dutchman, and an African, all at the same time."

"You think it's impossible to be all three at once?"

"It's not my place to speak on your patriotism, Mr. Van Zijl."

"Why do you say that?"

I shrugged in what I hoped was a nonchalant manner. Whatever I thought of him, I didn't think it was wise to say it as plainly as he apparently wanted me to. I only said: "You're very lucky. To belong to the world so freely is a very rare thing, a gift."

"But you also think it's impossible, don't you? You think it's naïve, almost fantastical."

"Does it matter?"

He shook his head. "I'm not sure. With some people it does,

with some it doesn't. With you, it will depend on what you think of my story."

"The necessary story." I nodded. "My curiosity is growing."

He chuckled. "Well, when I was a child I visited a museum with my father. We saw many things there, many wondrous things. Towards the end of the day I saw the head of a king, encased in glass, displayed in what I thought was honour. I was hypnotised by him, by the audacity of his majesty, even in death.

"I wondered about his life, about the hints of wealth and foreignness engraved in his crown. I asked my father where the king came from. My father said Egypt. I then asked where Egypt was, at which point he said Africa. So when he and my mother devolved into . . . into . . ."

Sensing his discomfort, I said: "These are delicate matters, Mr. Van Zijl. It won't offend me if you leave some things unsaid."

He smiled. "Thank you," he said. "But they must be said. When my parents devolved into the harder years of their marriage, my mother booked us passage to Africa in secret, then snuck me away one night. That way she could punish my father by keeping me from him. I was his only male offspring, his sole heir. I'm inclined to believe that she also hoped to sway me to her side, and to still have family when the sordid affair of their marriage was done with. So we stole away to Egypt, where we admired the pharaohs and their tombs.

"I understood, on beholding the pyramids, that the king I'd seen back home didn't see death as an end, but as something else. You can't dedicate so much of yourself to a tomb if you see death as an end. It's futile. Whatever comes after this life must be greater, at least, as the king might have seen life. Yet mere centuries later someone saw fit to remove him from his threshold to eternity. They sealed him in glass and summoned the crowds to witness his disembodiment. He never reached the heaven he had so pursued." The soothing smile vanished from Mr. Van Zijl's face, and in its place rested the firm sourness of regret.

"It broke my heart," he went on. "But I was a child. My heartache was fleeting. And with that, the call of our journey interrupted my grief. From Egypt, we trailed our way through the rest of the continent. We rested in Timbuktu to see the mysteries famed to dwell there; then trekked south still, through the Congo, where we greeted the gorillas.

"Then farther south, through the life-filled plains of the Serengeti, where the world stretched endlessly to the horizon, far, far through places whose names I can't recall, and even to the bronze dunes of the Namib, where the desert greets the sea like an old friend. Under the blazing sun of Africa, we teetered here and there and everywhere, until at last, we came to the very end, to a place where two oceans meet and the sea had birthed a mountain."

Mr. Van Zijl ended his rhythm unceremoniously. I was jolted out of the trance he'd woven with his words. I found that I missed the sonority of his voice, the passion with which he spoke, and the poetry and theater of it. I imagined him delivering the seminal soliloquy of some tragedy, willing himself to transcend his shortcomings—be it panic or ineloquence. It seemed that he was reliving his fondest memories, and he strived to convey them faithfully. Fleetingly, it made my heart flutter.

"Did you know that the ancient natives have a different name for it?" he said, suddenly.

"Do you mean Table Mountain?"

"Yes. I learnt from a man who fancied himself a poet that they call it Hoerikwaggo—the mountain of the sea. Somehow it hadn't occurred to me that the natives might have a different name for it." He sighed. "Did you know that they have a legend for the cloud-cloth that sometimes drapes its plateau?"

I shook my head. "No."

"They do. But the thing is, the people have since been displaced from there. Along the way to new places, places that were far from the mountain, they lost the legend, or hid it away from invaders. No one that I know remembers it. No one has yet told it to me."

"And the legend is lost forever," I said in a whisper.

"I prefer to think otherwise," said Mr. Van Zijl. "But you're probably right."

"How sad."

"Yes. But the Cape Malay have a legend of their own."

I smiled. "A story from an enslaved people; I'd like to hear it."

Mr. Van Zijl smiled brightly too, the green of his eyes sparkling. "Well, depending on the faction telling the story, the details are different, of course. At its core, however, every legend about the mountain says this: the cloud-cloth was born from a wager set between the Devil and a retired pirate named Captain Van Hunks. They, Satan and his sinner, once sat together like gods on the mountain, duelling to see who could smoke the most. To this day, their smoke can be seen as a cloud."

"Does no one ever win this wager?"

"One is the Devil himself, the other a retired thief," said Mr. Van Zijl, chuckling. "I don't imagine they conduct themselves with much honour, if any at all."

"And so the wager goes on, into eternity?"

"Oh yes," said Mr. Van Zijl, nodding. "It seems like a futile fate, doesn't it?"

"It seems like an unnecessary chore," I said, "to crouch eternally in the company of an enemy and smoke until the very smoke from one's pipe casts the world into oblivion. How shameless and horrific your story is, Mr. Van Zijl. Do you have another one?"

"Well," he said, chuckling again, "there *is* one about the Ghost of Verlatenbosch."

"A ghost?"

"Oh yes. They say a boy was deceived into playing a flute that was once played by a leper. Hence the boy became a leper. He lived the rest of his life hidden in the forest, where he died with only his music to lift his sorrows. To this day, when evening falls, the haunting music of a flute can be heard in the breeze, whispering through the trees on the slopes of the mountain." He clapped his hands once, I jumped, and he laughed and smiled cheekily. "I frightened you, didn't I?" he said.

I shook my head profusely. "You're scandalous, Mr. Van Zijl."

"The story is getting out of hand," he said, still laughing. "I'm sorry about that." He slowly resumed his serious demeanour and continued. "What I'm trying to say, Miss Miller, is that everyone has a story to tell, every person you meet. Places aren't different in this regard. Every place has a heart. Every place is alive."

He loves Cape Town, he said. He loves the Cape people. He loves their tales and myths and strangeness; for who else could look at a mass of rock jutting from the sea and conclude, all at once, that the massive pile was ghost and god and child and nothing and mere mountain, and everything that was beautiful about their world? Who else if not the Cape people?

Then he said something else, and when he was done, I had no choice but to love him. This is what he said: People can belong to a place because it births them, or it enslaves them, or they've borrowed it. It doesn't matter how we're tethered to a place because we each leave a mark there, like an echo sounding after the call has died, or a chasm carved by the wind. We each leave a piece of our heart. Through time it travels to tell its holder's tale, both guarding and revealing the past. This happens in Cape Town, he said. The city is like a mother whose children are the wandering souls of the world. They travel there lost, but once bound within its bowl, they cannot leave.

Yes, it's common for mountains to hold up the sky, for seas to rage against shores, for pretty flowers to bloom—for life to propel itself in clichés and repetitions, it's common. These are signs of nature, immortal, immortal. But Cape Town had sheltered the enslaved and borrowers alike, enslavers too. It couldn't spit anyone out, or it was unwilling to. If it sheltered a man it hadn't birthed, he said, a man such as himself, then it was obligated to love someone like me.

More or less, paraphrased, that is what the strange man Mr. Abram van Zijl said to me.

I watched the side of his face revealed to me, his left. The stiffness in his jaw suggested that his teeth were clenched, and his eyes, I surmised, stared into nothing. I decided right then and there that I loved him. What else could the throbbing pang in my heart be? I decided, too, that I'd never love anyone else as purely and unequivocally. It might seem haphazard to someone who doesn't know me. It might seem callous to simply decide that I love a man, to not sing poetry and swoon—to simply decide that I love him.

Yes, I *do* believe he's naïve. He hasn't lived the harsher realities of the world. Such is his life, that he can easily belong to the world and boast as much. The world as *I've* lived in it is not as he has found it. I cannot call him a fool, nor can I resent his naivety, for he has lived his reality. But I have to love him. How can I not when I never have to justify myself to him, when I don't need to narrate my tragedies? And it's because he's naïve that I don't have to; that he can say something so simple and make me feel unburdened. I know a city can't love me. But how can I not love him?

My mother once told me that when she first met my father, she knew that their lives would be forever entwined. She said she couldn't predict the manner of that entanglement, nor could she then deduce, on their first meeting, that she would fall in love with him. But she felt as though the fates whispered a secret to her; gently, silently, they revealed some intangible thing from her future—and so her present unfolded with a resonance that transcended time itself.

My mother's transient transcendence is the best way I can explain my own. I knew, even in my confusion, that I was at the brink of something I didn't quite understand. It frightened me. It made me falter. I didn't want to open my heart. I didn't want to break it. The bereaved seabird of earlier moments chose then to begin again its lament. It wailed long and loudly, calling, calling for its kin's embrace. The wind whistled eerily. It blew colder than before, ruffling strands of our hair into our eyes, draping us with the cold, at the same time leaving us bare to one another.

I felt my hopes and dreams within reach, grazing lightly at my fingertips. But I was afraid to seize them, for if I did, they would slip away. And the wind still whispered its eerie whistles, as though carrying the wisdoms of the fates, as though gently revealing some intangible truth from my future. That wind called my name. It lulled me. It rooted me deeply into that moment and I felt . . . I felt that I had no choice but to live it because I had done so endless times before and would do so endless times to come.

But it was only a fantasy, a deceit concocted by my tired mind. The wind couldn't speak. It couldn't foresee fortunes, nor reveal them. Shaking myself out of my foolishness, I said, "Thank you for your stories, Mr. Van Zijl. Can I repay you with one of my own?"

He smiled. "I'd like that," he said.

"You see, when I was a child and the so-called Russian flu swept across the world, my father got ill," I started. "He knew he was dying, so he called me to his side to tell me a story about the Children of the Sky God. This is how it goes."

Miss Alisa Miller's
Journal: 1913

Thursday, 1 May

I daresay my mother thinks my letters are designed to lure her into what she refers to as "curiosities best left unsatisfied." She persistently asks about the hot climate, yet continued her complaints even after I told her we're entering winter. In her last letter, she wrote:

"Mr. O'Brien has informed us of the endless plagues that infest that place—such insects as have yet been named; a bite from any one of which, I'm told, is likely to induce death or worse. He has been so faithful in every account of his other travels, dear. Hence, it serves no purpose to question him, nor to test his assertions, firm as they are. Does the infamous, relentless heat, rumoured to catalyse these pestilences, not inspire your return home, Alisa? It is overdue, and your father does so dearly miss you."

All her letters have been rife with worry and other unsaid things. They all indicate that she thinks I'm foolishly hopeful. "Are you sure this man wants to marry you?" she all but asked. My father expressed a similar sentiment, though subtler and a touch more delicately.

He wrote: "I've enquired after this Mr. Abram van Zijl. As far as my man can tell, there is no ill-repute associated with his name. He sounds a respectable man, my dear. I dare confess your mother approves. If it's my blessing you want, know that you have it. But know that as your father, it's my duty to question his intentions where you're concerned.

"Until such a time as I am acquainted with him and convinced of his goodwill, I must execute this duty as industriously as possible, without marring your pending nuptials. I hope you trust me in this matter as you have done in all others. And please, dear, write more often. Your mother worries."

As ever, they're both eager to reveal the other's overstated misery, but neither can admit their own. Anyhow, it doesn't matter since they'll be travelling here. They've secured a berth on *The Black Swan*. She's a fast vessel; granted fair weather and the captain's aptitude, I'll be welcoming my parents in a fortnight or less.

I expect that my mother will play the part of a mildly disapproving parent splendidly. She'll want to be coaxed into accepting Bram. She'll want to find faults she can fix, things to worry over, to lament, then flippantly dismiss as wholly unimportant in the general scheme of things. Of course, I'll play my own part of a rebellious, lovestruck bride just as splendidly. I'll have to take care not to overdo it, since I am rather too old for such games.

But traditions must be observed, if only some of them. And I've always so wanted to be fretted over in this frivolous sort of way.

As soon as she's convinced of my devotion to Bram, but more importantly, of his to me, I expect my mother to fully take the reins of the wedding preparations. Well, I say it's a wedding but really, that's very generous. There'll be a ceremony, but nothing lavish, nothing traditional. My parents won't care about the smallness of it; their own wedding was such a sorry thing, or so I've heard. My father was an upstart, my mother, a poor farmer's daughter—polite society didn't call on the gates of heaven when they got married.

But I know they'll be happy. This is a domestic triumph they'd started to think wouldn't happen. I know they'll also be sad because Bram and I will be settling here. I'll be so far from them. It will break their hearts. But I'm happy here. I'm truly happy.

[Missing Journal Entry Text]

[Exact date unknown]

of the books Yuri sent to me. I'm very interested in what he thinks about the revolution. Is it practical? Can this new world be sustained? Is the age of monarchies truly coming to an end?

In any case, Bram and I plan on visiting the wilds of India at some time in the coming year. He wants to travel to the northern tribes of South Africa after that. He's quite fascinated by the people bordering Southern Rhodesia. He speaks of rain queens, ghost mountains, and stranger things. There is magic there, he said.

We sat under some weeping willow near the vines. The midday sun shone brightly, without mercy. The rays streamed through the canopy, and every so often, I saw his eyes twinkle.

A breeze blew with a silent rhythm unheard by us; it whispered to the leaves that danced around us. In these moments, when his happiness is greater that his misery, I'm glad to be reminded of his true self.

Softly, he brushed my hand with his. If pressed to do so, I could recite the colour of every flower that bloomed in that moment; the song of every bird flying above, the majesty of the Boland Mountains floating in mist, gliding somewhere on the horizon.

He has given me more than even he realises; this, all while losing his family. They have committed themselves, to varying degrees, to the idea that Bram is afflicted with a profound form of madness. They think I'm a symptom of it. As their chosen cure, they have shunned him. None of his family and friends have promised to sail for the wedding. His eldest sister might have come, but it seems that her husband might take her attendance as a personal affront.

As for his parents, his mother has chosen this moment to re-member that once, in Windhoek, an African man nearly stole her purse. His father has suddenly become distressed by this inci-dent, and as a result, he, too, has remembered old (and rather un-specific) crimes committed against him by Africans. It is perhaps an irony that the news of our pending marriage might mend the long-suffered estrangement between Bram's parents. I'm inclined to be moved by this. It has been such a convoluted story; to have such an unpredictable ending is somewhat fitting.

The only friend Bram still has is a man named Johannes Joubert, whom I met briefly. Even he looked somewhat peeved by the prospect of gaining me as an in-law of sorts. But unlike Bram's family, he is here in Cape Town. As such, he can't feign an illness that prevents him from crossing the sea, or a prior engagement that he absolutely must attend. And of course, there is Mr. Ivanov.

It saddens Bram, I know—to suddenly find himself stripped of bonds he'd imagined unbreakable. It breaks his heart. It fills me with fear, for I now wonder, as my mother did: Does he truly want to marry me?

A marriage with me will separate him from that other world he proudly claims. He has arrived at a proverbial crossroads and a path he must choose. To go one way is to shun the other, deny himself whatever fruit lies that way. It's not easy for him; unlike me, rejection has never hardened his heart. He never swallowed the bitterness of pending disappointment. And now, at only twenty-seven, he's too old, too late, too unadaptable, and yet he must adapt himself to heartache, disillusionment, and near-solitude.

We are kindred in this. I'm also standing on some proverbial precipice of *my* journey. I've learnt that in South Africa, my new home, the division of the races and classes is subject, among several other factors, to geography and colonial allegiance. I suppose one needs to travel the rest of the world before asserting this as the absolute truth. But as far as I can tell it is at least true of the Caribbean, Great Britain, much of the Americas, and Southern Africa.

You see, to my father's staff I was the master's daughter. Given my race, this caused confusion. Everyone got used to it with time, however. I became an anomaly that people considered with a reserved sort of politeness, an indifferent sort of contempt. In South Africa, however, I'm a different species. I'm Black, so when people look at me they immediately assume that I belong here, that my parents surely came from here. Yet when I speak, I immediately declare myself as something entirely different. Further, when one factors in my class, I become even more separated from the greater majority of South African natives.

I've since reassessed my position of homelessness. More precisely, as I once told Mr. Ivanov, neither England nor Jamaica were home to me. Looking back, I now see that in some way Jamaica *was* my home. But as a child it didn't seem like it. There were whispers of Africa—a far-off land some of us dared to dream. It seemed like a mystical place abundant in Black bodies and faces that resembled mine yet walked with a pride *I* lacked. This Africa they spoke of, it was where I belonged. Africa wasn't just a dream, it wasn't just a place; Africa was heaven.

When a slave died their soul went back to Africa because that was where we belonged. When the soul reached Africa it was greeted by the ancestors in the spirit realm. And once the soul was greeted, it waited for other souls of departed slaves so they, too, could be welcomed home. Every soul did this duty until it was reborn purer, again and again, because life is a stream that flows and flows endlessly into many bodies. In this way a deceased mother could return as your child, a lost slave could redeem a brutalised life; but first, the soul had to be returned to Africa. It had to be washed there, it had to touch paradise, home, heaven. And Africa was heaven.

My father dreamt of going back alive so he could thank those ancestors so patiently waiting for him. He wanted to say: "Thank you for not taking me away from my mother when she begged you. I lived my life well, but I need a new name now. I don't want to be Twentyfive anymore. I need a new soul."

In the end he died before he could return; only his soul went back. His body, they buried in exile. Although he hadn't bequeathed his dream to me, I inherited it anyhow. I dreamt of coming back to Africa. I dreamt of coming back alive. I dreamt of coming back as though I, and not my ancestors, had been stolen from it. I never considered where in Africa I would go, which generous nation would claim an orphan child.

From all this, I surmise that Jamaica must be my home. After all, it was the land of my birth, and isn't that the greatest claim of patriotism? Whatever the answer, I know I can't own the Caribbean the way my adoptive father can: not land, not property, not even my name. Yet I imagined, in my naivety, that I could claim Africa. It had given me my skin and what a field overseer once called an inherent barbarity, illiteracy, and obedience. These things I understood and these things Africa had given me; through time, across the seas, Africa had reached out and marked me as Her own.

That mark isolated me more sharply than any other trait. My peers saw me first as African, and as a peer second, or never. To belong to Africa meant I couldn't belong to the rest of the world or another part of it. So many times I've heard the words, "Go back to the jungle," because to everyone else Africa isn't a dream or heaven. It's a jungle. It's only a place.

To me it's yet another place that doesn't quite belong to me, where I don't quite belong. I can never claim it as others can: not its history, nor its kin, nor its full identity. Further, Africans who were never stolen away, whose stories of belonging to this place sound louder than my mere whispers—they don't own Africa the way Bram and his cronies do.

Drawing from my own discontent, I conclude that it can't please them to belong to a place by half measures. They're bound to revolt, to reclaim an Africa that is familiar to them. And surely, both the English and Dutch realise their governance cannot be sustained here. As I try to befriend the people of this place, to learn their untold histories and to unlearn those I took from my books, I think I'm beginning to understand Mr. Ivanov's position on the advantages of an independent Ireland. I can't accept the colonial benevolence claimed by Rudyard Kipling. I've witnessed the evidence of its falseness in every place that has adopted me however briefly and begrudgingly.

Mrs. Alisa van Zijl's
Journal: 1927

Wednesday, 30 March

I've set about righting my affairs in this place, and while gathering my things for our possible journey I found this journal, which I apparently kept from 1912 to 1915. This is from the time of my departure from England, to when Bram and I met Gloria. I never filled the journal to the very end but for one reason or another I started a new one in 1916.

I can't say the confusion and anxiety caused by the Great War are to blame for my forgetfulness, since I seem to have flippantly started yet another one in 1917, with no explanation in either journal for the sudden change. It might be the case that I simply misplaced it and I'm only finding it now. That's possible, because I've been looking around to see where I've put the ones I kept before 1912; it seems that I flippantly discarded those ones as well. It's very worrying. This now seems like a habit I've acquired—to start stories and not finish them. It's only right that I close this one, that I complete it. It seems a fitting end to my stay here.

Something else I found while rummaging around, beneath the suitcase I packed when coming to Africa, was a Bible my mother gave me when I was a child. It was buried there with other neglected relics like scraps of the story about the Children of the Sky God.

I remember that story—I've always wanted to expand it. The Bible, though, was such an old thing, such a forgotten thing, that it shocked me to be reminded that I owned one. I suppose that given my devout upbringing, it was only right that while digging for the scraps of my life, I find gods I had long since buried.

It dawned on me right then, holding that Bible, that fourteen years have swept by since I left England. My youth has passed me by. Now, embittered by my failures and nearing middle age, I wonder: Where has the time gone? What have I achieved with my life?

It's not easy to look at one's life and find that not much can be salvaged from it. When I travelled here, when I wrote this journal, I had so many ideas, so much vigour, so much hope. I can hardly believe that I once had such simple dreams as travelling to India, seeing the samurai, finding a home, finding Africa—heaven.

Ah, heaven! It was such a fickle dream that it flickered away when I touched its tip. When I glimpsed it, it evaporated, like a phantom someone had whispered up. I was too easy to please. The taste was enough to lull me, and the years swept away until a Bible mocked me back to life. Why didn't I go all the way to West Africa? Surely heaven is there, no? Surely I should have walked that proverbial extra mile to hold on to heaven, even if for a heart-beat. Surely then, having held it longer, the years would sweep away more slowly, tenderly, and time wouldn't feel so heavy.

In any case, Bram has suggested that we leave South Africa. Jamaica, England, the Soviet Union . . . he says we can go any-where I like. We could visit Yuri; it would be interesting to see the new Russia. All I have to do is say the word and we'll sail away. I could finally go to West Africa . . . I suppose I could finish another thing I started. Wouldn't that be something?

But on the other hand, wouldn't it be another exercise in futil-ity? Are the nations of West Africa not caught up in colonial sagas of their own? If I went there would I be home? The matter of my African identity isn't as simple as my skin. I've been tried in that regard and proven false. So, if I went to West Africa now, would I be home?

It's quite frustrating because Europe has already rejected me as completely as I rejected it. I can't call myself an Englishwoman. But Africa doesn't recognise me. It means I can't be that either, whether in the south or west of this continent. And if I, a woman black as coal yet so deeply initiated into the ways of Europe, can-not find a people who can accept me completely, what's the fate of my mulatto children? I can't belong anywhere because this place is in my blood. Yet I can't belong here because my blood is not enough.

If I, a woman black as coal yet so deeply initiated into the ways of Europe, must dance between such contradictions, what will happen to my children? They only half-inherited their father's skin. What will happen to them? The world is filled with places they must sit, where they must be, where they must go, but more importantly, where they must not. Big places, small places . . .

so many places scattered all around the world, scattered everywhere, and these small girls must learn and remember all these rules.

I've cursed them with my skin. I've made them fugitives of my skin. I selfishly brought them into a world filled with men who sit in rooms and decide who can and can't be one thing or another, who design the world as they want it. South Africa is no different in this regard. It's a very complicated place; it's not easy to understand. However, the fundamentals that led us here are so very rudimentary, that even a child could offer a sound analysis. I cannot proclaim myself an expert on the subject, but I'd venture that stronger civilisations always use the same strategy to further weaken their weaker counterparts. It can start with something as simple as fields, fields meant for a way of life, simple fields. Gloria told me that once.

It starts with a field that doesn't belong to a people anymore. So the people flee and scatter to feed themselves. So the field becomes obsolete, the clan evolves, they evolve too well, so well, in fact, they must now enter the room where men sit and decide. So the taking away of the field must evolve as well. Something else must be taken.

So the sense of self of the scattered, the newly arrived in the room, this simple thing must be taken. Wasn't that the reason the first men built that room to begin with? Wasn't the taking of the field supposed to prevent this? Well, it doesn't matter because this can be fixed; after all, a fundamental of evolution is its reliance on mistakes, its persistence in hammering them into perfection, in exploiting them to thwart unforeseen, undesirable results. If the clan evolves again another thing must be taken, and taken and taken and taken again, and like that it carries on.

Bram says we should not worry because we are married and we have the documents to prove it. He says the Immorality Act is an exercise in frivolity on Parliament's part, that it is too abstract to actually affect our lives. This seems like denial to me. The South African government can surely be accused of several atrocities, but it cannot be accused of frivolity. If nothing else, they're a thorough organisation. There's no such thing as an abstract law that wasn't designed to affect people's lives. He must at least suspect this, since he was as panicked as I was upon finding that the law had been passed. He should know that something as simple as the taking away of a field can, one day, end with a woman exiled to the wastelands of her own society. That was how we met Gloria, after all.

So this can only be the beginning. This is the foundation of something much bigger. And to think that it can start with something as simple as a field. Then it tumbles and coils and evolves until one day, a girl is born into a country where she can't be a citizen.

But I suppose I can console myself with the fact that we *are* married. I can set about righting my affairs in this place, bidding it farewell. It's strange, I hadn't even realised I had started thinking of it as home; and I must say that it has made me sad to have to leave it now.

Wednesday, 6 April

It rained in the night. Even the heavens mourn the souring of my life, it seems. The air is chilly from the wind, and the day dark; yet I must sit beneath this weeping willow to soothe away my woes.

Just now, the breeze grew colder, and more clouds gathered. I'm not a woman who seeks meaning in the coincidences of nature, but it seemed, at least briefly, that my mood swung and drifted and ebbed and re-merged with the fleeting resolve of the winds, that the world wept because I did, because I bent it to my will.

Since I found this journal I've become consumed with it. Even more than that, I've had to rethink a few things about my past. It's both a blessing and a curse. On one hand, I no longer trust my memory, so this journal serves me well. For instance, I remember my time on *The Black Swan* very differently. I remember meeting Bram differently; I don't remember half of what we said, and what I do remember is either a simplification of itself or a distortion.

On the other hand, I'm filled with regret because I'd forgotten so much. I've resented Bram for too long, it seems; so long that I've forgotten how much I love him. I want to say that I resent him because of the freedoms he has enjoyed here, freedoms that were denied to me. I want to say that he became cruel, because that would make it easier to still resent him. I want to say he betrayed me. I want to say so many things but I can't; they wouldn't be true. I don't know when this happened: at some point in our marriage I started resenting him.

We grew apart and I simply didn't know how to be free with him anymore. Well, that's not exactly what I mean but it's the best I can do to explain how I've felt. I must conclude that my memory has been polluted by time and my failures.

I'm so thankful to have found my thoughts again. It's given me a bit of peace. I feel easier about what I must do now. It might seem callous or haphazard to someone who doesn't know me, but I know that I've gone as far as I can go. I've held on for so long, so long, but I'm tired. Bram gave me relief but now I'm tired.

I've become a burden to him. He even believes the rumours. He believes I've betrayed our marriage with Yuri. Although this thing I didn't do, I could beg for his forgiveness, for I feel that I must repent for *some* crime, any crime, it doesn't matter which. I could beg and Bram would forgive me. He always forgives me. Always.

But this disease that eats me, it will not let me be. I can love Bram unencumbered for the fleeting moments of my sobriety; but soon, the darkness will eat my mind and heart and even my smile. It will eat and eat and eat, it will poison his heart. He will hate me again, and the hatred will drive me to near-madness again. In time my sadness will bleed deeper and deeper into my heart, and his love will fade, blossom anew, and fade. Like that our tragedy will continue.

I couldn't spare my daughters the burden of my skin, but I must spare them *this*—this thing I must do. I can't leave them behind. They would be shunned. One tragedy they could survive, but not both at the same time.

It breaks my heart because I don't want to be weak. Yet the darkness engulfing my heart grows and grows; new seeds it sows, it nurtures. And renewed, they grow to repeat their sequence of attack. Oh, how it frightens me: this state of living for the sake of living. How swiftly my futility flows into a darkness so tireless in its toil—deep, deep into my skin until nothing else is left. It might be easy for someone who doesn't know me to assume that the premise of my decision is as simple as death itself. The truth is I don't want to die. I only want the pain to stop. I want to rest.

My mother once told me that to kill oneself is an unforgivable sin. I surmised, after brooding on the matter a long while, that I needed to see the words myself. Suddenly, my old Bible became useful. I searched for the verse that condemned suicide. After a few hours it dawned on me that I had never appreciated how elaborate the book is. It's so very massive, and I found it tiresome (and impossible) to find the precise verse I was looking for.

I searched, too, for a verse condemning divorce; but after another two hours of no enlightenment I concluded that abandoning religion in my youth was a graver mistake than I anticipated. Thus, defeated by my own apathy, I wallow in an old journal I once discarded.

I had hoped to give the journals I kept over the years to my parents, to make them understand how I got here. But I've decided that the unnatural longevity of my misfortunes must end here, with my death. I must take them with me. I must take everything I can with me.

Something else that's been consuming me is this: I'm trying to remember my father's face, his voice, the stories he told near his end, the bright smile only matched by the sun's majesty, the dark skin that glittered in light, the limp of his left leg, his nearly hunched back as he walked to the plantation, the scent of sweat sticking to him—even the ordinary things, I'm trying to remember them. The corners of his eyes crinkled when he smiled, for he was aged, and the sun had burnt him well. These things, I think, mark the beginning. But these things, you see, I lose to time.

[Annotation to the entry of Wednesday, 6 April]

Gloria asked me a very strange question today. She asked if either of my deceased parents died with any unfinished business. "Or a grandmother, or a grandfather, or anyone in a rumoured clan," she said. I told her that I couldn't think of anything; at which point she nodded thoughtfully, bit her lower lip, and retreated to the kitchen.

I thought it was just passing curiosity on her part, but now that I think about it, when she first came here she sometimes asked these sorts of strange questions, like whether I'd ever thought of perhaps naming the girls after a grandmother somewhere in my past.

Anyhow, I've been thinking about it all day and I realised that my father never told me the other stories he promised. Also, he never came to Africa. These don't seem like instances of unfinished business to me, though. They just seem like things my father never got around to doing, in the same way that I never got around to seeing the samurai or going to West Africa.

What's troubling me, now that I think about it further, is that the last time I had a dream with shadow hands and snakes was right before I left England. I've had other frightening dreams since then (like the one with the rabid dog and the one with a python swallowing me). They recur, of course, like all my dreams do. But the shadow dream itself, I last had it sometime between January and 27 March of 1912. I noted this very fact in this journal. It's funny, when I married Bram I thought that he might have been the cure; I realise now that I was naïve and wrong.

It seems silly, but I now wonder if something as simple as promising a story to a child and not telling it, or wanting to return to the land of one's ancestors but failing to do so, can be so potent as to haunt the generations that come after. In coming here, did I unintentionally inherit something far more profound than I understood? Did I fulfil some cosmic fate that I didn't even know I was bending myself to? Also, if I completed one fate, it's logical to assume that I might have failed in completing another. It's really rather frightening, if I must be honest. I felt chills all over my body when I started to think along these lines.

I don't know what any of it means, but now that I'm at the end, I feel that it's important to understand why and when the dream started, why it stopped, and what it meant. Oh, how I wish I could talk to Bram about these things.

It would also be so helpful if I had my earlier journals. That way I could start at the beginning to see if there was something I missed. My own unfinished business

The Small Black Book

A lisa's words ended there. Abruptly. Incompletely. Lingering with foreboding prophecies.

Abram concluded that he should have left them untouched, preserved in the past. Alisa belonged there as well. But like the mark given to her by Africa, her poison and beauty and scent had stretched through time to touch him. She was like a ghost that refused to leave him, like an illness that couldn't be cured, not by any remedy he knew; certainly not by time, because time had folded itself to catch up with him. He couldn't change the fates already passed, nor the order of time. He was only a man.

Even in her death, she wanted to spread her fear to him. She wanted to infect him with her fickleness. Now he had to live the rest of his life wondering about her unfinished business, about some malevolent curse she had unwittingly unleashed. Oh, Alisa, why couldn't she simply rest in her grave? She had wreaked her havoc so efficiently. Couldn't she leave him alone now?

There was a time when she liked to tell him about her childhood. She spoke about the warm summer heat that bathed her skin in sweat, about the taste of overripe mangoes and a foreign spice splashed into the meagre food her father fed her. "I like to think I was happy," she had said. "I like to think I didn't dream those things." But of course, the tides had turned and in the end she couldn't even tell him something as simple as the details of a dream. She had harboured everything within herself until she had no choice but to befriend the shadows haunting her.

The small black book had knitted her grievances so intricately into each other that by the end of his first reading, he felt overcome by regret. He thought *What has my life come to?* He longed for the walls to echo his cry—to extend their stoic presence, hug him, and dispute the fateful futility so tragically narrated by Alisa. But alas, the walls did not, for the cry was silent and the room filled with Johannes's youthful souvenirs.

There was no space for grief. There was nothing to be gained in self-pity, nor in regret. He closed the book.

PART FIVE

Children of the Sky God

Marula

The sun had passed its zenith. For the sake of decency, Abram at last rose from the bed. He walked to the window and looked outside, where a *marula* tree shed its leaves as well as the last of its fruit.

Dido had gone with her band of cronies to the river, where apparently there were playful monkeys to be seen. When they were not enthralled by the mysteries of the river, Dido and her friends, two farm boys named Justice and Maleka, liked to sit under the *marula* tree and gather the fallen fruit. It was sweet to the taste; Dido declared she couldn't recall anything more succulent.

Josephina had told them that once fermented and distilled, the fruit produced an alcoholic brew. "What is the drink called?" Abram asked. It turned out there were two answers. It was called *maroela mampoer* in Afrikaans, and something entirely different (which Abram forgot) in Josephina's language. She had given a shy smile and looked at her hands as though some fascinating spectacle unfolded itself there. "I make it for *Baas* Joubert when the fruit has ripened," she said, in Afrikaans. "If Sir liked, I can make for you as well. I will tell the children to gather the fruit." With that, she bent her right knee out of respect, and promptly returned to her chores.

The children had since spent their mornings filling buckets with *marula*. Oblivious to the alcoholic nature of the promised drink, Dido told Abram: "We must ask Miss Josephina to show us how she makes it. I will gather more fruit to take with us. That way we could drink it wherever we went."

Abram laughed. "It is like wine," he said. "Children must not drink it."

Dido contorted her face in thought. "Miss Josephina is like you, isn't she?" she said. "Only she doesn't sell her wine, but gifts it to people she loves. Should we tell her to sell it? If she did, she wouldn't live in her small hut with her husband."

"Yes," he said, smiling away the things he couldn't yet say to her. Things such as the impossibility of Josephina's venture into business. It would break her heart.

In her innocence, Dido had bounced to the tree, to indulge in the fruit before starting her chore. Abram now walked to the tree and picked green *marula* from the ground. They were bitter, and he preferred them to the ripe, yellow kind. There were also stones scattered among the fruit. As he had learnt, when the flesh of the fruit was finished, the stones were put in the sun to dry. In winter they were cracked to yield nuts, or planted to sprout more trees, or stowed away, or the children carved holes in the ground to play games with them—the stones were moved in and out of the holes much like chess pieces were moved around a board, or so Abram surmised.

He crouched down to pick the fruit not yet rotted by neglect. Immersed in his chore, he didn't see Josephina approaching.

"Good afternoon, Sir Van Zijl," she greeted.

Although her voice was as soft as ever, and her manner gentle, her presence startled him. "Good afternoon to you as well, Josephina," he said, standing up.

"May I bring your food now?"

"Thank you, Josephina, but no."

"Should I keep the food for later?"

"You may. Thank you."

He expected her to leave him to his idleness, as she always did after wishing him a good day or bringing him food. She didn't. Instead she fiddled with her hands while glancing around. She said, "Must I check if *Baas* Joubert wants your company?"

Abram smiled at her. She must have sensed his uneasiness in Johannes's company. He guessed from her shaking head that she was chiding herself for her unsolicited openness where her employer was concerned.

"The northern Transvaal is not a place of treasures, sir," she said, abruptly. "No one comes here. Everyone goes away. They go to Johannesburg, where gold is said to litter the streets. They go to the Cape and Natal to see the sea. They go north from here, to Uganda, to other places. They all go away. This is not a place for travellers. We, who remain here, know only the news of cows and fields and the harvests we reap from them.

"That is how *Baas* Joubert finds himself with his many books. I do not have the gift of reading so many languages myself. But I know the tales of books are not the tales of the living. You are a living man, and . . . Sir, sometimes it is better to hear the things of the world from the living. Can I check for him, if you want his company?"

"No, thank you, Josephina," he said.

She retreated into her submissiveness, bowing her head and fiddling with her hands, as she was wont to do. "I must return to my chores," she said, turning to leave.

"Can I ask you something?" said Abram, stopping her.

"Yes, sir," she said, turning back to face him.

"Do you know if John . . ." Abram suddenly found himself lost for words. He didn't know how to ask the question without revealing Johannes's secret, if a secret it still was. He cleared his throat, taking a moment to gather his thoughts. "Has he courted any ladies from the nearby farms?"

For the first time since they met, Josephina looked Abram in the eyes. Her eyes looked frantic, and her lips were pressed together as though, by the will of her bones, she could swallow away the secret now between them. He could tell her it didn't matter—that she could be on her way; but that would arrest his mind in that perpetual state of unknowing so lamented by Alisa. He thus allowed a natural end to the silence between them.

Josephina had been standing near the edge of the tree's shade. To answer him, she abandoned the sun's warmth and stood closer. From time to time the branches swayed this way and that, and with them, the leaves; some gently, and some fatefully, as they abandoned the safety of the tree to drift to the earth below.

"As I know it, sir," said Josephina, "there have been no courtships."

"Then you also know that John chooses his isolation. I know you mean well, Josephina. You want to save him from what you think is loneliness; but it is not loneliness. John is consumed by the hatred of his own heart. He hates everything and everyone. He hates himself, even when he shouldn't. He dares not surrender this hate for fear that he will become a lesser man. It's not an easy thing to love a man like that, Josephina, to wallow, eternally, in his bitterness, as he does."

"That may be so." Josephina smiled her toothless smile. Even in her old age, she looked much like a child. Her shy demeanour added to the effect, and the way she tilted her head to the left, being deaf in one ear, made her look persistently curious.

"But, sir," she continued, "this is not a place for travellers. I have grown old with only the harvest to tell the years that pass. Even my enemies have turned friends. I see them at sunrise, at sunset, and in winter we say to each other, 'Oh, the air is cold, cold, cold.' The winds rise and we say to each other, 'Oh, the winds are harsh, harsh.'

"You live your life hating a face but come morning you seek that face to say: 'Oh, the land has dried. This heat and dust, it kills my skin, I tell you—it taints my blood. We need the rains. We need them now.' There comes a time when you look at the face and know in your heart you can't hate it anymore. An enemy becomes a friend in a place like this. If they pass on, you wake in the morning and find you cannot sing your troubles to anyone. They grow heavy in your heart. It is not easy to hate a man—to wallow, eternally, in his bitterness, as he does."

She shrugged, maybe to surrender to some futility she couldn't quite explain, then laughed in discomfort. "This place is my home, sir. Even when I do not want to, I have to love it. I have no other home. This is where I belong. If the people of here wallow in bitterness, we all feel it, as it poisons all of us."

The pretty spark of her eyes turned dark just then, and her smile was swallowed by the creases of her age. A sudden sadness that wasn't there before came over her face. For a heartbeat, she reminded him of Alisa. "I must return to my chores, sir," she said.

"If you can, Josephina, please see if *Baas* Joubert might want my company," said Abram.

"I will, sir," she said, turning to leave. "I will."

With the sun gliding farther west, Abram thought it best, at last, to trim his beard, tidy himself, and pack Alisa's journal at the bottom of his suitcase.

Orion, the Hunter, Was Swallowed by the Horizon

To say of Johannes Joubert that he was frugal in forgiving those who, in his eyes, had trespassed against him, was a severe injustice to his stubbornness. The man was convinced of his rightness in everything. As Abram saw it, time had let him settle into an indignant sense of martyrdom. "The sale of your estate is going swimmingly, old friend," said Johannes. "You will soon be free."

That wasn't true, of course. Abram doubted he would ever feel untied from Cape Town. The place had been his home for two decades. Dido was born there, as was Emilia. And despite her hatred for it in the end, it was Alisa's home too. For the sake of being polite, however, he answered by leaning farther into his chair, sipping from his teacup, and saying: "This man, Alfred Aaron de Pass, he intends to continue the winemaking. He wants to restore the manor."

"Yes," said Johannes, pausing to take a drag from his pipe. "I must say, it was reckless to leave your fortune in the complete care of natives in the meantime. Mr. De Pass's stay in Windhoek might be extended. There's no knowing what chaos your employees will concoct."

"I trust my people," said Abram.

"Of course you do," said Johannes, waving smoke away from his face. "Anyway"—he coughed—"aren't you tired of this endless waiting?"

"No. I knew it might take time. What weighs on my mind is the fear that I'll be caught. I've been anxious over it." He sipped his tea again. Josephina had served it some time ago, too long ago, he judged. While Abram listened to Johannes passionately espouse the wonders of his vast tomato fields, the tea had grown cold. It was a blend of the rooibos plant, which Josephina had assured him was different from the Cape variety in both smell and taste. He was happy to find that Josephina was right. But Johannes wasn't fond of tea and Abram was left to battle the large pot on his own; out of politeness, he felt compelled to finish it.

He'd found that from time to time he could use the tea to gather his thoughts. Maybe that was the reason Josephina had insisted that he test the flavour. In case he wanted to pack it for the journey, she had said. Presently, having soothed his throat, he said: "You know, John, our estrangement was unfortunate even as it began. Don't you think it's time to end it? I came to you as a man stripped of his convictions, and you welcomed me despite yours. By that alone, haven't we proven the futility of these long years of our animosity?"

Johannes didn't immediately answer. The silence that followed was filled with the things neither man could say. It was a familiar sort of silence, long and troubling and speckled with longing. Abram decided the moment was ripe to exit the conversation and retreat to his quarters. Dido was surely returned from the river, and he wanted to hear her merry stories. "John," he said, sipping the last of his tea, then placing the cup and saucer on the table before him, "I must go back to my daughter. Good evening."

"No, no," said Johannes, raising his free palm, "sit. Please. I don't mean to offend you. You've simply caught me unawares."

Abram sat down. But finding that he and Johannes had nothing more to say, he allowed the lull of the silence and twilight and the tea to nudge him into contentment. It was a welcome feeling. From the moment he discovered Alisa's journal, he'd been consumed by thoughts of her, by guilt and much else that bled into his heart.

Unceremoniously, Johannes disrupted the lull. "Can you allow me a moment of impertinence, old friend?" he asked.

Abram smiled to himself. "Ask away, John."

Johannes gazed into the distance, where, currently, the sky was alight with the ceremony of sunset. Beneath the last glow of the sun, a cowherd ushered a herd of cattle home. He was a very thin man. He didn't wear a shirt. He carried a raised stick in his right hand, the better to guide the cattle where he wanted.

As the cowherd and his horde trod closer, they raised dust into the air. One, two, three, and more cattle bellowed, and the bells around their necks rang with the steps they took. The sound they made was the song of sunset. Speedily, the sun receded behind the cowherd as he wiped the sweat from his forehead and marched home to quench his thirst, or so Abram surmised. "How far do the cows go for their grazing?" he asked Johannes.

"Walter, the cowherd, he takes them to the veld near the lake."

"Which do you find easier to manage, the livestock or the tomato fields?"

Johannes prefaced his response with a heavy sigh. "There is nothing easy about this place," he said. "There are good summer years and drought years. The good years are shorter, it seems. The drought years remind us that nothing survives here except the heat and dust. Did *you* love your winemaking?"

Abram kept his gaze on Walter's progress: he was then turning at a fork in the road, away from the house and onto the road that led to the servants' quarters. By a whistle and a call to the wayward cattle whose names he knew, and the brandishing of his stick, the herd turned as well, to lead their master home.

"I enjoyed the stories told by the workers," said Abram. "I enjoyed the beauty of the fields. The wine itself was unremarkable, not nearly as good as what comes out of the Groot Constantia Estate. But it was a legacy I once hoped my daughters would refine with time and a better passion for the trade. I excelled when it came to our finances; although even *that* isn't something I could profess to love. It was necessary. But I don't think I loved it."

"Yet you carried on with it."

"As you carry on with this place of heat and dust, as all the people here do."

"Maybe we should rush to the gold pits of Johannesburg."

"The noise alone will drive us mad."

"Maybe, but we must now live without knowing."

"That, I can do," said Abram.

"Regarding my impertinence, Bram, can I ask why you never divorced Alisa? What made you endure her bitterness all these years?"

By then, Walter and his cattle had disappeared to their journey's end. The only reminder of their passage was the dust they had raised, and their footprints. The dust danced in the glow of dusk like the last sunrays, dying and fading and flickering back in desperate resilience. Finding the scene tedious, Abram finally said: "I loved her."

Although they were few, there were days when she loved their daughters. Days when she stood beneath the stars and laughed into the night; when she said to him: *This is not how I want to be.* Abram felt tears quicken themselves in his eyes. "I loved her," he echoed.

Johannes turned to fiddle with the contents of the drawer near his seat. When he turned back, he held a sealed bag of tobacco. He emptied the ash from his pipe, stuffed it with the fresh batch he had retrieved, and lit it with a cough and a shaking hand. "And she?" he asked, smoking from his pipe. "What was the reason she didn't leave?"

"She could divorce me, yes. And maybe she wanted to. But when that was done, where would she go?"

The darkness of evening was then shrouding them, but Abram could still see that contemplation had overcome Johannes's eyes. "You were bound together."

"Yes," said Abram. There was more to be said, of course. Alisa's sadness was like a disease. It came in cycles, like the seasons or the phases of the moon. Today she was happy and jumping with it. Tomorrow she refused to leave the darkness of her room. So in cycles Abram loved and hated her. In a trap of her own madness, she loved and hated him. She was easier to understand when he thought along these lines; that was what he should have said to Johannes. But those things belonged to him and Alisa, and even Dido, who carried her mother's pain in her skin and heart and a small black book with a burnt spine. It wasn't right to share those things with Johannes. They were sacred. Johannes would taint them with his hatred.

There was a knock at the door, and Josephina entered holding a lantern that she placed on the windowsill. "Your food is served, *Baas*," she said. "And yours, sir."

"Thank you, Josephina," they chorused.

"Has Dido come back?" asked Abram.

"Yes, sir. Not long ago." She slightly bent her knee before leaving the room.

"Well," said Johannes, standing up. He removed the pipe from his mouth and held it aloft. "I expect there will be another telegram tomorrow. The whole affair will be done before the end of the week. I daresay you will leave as scheduled. If there's nothing else, Bram, I must dine."

Abram stood up as well. "Thank you for your help, John," he said. With that, he made his way to the kitchen.

"Oh, Papa!" exclaimed Dido, upon seeing him. "You look handsome again."

Abram chuckled. "Do you think so?"

"Yes." She smiled. Her skin was patched by a darker shade in places; it was mud and dust, he realised. Often, she came home cloaked in dirt. And often, Abram needed to coax her into a bath because, after eating her supper, she soon fell asleep. And always, she begged: "Please, Papa, if I rest only a little I'll take my bath when I wake up."

"When you're done eating, please go straight to your bath," said Abram, "else the water will be cold." He sat beside her, tickled her under her shoulders, and said, "The cold water will prickle your skin and prickle it here and there and there and there and you'll turn to ice."

Dido laughed, contorting her body to shield herself, and tried to shake herself away from his reach. Her laughter hindered her, so Abram found more skin ready to be tickled, further exciting her into her frenzy of laughter. "Please, Papa, please stop!" she said. "I'll go. I promise."

"All right," he said, reaching for the cutlery Josephina had set for him. "But if you don't keep your promise, just remember I'll tickle you out of your sleep."

"You wouldn't."

"You dare challenge me?" he said, failing to keep the smile from his face and laughter from his voice.

Smiling widely, with nearly all her teeth showing, she shook her head. "No."

"Good. Now tell me what you did today."

She dove into a story about Mamolapi, a water goddess who was said to be both a fish and woman.

"Like a mermaid?" asked Abram.

"Yes. But Mamolapi lives in the river, not the sea. She has many children. But all her children have been stolen from her, see. She looks for them always. If she sees something that looks like water, something like a house roofed with unpainted corrugated iron, which shines in the light of sun, then Mamolapi will destroy that house because she thinks the people there have stolen her children and hidden them in false water . . ."

He listened as the story of Mamolapi changed into that of

a monster man named Mphukudu, who was tall and pale and snatched away people and no one ever saw them again; then into the tragedy of a young girl and her defiant sister whose names Abram would never be able to recall. And on and on they went, fading in and out of each other with the effortless abandon that only Dido could achieve.

As usual, her words flowed into each other without rules of syntax and punctuation, without restraint. She said everything as a single, long word; pausing only to catch her breath. Maybe like her mother, she thought there would come a time when those who listened to her wouldn't listen anymore, and so thought to keep the listeners intrigued while she still had the chance.

Abram listened as the legends she recited were delicately fused with her own imagination. "It's all very fascinating," she said, pausing to confirm that he was attending. "Let me tell you what else Mamolapi can do."

He nodded, as she returned her hands and eyes to her food, then insisted that before continuing with her knowledge of Mamolapi, she had to, absolutely *had* to tell him the different ways one could tell whether a locust species was edible or not.

"There is an anthill," she said, "over way by the river, but really it's not an anthill but a place where termites can be found. Near there, that's where Justice says the tastiest locusts can be found. Tomorrow we're going there and he's going to show me how to catch them. He says it's easy but he also said he could catch a monkey. He was lying about that. Not even Maleka can catch a monkey. Maleka has very fast legs, see." Deciding that she was too tired to carry on, as supported by her yawn, she said, "Well, Papa, I think I'm tired now. I have to go for my bath. Is it all right if we continue tomorrow?"

"As far as I know, stories never rot."

"I promise not to forget everything I didn't tell you." She slid out of her chair, kissed him on the cheek, and hopped her way to her bath. "Good evening," she called, her small frame disappearing beyond the kitchen door.

"Good evening."

With that, Abram was abandoned to a silence that was intermittently broken by the chirping of crickets somewhere in the darkness. He finished his supper of roast chicken and potatoes with gusto. Then he stepped outside into that darkness interrupted by the calls of owls hiding near and the twinkling of stars far away. The seasons were changing, the world was turning again, and the stars rose and set with the turn.

Abram stood near the *marula* tree and watched and listened to the things of the night. They came to life in the shadows. They buzzed and howled and sang their misery; their misery and joy and secrets. Shyly, they crept and crawled and hid and sang again the song of night. And still the stars twinkled above, and the moon crossed the sky from horizon to horizon, following the sun but failing to make known the things that crept and crawled and hid.

Smoke wafted from where the servants had built their huts. It carried the scent of spices, roots, and other edible things in their pots. Abram wondered if the workers, too, listened to the night things and heard a song, or if they were uninterested in these trivial mysteries.

That made no difference to him. He wanted to capture the mood and rhythm surging through that place. He wanted to inhale its secrets—neatly woven into these ageless survivors of time, given and taken, and given again to the descendants of the soil. He closed his eyes and listened to the soft ringing of a cowbell whose keeper had not yet rested, to a woman who called her children to a meal, to the flutter and frolic of each survivor's pursuit.

They were simple things, the symptoms of life, memories echoing from his youth. They were beautiful, fleeting, and slipping away from him. His thoughts went back to Alisa's journal. He felt crippled by her. It was true that he hated her. But what the charred and blotted pages didn't say—for those tales were stolen by the fire that stole her—was that he loved her. Even at the end, he had loved her. But she was gone. He couldn't tell her these things. She was gone.

Safe in the cover of darkness and solitude, Abram didn't resist the tears that sprung from his eyes. With his eyes closed, he raised his hands to the sky. "Forgive me, Alisa," he whispered. "This is not how I want to be."

The tears teemed freely. They flowed impatiently, eroding his face with their heat and salt. For a time, more than a heartbeat, he stood near the tree to let the tears drain as they would, from his bleeding heart.

There was pain and pain and more pain. His heart bled and bled and bled some more. It felt unending, and Abram tried to catch those things of his youth slipping away from him. They eluded him. They swept through the night seamlessly, away from his memory—wafting from his reach with the smoke and the glide of the things that crawled and crept and hid away.

He couldn't catch them. He couldn't relive them, nor pack them beneath the clothes and papers he had packed away for his journey. So he breathed deeply, and felt that the tears would fall no more. He lowered his hands and wiped what was left of the cascades. Briefly, he felt someone watching him. When he looked around he didn't find anyone. His heart beat faster. When he looked around again he saw Dido standing in the doorway of his quarters.

She sprinted to where he stood and he greeted her by lifting her from the ground and keeping her in his arms. Although she was tired, for she rested her head in the curve of his neck and yawned, she stayed awake.

Together they silently stared into the night, watching as Orion, the Hunter, was swallowed by the horizon, and the Southern Cross announced the pending arrival of the colder months. As the hour grew later and later, and the air cooler, Abram placed his daughter on the ground and took her hand in his; together, they trod to their hovel to rest their weary bones.

Tale of the Rain Queen

Bram and the girl stood near the window. Johannes had taken great pains to secure the girl's present ensemble: a white shirt, and a jacket and trousers that nearly matched the shade of her skin. If he didn't know her, he might have thought she was a boy. She smiled when he entered the room, tensely, but somewhat prettily. "Good morning," he said.

Bram and the girl chorused back the greeting. Then Bram immediately plunged into gratitude and farewell: "This is it, as they say. You've been a true friend, John, a true friend indeed. We must now thank you and be on our way."

Johannes felt a sudden need for his pipe. He walked to the drawer to retrieve it. He lit it like he always did, with great patience. He felt his guests' eyes firmly fixed on him, maybe in awe, maybe with revulsion. He didn't care either way. All he wanted was the relief of that first wisp. Once achieved, he said to Bram:

"I was glad to be of help, old friend. I trust that the passage across the border has been secured, the man will be waiting for you."

"Oh yes," said Bram. "The nuns and Gloria have been very helpful; as have you, of course."

"I suppose you've decided where you will go."

"Not yet." He draped his arm around the girl's shoulder and, it seemed to Johannes, prompted her to say something.

The girl said, in her singsong way, "Thank you, Mr. Joubert. You've been very kin, so kind—"

Johannes laughed from shock. "Kind, you say?"

"Well," she continued, her voice slightly afflicted with a quiver, "you told me the tale of the Rain Queen. You did it well, sir. It made me happy."

The girl looked to be speaking earnestly. Johannes was oddly delighted by that. "As I remember," he said, "we ended the story at something of an impasse. Can I ask if your thoughts on the matter have changed?"

"Well. I don't know yet. Can I ask you a question?" As she spoke, she stepped on her left foot with her right and tilted her head to look at Bram. It might have been approval she wanted, Johannes never knew; all he saw was the other man's growing interest in the conversation.

"You can," said Johannes, after a pull on his pipe.

"Did the chief ever see his daughter again?"

Johannes looked at Bram. "Do you have a moment, old friend? It might be best if you sat."

Bram nodded to the girl and both took their seats, with the girl claiming her father's lap. "Don't take too long," said Bram. "I don't want us to miss the train."

Johannes took his place near the drawer; he crossed his left leg over his right, rested his free hand on his lap, and cleared his throat. "Don't worry, my friend," he said; and to the girl: "Where did we end?"

"You told me that the queen's magic couldn't follow her to her father's valley," said the girl. "You also said the queen's father was nearing his death. That was when we eh . . . uh . . . reached our impasse. You asked me if I understood the story."

"Oh yes, I remember," said Johannes. "I suppose I must resume here: after I met the chief, I left his valley. I went south, where his daughter ruled. I came to a valley much like his. Their bonds were built in the currency of cattle; their huts were built from dung and mud and their people were simple. Their fields, however, were rich. I met with the chief of that place. He was a younger man who was born in some famed year of a great harvest. They called him blessed for it. He invited me to his hovel, and there, I asked about the Rain Queen. 'I'm traveling now to see her,' I told him. The young chief asked what I knew about the queen. With pride, I told him the tale once narrated to me by the old northern chief. 'You see, my good man,' I told him, 'I know a lot about her. I only want to see her with my own eyes, to witness her wonder.'

"The chief laughed. I must confess that I briefly thought he was mad. Then, as abruptly as he'd begun, he stopped laughing, stamped his staff on the ground, and handed me a coin. It was a florin that, by its inscription, was minted in 1849. It had Queen Victoria's crowned effigy on one side and four shields on the other.

"The chief pointed at Queen Victoria and said: 'I have been told stories about this woman. By men like you, missionaries and hunters. I have been told that this woman, who was seas away and unknown to me, worked vigorously to lift me from squalor, ignorance, and barbarity. Tell me, visitor of mine, have you met this woman? Has she entrusted you with this mission?'

"I was then convinced his people should have called the young chief mad instead of blessed. I thanked him for his hospitality and begged his leave. But in response, he stamped his staff and said: 'I will arrange a guide for you to the Rain Clans, if that is what you want.' Seeing his renewed kindness, I expressed my regret in being so easily offended. 'I'm not an Englishman,' I said. 'To be thought of as one is an insult.'

"We sat at length after that. I learnt that he was a man who laughed easily. When the time came, I said farewell to him. And a week later I arrived at my journey's end, the territory of the Rain Clans. The Rain Queen admitted me to her court with grace. Naturally, I asked about the secret of her talent for rain-giving. I suppose just as naturally, she smiled politely and told me it was a secret meant only for her people. I then asked if she missed her father, her home, her people, and all that she was before ascending to her throne.

"She asked me: 'Which father? Which home? What people? In short, what account of my tragedy brought you here?' In shock, I further asked whether in the years following her abduction she forgot the details of her former life. But again she said: 'Which life do you speak of?' At that, I narrated the tale once narrated by the old chief. The queen nodded thoughtfully. Then a silence grew between us—long it was, long and filled with my swelling doubt in the matter.

"She watched me with pity, as though conveying some profound wisdom with her eyes. Her calmness at my confusion unsettled me, and her hope that I would grasp her silent message frightened me. So we sat untouched by the happenings of the world for what felt like an age.

"Soon the moment ended, and it was then, in that eerie silence, that I was lifted from the oblivion of many years. When she saw the truth change my face she smiled knowingly, the first such expression I saw on her face. It was lovely to see, lovely and as rare as her talent. Still enchanted by her mystery, I finally nodded my understanding.

"I then left her valley. On the journey home I crossed the mountains where ruled the young chief. I thanked him for his wisdom and journeyed to the old chief, where I thanked him too. And that is how it ended . . . as far as I know." When he finished, Johannes found that both Bram and the girl were quite arrested by his tale.

"This journey of yours, John," said Bram, "was it before or after I married Alisa?"

"It was after."

"Is that where you found Josephina?"

"Yes."

"Why?"

After Johannes and Bram had their falling out, Bram went north with his wife. Johannes had followed them and gone north as well. He'd needed to understand why Bram could so easily betray a friendship that had endured so much, a friendship that had survived a war, the barriers of politics and ideology, religion and so much more. Everything that Bram had done, Johannes had tried to do because, if he could understand him even for a second, the pain of losing him might feel bearable.

Johannes had immersed himself in Africa. He found that he

loved it. He tried to hunt. He found that he didn't like that at all. He then immersed himself in wine and history and business and many things his friend had immersed himself in. In the course of his numerous immersions he had collected several natives he later employed, natives such as Abram had collected. Then, when he was done immersing himself, when he emerged back into his own self, he reflected on his heartache and found that he wasn't sufficiently heartbroken. He needed to be far more pained. He realised, at last, that he was a man who loved another man. A man who, though he loved another man, still understood the depravity of the fact.

Here, because Johannes never wavered in his convictions, he resolved to immerse himself in an entirely original endeavour. He banished himself to the Transvaal and proceeded to live the rest of his life repenting. He couldn't say any of this to Bram, of course. As the one who ended their friendship, Bram wouldn't understand.

But even in that resolve, Johannes felt the regret of many years wash over him and leave him cold and bare and alone as an empty sky. He inhaled a deep gust and said, simply: "Because I wanted to." He wanted to say more. He felt like a man at the brink of revelation. It was within reach, but like a fool or coward, he was letting it slip away. It wouldn't come again, he knew. But there was nothing to be done about it. Desperate, afraid, and hoping to eternally anchor Bram in their entanglement, he added: "Things aren't always as simple as you make them seem, Bram. We must obey certain rules if we want to propel ourselves into the modern century with a chance of surviving as an independent nation of civilised people. The world is divided, not by me and you, and not by the lawmakers. It's divided by nature.

"It's a necessary division that exists between a parent and a child, and *must* exist between a master and his subject. Although we are blessed with superior intelligence and every form of civilisation, we are a race at the brink of endangerment. It is our duty to rid those less fortunate than ourselves of their barbarity, their primitiveness, their heresy, and all forms of their depravity. If you travelled the entire continent you would see this.

"Although contact must be made, for how else can we dispense this magnanimity entrusted to us, it must be controlled to its smallest degree. In a world where division is demolished, where the subject can mingle with his master as an equal, how can we prosper? Tell me that, old friend. One can't be both at once. He must be either leader or follower, civilised or not; to play both roles would lead to failure. You should have listened to me, Bram. You should have listened to me from the beginning. There can't be two Europes in the world. Africa must be saved from homogeneity," he finished, then puffed from his pipe as he waited for a rebuttal.

But, as he'd expected, Bram simply nodded and said, "Then I must retreat from this battle knowing that even you, John, who loved me dearly, deserted me in the end. I thank you for the refuge. And I do hope when next we meet it will be as friends still. Goodbye."

With that, Bram stood up and took the girl's hand in his. She, apparently still intrigued in the argument now concluded, said: "I understand, Mr. Joubert. I think I would have understood if you told me the whole story the first time. It's a good story, a bit sad, but I think I like it. Thank you for telling it to me." She smiled so brightly, so purely, that Johannes was briefly fond of her.

"What is it you think you understand?" he asked her.

It wasn't the girl who answered, but her father. "It's very simple. The queen was both myth and truth," he said. "The old chief was not her father, but the story he told was true. She belonged to all her people, and to none at all. You, a mere traveller and therefore foreign to their truths, wanted only simple truths. But nothing is pure with legend, and their secrets were theirs to keep, not yours. You're the one who should have listened. You're the one who didn't understand."

"That's all good and well," said Johannes. "But I want to hear what the girl thinks."

Her forehead creased in great thought. Finally she decided: "I think my father is right."

"That's what you think?" asked Johannes, smiling.

"Yes, I think so," she mumbled.

"Then I suppose that in the end, Dido, we see things the way we want to see them," said Johannes. "You say a thing can be both true and false at the same time? I say it cannot. Who is right between us, and who is wrong?"

"Does it matter?" she asked.

"It does," he said. "It does."

That was the end. Despite Bram's earlier promise of reunion, Johannes knew it was the end of their friendship too. When next they saw each other, it wouldn't be as living men, but as ghosts either haunted or aimless. Or, maybe the theists had it right and there was a heaven. Somewhere beyond this world, there existed another, better world. And there, among the stars, they might meet again.

He felt that he needed to say more. But he felt, too, that he could not, for the flash of epiphany was swiftly slipping away, faster, faster, to depths he would never dare to explore. He cleared his throat. "Goodbye," he said.

"Goodbye," said Bram and the girl.

As easily as that, Johannes was out of time.

Around the Bend
and onto the Dirt

Abram's eyes sparkled with tears that never touched his face. He had settled in South Africa at an opportune time in his youth. He had loved it. Then one day he left his contentment behind, taking only his daughter and the chosen things that hadn't burnt in Alisa's fire.

Flight from a place was like ripping a heart by its roots and carelessly planting it in salted earth, where nothing grew. That's what he felt in that moment. He walked to the car with Dido's hand in his. The driver was ready with a smile to greet them and assurances of his good driving. Josephina hugged Dido, then, pulling away to lament how dark her skin had become, she added, "I will miss you, Dido. I will not forget you."

"I will miss you too."

"Don't be sad, now," continued Josephina. "Do not leave me with a sore heart. Do not taint your path with tears."

The scene was interrupted by the two boys, Justice and Maleka, who arrived abruptly, breathless from running. Josephina said, "See how loved you are, Dido? See what joy you brought to us, and what pain your leaving has left us?" Josephina's face became dim. She bowed her head in shyness. "May you travel an easy path, sir," she said.

"And may you live an easier life, Josephina," he said.

Maleka and Justice, who had been rendered speechless by their fear of Abram, and by sadness, simply waved and said: "Go well."

Dido waved back. "Stay well."

At that, Abram and Dido finally boarded the car. As the door closed, Abram whispered: "Goodbye, John. I will miss you."

Johannes, however, was behind his study window, smoking his pipe and exhaling the smoke onto the pane, staining the glass, clouding his vision and further agitating his throat. He couldn't have heard Abram. Hurriedly, the car drove around the bend and onto the dirt road leading away from the farm.

To the west, Dido said there was a termite hill, and beyond the termite hill there was a field where the fattest locusts could be found. Beyond that field, she said, there was a nameless tree where lived a man so tall his face couldn't be seen. It was said he could reach the clouds.

"He's a ghost-man, see," said Dido, her eyes flitting this way and that, as though afraid of the spectre's presence. "His skin is grey with death, his eyes black with wickedness, and his teeth red with blood. He eats children. Maleka told me not to go to that place. He told me to keep my eye away from it." She immediately averted her eyes from the infamous place, lest the ghost-man sense her defiance and cast his evil eye on her.

. . .

The river monkeys were a troop of monkeys that lived in the trees and caves near the river. This was just at the base of the mountain, near a bend that, if you turned right instead of left, if you walked slightly in the direction of the lone jacaranda that bloomed late every year, like all the things of that place—if you followed that path, it would lead you to a sacred baobab.

A man stood near the baobab. In his opinion the tree looked upside down. Its thin, hungry branches clawed at the sky like roots. The man had the sort of lazy tongue that struggled to enunciate guttural words. He'd personally prefer another word to describe the branches; that is, once he found the word. A tree was a tricky thing for so many other reasons.

For example, and the man had started many debates over this, you couldn't stand *behind* a tree because a tree didn't have a front to begin with. But just then, he had to concede that maybe he *was* standing behind a tree.

A car came from the south, along the dirt track leading from the Joubert Farm. Usually a group of five children or so came from there. They always turned left at the bend and followed the path to the river, where lay the promise of the famed river monkeys. But that morning the man expected a car that had a white man and a mulatto girl as its passengers. At least, that's what the telegraphist had said. "Ah," he exclaimed when he saw the car. He had to leave the valley quickly. He needed to alert the officer at the border as soon as possible.

· · ·

In that same moment, two children were headed to the termite hill in search of locusts. One of them, the younger, saw the man as he stepped from behind the tree. The boy was frightened. He stood frozen for a moment.

His brother was annoyed because this always happened when their mother sent them off for field chores: the younger boy always lagged behind. "Let's go, eh!" he said, clapping his hands. The boy who had seen the tall, pale man finally woke up from his shock. He nodded towards the baobab tree and said to his brother, "Mphukudu was hiding behind that *moboyo* over there."

By the time the elder brother looked, the man had disappeared and the first boy was unsure he'd seen him at all. A bird flew into the sky as though it had suddenly been disturbed from its sleep by a creeping presence. Then another bird followed it, and soon the silence of the savannah was filled with things fleeing from something that the boys couldn't see.

Now afraid, the boys quickly ran in the direction of home. When they told the story of why they had returned without catching even a single locust, their mother clapped her hands once over her head. She sucked her teeth and said, "You know, when other women were given children, me I was given a punishment. Which Ancestor have I offended, oh? Please tell me so I can find a cow and slaughter it before I go mad." Sadly, no one found a cow for the mother. She was forced to go to the neighbour's homestead to ask for vegetables from a small plot there.

"Isn't it your sons went to the termite hill today?" said the neighbour. The mother was forced to relive her punishment by telling her children's story. When she was done, the neighbour laughed and laughed. "Ah," said the neighbour. "Don't your sons know that Mphukudu is just a story told by the elders to frighten children from wandering too far from home?"

The mother said yes, her children should know this. They really should, eh. But isn't it that when other women were being given children, she, apparently having offended some unforgiving Ancestor, was given a punishment instead. She shrugged in defeat and went to the plot.

· · ·

Some way off in the distance, away from the woman who was foraging for leaves that wouldn't taste bitter from too much summer, Abram and Dido were now in the tropical belt, on the foggy slopes. The fog was so thick that it wasn't easy to see very far ahead or behind. Samson, the man who drove the car, assured them that this sort of weather was very common in the mountains. They didn't have anything to worry about, he said. He had done this many times.

What worried Abram wasn't the fog, though, it was the sharpness of the turns in the road. They were numerous and sudden, and often, the car seemed to be teetering at the edge of a cliff. In these moments, Samson was silent with concentration; Abram, remembering Alisa's foreboding prophecies, was anxious; and Dido was perched near the window, trying to see how close they were to the edge of the mountain.

"The trees are so tall and the leaves so thick," she said. "It doesn't look like autumn. It doesn't look like Cape Town." Abram mumbled his agreement.

Once Samson delivered them out of the bends and the fog, Abram sighed with relief while Dido slumped into her seat with disappointment. They now passed thinner, shorter trees, all of them wilting from the start of autumn. How long had they lived there, he wondered. How strongly did their roots entwine and etch themselves into the earth, or did they rot with the passing of time? If taken by their roots and planted again in soils far away, would their roots grow and entwine and etch and rot just as easily? As the car carried on, the trees grew thinner and thinner, and shorter and shorter. Their canopies became flatter as the lushness of the valley receded behind them. The arid expanse of the savannah opened its arms wider and wider.

There were also wild dogs and rabbits, flightless birds and crickets and wayward bucks and snakes. They were alone and untamed and wandering from this place to that one, or hunting, or being hunted, or merely resting their hides from the heat of the unyielding sun. There were oases of life in the barrenness. In the barren places, it seemed to Abram that the living things were dying more swiftly: the leaves there were browner, as though the autumn winds blew harsher. Or maybe the summer sun had burnt hotter.

The animals there hid themselves away. They lent the plains to migrating people who went from here to there to there—away from something, towards something else. Some had shoes on their feet, some did not; but each one briskly trod away from his or her poverty surefooted.

They carried their possessions preserved in paper and plastic, then bound by ropes and balanced in heaps. The women carried children on their backs and piles on their heads, and they followed the men, who carried their loads in their hands. The clothes they wore clung to their bodies. The sun beat against their skin until sweat and salt poured from their pores and onto their threadbare modesty.

South, they were headed. Abram imagined that the men would board a train going to the mines. The women would follow. Or there might be a farm nearby where they were promised work. But the northern Transvaal had not been kind to them in many years. They might think the mines would be more prosperous.

He imagined the patter of their feet; the harsh places that had birthed them, then cast them onto the salted earth they now pursued. He wondered about the treasures they carried with them; if they were, in fact, treasures and not burdens. And he wondered if they wondered about him.

Did they pity him, for unlike them, he was northbound? Some craned their necks to peek into the car as it passed them. But once their curiosity was satisfied, south and south they went on, past the baobabs and the hills, their heads never turning back to the sad white man who held a Black child in his arms. Soon the hordes dwindled and only stragglers could be seen. They didn't carry loads, nor were they followed by women or children. They walked more briskly and faded into the horizon faster, the weightlessness of their lives aiding their flight.

Quickly, far too quickly, they vanished into the distance.

Leaf of the Willow Tree

The leaf, browning with the turn of the seasons and newly fallen from the highest branch, gently floated in the breeze. It landed on the mat forged by the assembly of its fallen kin.

The keeper of the willow tree was departed. She was stolen by flames. Her pilgrimage was ended. There had been another keeper who recited the names of stars as the southern people did. Although *she* was still alive, as told by the wind, she was also departed from her post, stolen by the road and taken to places unknown.

A call echoed from her. It was a child-voice. It begged for refuge from a nameless people somewhere in the world. The wind of singing voices heard that call. It was passing by chance over an old hill at the edge of a continent. Being the wind of singing voices, it was compelled to catch the child-voice before it drifted away. The wind then carried the echo this way and that, from this mountain to that one, to the skies, the valleys and rivers, the trees, the falling leaves and other rotting things, back and back in time, and back again.

The ears it sought were scattered. They were in this place and that, beneath this earth and that, beholden to these people and those who came from over there, to every place and no-where at all, to every god and none, to nothing, to everything. The wind knew this, and carried the voice this way and that and back again.

Patiently, it sounded the child-voice to every place and time there was. It received the voices that returned with echoes of their own. It listened to them, to every tale and rumour, to names given to nameless people, somewhere in the world. It gusted stronger and lifted the leaf from its rest. The dust devil rose from the burnt east wing gable. There was ash there, ingrained in the sand. The devil unearthed it and carried the ash to the north and the west, and north and west again, to a place that was once known by many names but was now called West Africa. Whispers told of a people once bound to that place. Centuries ago, they were stolen and scattered by the tides of the Atlantic. They lost the names of their ancestors. An orphan people, they were. But the bones of those ancestors still lay in the crags of their cradle land.

It was there that the wind travelled. It scooped the ash and dust devil. Together they spun through the desert dunes, through the paths of hills and the tides of winds wandering to this place and that one. Here and there, the wind carved its way. In soft whistles and whispers it signalled its passage, and every other wind lis-tened. Some tides begged for ash from the wind and promised to deliver the bounty to other rumoured cradles. The wind thanked them and whirled away.

At last the ash came to the far place where waited the grieving souls of the ancestors. There was a place there, a castle where you could stand and see the endlessness of the sea. It went on and on, like the journey. Someone had had the idea to name it "The Gate of No Return." Once they had passed the threshold, no one was meant to come back.

But you can't name a place, or so said the wind. A place belongs to itself. If you listen it will whisper its name and gods and past to you. It is an eternal thing, and people are so fleeting, so quick to die. So how can people name places? This is why a people who don't have a river can't have a river god, a people who don't know eagles can't have an eagle god. But have you ever met a people who didn't know about the Children of the Sky God, a people that didn't narrate some version of how the sky came to be? The San knew all of this, said the wind; but other people hadn't listened to the San in a very long time.

So through that door, that gate of no return, the wind slipped through, brushing past a history that people only whispered now. The wind slipped through there and whirled and whirled to call forth the ancient people of that place.

A breeze wafted from the sea—in welcome, said the wind. The woven voices once elusive in their call now called louder, in sacred words and sacred songs. They swept the ash from the wind. They whirled and whistled until the wind knew the journey was ended and the task completed. The child-voice was home at last.

The echoes rose and receded in rhythm. They erupted into laughter, into chants and songs and a hubbub of secrets the leaf couldn't know. In the joy of her return, they called the child-name to every time and place there was, through the whispering winds, through the world, here and there and back again. Over yonder on an old hill at the edge of a continent, they found the soul that was stolen by flames. They found the child that was stolen with her. *Welcome home*, they said, or so said the wind.

And the leaf of the willow tree, now withered by the labour and dust and whirl of the road, gently floated to the ground. There, it rested.

ACKNOWLEDGMENTS

Writing this book took many years, airports, and cities. It was a very lonely process, but in no way did I do it alone. I would like to express my sincerest gratitude to the following people, without whom this would not have been possible, nor as fruitful:

Bridget Impey, Nadia Goetham, and the entire Jacana team for pinching me as I lived through my dream. Xuejun Jian, for being insane with me, for dreaming these impossible dreams; if you hadn't housed me on my visits to Cape Town, I wouldn't have written this. Xolile Mtembu, for reading the first draft, because I'd given up and you made me hope again. And my family, I guess, even though they still make me wash dishes—all of their love is written throughout this book, their names too.

A NOTE ON THE COVER

Scatterlings is filled with lyrical folklore and rich with pre-apartheid South African history. The joy of reading paired immediately with immense (self-imposed) pressure to ensure the packaging matched the interior's depth.

I felt it best to establish a cultural connection with the cover's art, so I researched historical and contemporary art by South African artists and discovered the work of Marsi van de Heuvel. Marsi's art completely moved me. Through an incredibly slow and meditative process, she fills pages with one-directional inked lines that can take up to two months and one hundred fiber-tip pens to complete.

I commissioned Marsi to create an original piece, the center of the art forming the African continent to complete the title: *Scatterlings of Africa*. Inside the silhouette a weeping willow tree appears where Alisa sits, the color contrasting with the dark background as beauty emerges from ashes.

—Stephen Brayda

Here ends Rešoketšwe Manenzhe's
Scatterlings.

The first edition of the book was
printed and bound at Friesens, Canada,
November 2022.

A NOTE ON THE TYPE

The text of this novel was set in Dante, a typeface first developed by German-Italian printer and type designer Giovanni Mardersteig (1892–1977), founder of the private press Officina Bodoni. Officina Bodoni quickly gained a reputation for their high-quality printing, and Mardesteig approached typefaces with the same perfectionism. Dante was released for mechanical composition in 1957. The digital version, which you see on this page, was redrawn by Monotype's Ron Carpenter and released in 1993. Dante is an exquisite, balanced serif font, making it perfect for print.

HARPERVIA

An imprint dedicated to publishing international voices, offering readers a chance to encounter other lives and other points of view via the language of the imagination.